# BADD
# MOTHERF*CKER

## A BADD BROTHERS NOVEL

Jasinda Wilder

# BADD
# MOTHERF*CKER

# ONE

## Dru

I SMOOTHED THE RUCHED WHITE FABRIC OVER MY HIPS AND sucked in a breath; the dress was crazy tight around my chest, which did wonders for my cleavage, but left me unable to draw a full breath.

"I can't really breathe," I said, once again attempting to fully expand my lungs.

"It's only for, like, an hour," Annie said. "Soon as the service is over, you can change into your party dress for the reception."

"Yeah, I guess," I said. "Who breathes on their wedding day, anyway?" I joked.

Lisa, another of my three bridesmaids, put the finishing touches on my hair, tucking a few strands into bobby pins and leaving a few strands loose around my face. "My wedding dress was so tight I nearly passed out during the service," she said. "Not breathing on your wedding day is a time-honored tradition."

"Well...fuck that tradition," I said. "I like breathing. Breathing is nice."

Annie was in front of me, touching up my makeup. "That cleavage is nice. Looking hot on your wedding day is also nice. Breathing? Meh, it's overrated."

I tried another breath, feeling my breasts swell against the constraining material. My head spun, and I was glad I was sitting down. I was just dizzy from nerves, that's all. I *was* nervous, that much was true. But I also legitimately couldn't breathe. I was scared out of my mind. I loved Michael, I really, really did. I loved him. I was ready to get married. I was ready to become Dru Connolly-Morrison. Mrs. Michael Morrison. Dru Morrison.

God, none of those sound right.

But Michael insisted I take his name, even if it was hyphenated. "I'm traditional that way," he had grumbled.

I *liked* my name, though, and I didn't want to change it. Dru Connolly: it had a ring to it. It was a strong name and, more importantly, it was *my* name.

Breathing was becoming harder and harder with every passing moment—or maybe it was just the fact that I was close to hyperventilating. I tried to slow my breathing down, but my lungs didn't seem to be getting the message.

"I need to see Michael," I said.

He always had a way of calming me down when I started panicking and overthinking things. He'd kiss me and hold me and tell me it would be okay and, somehow, things always worked out. Not always how I wanted them to, or how I expected them to, but… they worked out.

This wedding would work out, and the marriage would, too.

But…I wanted more than just for my marriage to WORK OUT. I wanted it to be amazing.

Annie and Lisa exchanged glances. "Um…well… you know it's bad luck for him to see you in your dress."

"I'll cover up or something. Can you just go get him?"

Another glance between the two ladies.

"It's just nerves, hon," Lisa said.

Annie zipped her makeup bag closed. "Just take lots of shallow breaths and focus on walking down the aisle. You'll be fine."

I looked from Annie to Lisa and back, feeling, perhaps unfairly, like they were hiding something, or avoiding. Something. I wasn't close to either woman, since they were the significant others of Michael's best friends, Nate and Eric—Lisa was Nate's wife, and Annie was Eric's girlfriend. There was one more groomsman, Tony, Michael's cousin, and one more bridesmaid, Tawny, one of Lisa's friends, added just to keep the sides even; I'd barely met Tawny, and didn't really care for her all that much, but you couldn't have two bridesmaids and three groomsmen, right?

I sighed. "I just need a few minutes alone, I guess."

"Sure," Annie said. "We'll go help Tawny with the flowers."

I frowned. "Help Tawny with the flowers? I had the flowers professionally arranged, and I checked them myself this morning."

Lisa hesitated, and licked her lips. "I...she's just double checking. You know, just...to be sure everything is golden."

I honestly didn't care what Tawny was doing, so I just shrugged. "Whatever. I just need a minute. Thanks, ladies."

"Sure thing, Dru," Lisa said, and then she and Annie were out the door, finger-waving at my dad as they passed him.

I really didn't have any girlfriends of my own, not anyone I truly liked or trusted. I didn't trust anyone but my dad.

And Michael. I trusted Michael.

Michael was amazing.

Handsome, successful, kind. Worked in marketing for Amazon. No beer belly, had all his hair, went to the gym two or three days a week, and could last longer than five minutes in bed. What wasn't to love?

I had to see Michael. If I saw him, all my doubts would be erased.

That's how it always worked.

Michael was a stickler for tradition, so I knew he wouldn't want to see me in my dress before the moment I walked down the aisle to him, so I stuck my head out of the door of the Sunday school room I was using as a dressing room. My dad was sitting on a bench opposite my room, scrolling on his cell phone. He was my best friend, and my namesake: he was Drew Connolly, and I was Dru Connolly. Maybe that was cheesy, sure, but he was all I had.

"Daddy?"

He looked up, smiling at me. "What's up, baby girl?"

"Do you have that stupid trench coat you're always wearing?"

He frowned at me. "We live in the Pacific

Northwest, Dru, so a trench coat isn't stupid, it's practical. So, yes, I do. Why?"

"I need to see Michael, but I don't want him to see me in my dress yet."

Dad nodded. "Ah, of course." He stood up, moved to a coat rack down the hallway and lifted his beloved, twenty-year-old tan trench coat off the hook.

I *hated* that trench coat. It made him look like he was trying to be a gumshoe detective in a late-forties detective noir flick. But for the moment, it was what I needed, so I put it on and buttoned it over my dress, and then did a twirl, kicking my heel up and posing… with zero percent sarcasm, of course.

"How do I look?"

Dad smirked. "You look great, baby. See? A trench coat is always fashionable."

I rolled my eyes at him. "Don't even get me started, Dad. Trench coats are *never* fashionable. Ever. Like, maybe for five minutes in the nineteen forties, sure, but that's it." I leaned up and kissed him. "I'll be back, and then we'll be ready to get started, right?"

Dad gave me the look, then. The one I hated. The look that told me he didn't quite approve of Michael, or the wedding, but was supporting me because I was his only child and he loved me. "If you're sure this is what you want, then yes, we'll be ready. Michael's family is here, all sixty-four of them." He grinned. "Rolando, Vickers, Johnson, Benson, Ayers, and Mickelson are all here too with their families, so we've got a few people to fill up our side. But if you're having any doubts, just say the word. We'll organize a getaway."

"I'm sure, Daddy. I promise." I leaned up and kissed him. "Now wait here, I'll be right back."

He sat back down, pulled his cell phone out, and resumed scrolling, content to wait as long as it took, as long as he had his Buzzfeed app to scroll through. "I'll be here, then."

Michael's dressing room was down the hallway and around a corner. His two best friends, Nate and Eric, were lounging on a bench like Dad had been, passing a flask back and forth and cackling about something on Eric's cell phone. Lisa and Annie were crowded around Eric and his cell phone, cackling right along and taking hits from the flask when it got passed around.

I strode up to them, and they were so involved with whatever they were watching that they didn't notice me. I was close enough to hear Eric's phone. It sounded like porn, and as I got close enough to see it, it looked like porn. Eric had his phone held away from himself, so everyone could see, his palms cupped around the back to reflect the sound. I stood next to Lisa and crowded in.

"What are you watching?" I asked, but I was able to see enough to know what they were watching.

Only, it didn't make any sense.

It couldn't be.

Eric did an actual double take: looking at me, looking back at the phone and then looking back at me in total surprise, which quickly morphed to panic.

"Shit! Dru, I—we—we're watching...nothing." He clicked the phone off and stuffed it in his pocket. "Don't worry about it. A stupid video my buddy sent me."

I was staying calm, so far.

It's not what I think.

He *wouldn't*.

Would he?

"That's not what it looked like," I said.

Eric shifted, looking to his friends to help him out.

Lisa glanced at Michael's dressing room door, eyes wide, and then looked back at me, speaking a little louder than necessary. "You want a shot, Dru?" She snatched the flask out of Nate's hand and shoved it at me. "Have a shot. It's Jim Beam."

I pushed past her, ignoring her and the flask, reaching for the doorknob.

"You're not supposed to see him before the wedding, Dru!" Lisa shouted, getting between the door and me. "It's bad luck!"

"*He's* not supposed to see *me* in my dress before the wedding, you idiot." I had never liked Lisa, I realized. She was vapid and stupid and now she was getting in the way of me seeing my fiancé on the day of our wedding? "Which is why I'm wearing the trench coat. Now get out of the way."

I heard it, then.

Michael.

Making certain…sounds.

Lisa heard it too, which was why she'd tried to talk louder than necessary.

I bit my lip, blinked hard, and forced my imminent breakdown aside. Turning to Eric, I held out my hand. "Phone, Eric. *Now.*"

He hesitated. "Why do you want to see it? You know what it is, obviously."

I got in his face. "*Phone…now.*" I used the hard voice I'd learned from Dad, the one with the snap of authority.

Dad was a cop, a former USMC drill instructor, and an overall badass, so he was an expert in what he called The Voice of Authority. He'd also taught me self-defense from the time I was old enough to walk, so I could hand most men their own asses in thirty seconds or less, and Eric knew it. Hell, he'd seen me do it more than once.

He dug his phone out of his pocket, unlocked it, and handed it to me—the video was cued up, on pause.

It showed the door behind me, the door to Michael's dressing room. It was cracked open, and the video was being shot through the crack. Michael was visible through the crack, tuxedo pants around his ankles. His bowtie perfectly tied, his vest buttoned up, his coat left open, white shirt hanging below the vest and coat.

In front of him, bent over the back of a chair, was Tawny, Lisa's best friend and my third bridesmaid. Yes, her name really was Tawny. And she fit the name, too: fake blond hair, big fake tits, skanky, had done a turn as a stripper. In the video, she was taking Michael's cock and, from the sounds she was making, she was loving it. Loudly.

I wanted to see what had been so funny, so I scrolled to the left to bring the video back to the beginning. The video had caught Michael as he tripped over his own pants and fell backward onto his ass, leaving Tawny bent over the chair, dress shoved up past her gyrating hips. Michael's erect dick flapped and flopped and wobbled as he toppled backward. Honestly, it was hysterical. It was funny enough that despite the circumstances, I actually giggled.

But I sobered quickly.

"He's still in there?" I demanded, tossing Eric's phone at him. "Fucking Tawny?"

Nobody answered, which was all the answer I needed; I'd seen enough, no need to confront him.

I wiggled my full-carat diamond solitaire engagement ring off my finger and sucked in a deep breath—well, as deep as I could, anyway—to fend off the meltdown for a few more minutes. I turned to Lisa, grabbed her wrist and pressed the ring into her palm. "Tawny can have him."

I turned and left, fighting off the need to have a total nervous breakdown.

Dad was still waiting on the bench, and he looked up as I stormed past him. "Baby? Dru? What's going on?"

I kept marching, and let Dad catch up. We were out of the church, and into the pouring Seattle rain in less than sixty seconds.

"You were right, Daddy," I managed, as I approached the driver's side of Dad's beat-up red '07 Tacoma—he'd driven us here, but now I needed to drive. I needed to get away as fast as possible.

Dad wasted no time hopping into the passenger seat, which was good since I wasn't waiting around. The second my ass hit the faded, ripped cloth seat, the engine was on and I was peeling out.

"Right about what? What's going on?" he asked

as I skidded out of the parking lot of the church and onto the main road.

Dad having trained me to drive, he was fairly relaxed despite my wild driving.

"About Michael, about everything." I sniffled and tried to stop the next one, because I knew once I let it out there would be no stopping it. "He—he—Tawny, he was—*SHIT!*" I slammed my fist on the steering wheel so hard the whole truck shook. "That piece of *shit* was fucking Tawny in the dressing room."

Dad's eye twitched, and his massive fist clenched. "Knew that punk was a slimy bastard."

"Yeah, you did."

"So now what?"

I unbuttoned the trench coat, shrugged it off, and handed it to Dad. "Now I go get shitfaced. After that? I don't know." I contorted in place, trying to loosen the bodice, and managed to give myself enough room in the dress so I could actually take a breath without it hurting.

Dad rested his meaty hand on my shoulder. "Pull over, baby-cakes. I'll drive."

I yanked the wheel to the right, hopped a curb, and skidded to a halt in a drug store parking lot. We did a Chinese fire drill, and when I was seated Dad took off again, albeit far more sedately than I had.

He glanced at me. "You gonna cry?"

I nodded. "A lot. I'm gonna ugly cry so hard, Dad, you don't even know."

He dug into his back pocket and produced an actual handkerchief. Dad, classic, right there. He's not all that old, since Mom had me at nineteen, but he acts like someone from a previous generation. Handkerchiefs, trench coats, and I'm pretty sure he has a fedora somewhere.

I stared at the handkerchief. "Do you use that on your nose?"

He shrugged. "Well, sure, it's a hanky."

"That's disgusting."

Dad stuffed it back in his pocket. "Suit yourself. But it's clean, you know. I have several, and I wash them. It's not, like, the same hanky with twenty years of snot crusted into it."

That got a laugh from me, because that was kind of what I'd been imagining. But the laugh was what broke me—I couldn't hold my feelings back anymore. It started with a single tear and a sniffle, which turned into a sob, and then I was full-blown ugly crying, as promised.

I took the hanky, gross as it was, and wiped my eyes with it, not caring if I smeared my mascara.

Pretty soon I was crying so hard I couldn't see, and I felt Dad pull the truck over. He unbuckled me and hauled me to his side, wrapped his thick arm around me, and held me close as I sobbed. He smelled like Dad and felt like comfort.

He let me cry for I don't know how long, and when I was finished, he took the hanky from me, wiped my face with it, and stuffed it back into his pocket. "Better?"

I shook my head. "No, not even close. But I'm done crying for now. Time to get hammered."

Dad took me to his favorite dive, a cop bar near a small rural airfield way outside Seattle. By small, I mean postage-stamp tiny. The biggest airplane anywhere on the field was a twin-engine prop plane getting loaded with crates; the rest of the planes were single-engine Cessnas, Piper Cubs, Beechcraft, and other single-engine private aircraft. He knew everyone there, since he'd been on the force for twenty years and had been going to that particular dive bar for even longer; it wasn't so much a cop bar as it was the personal, mostly private hangout of Dad and his cop buddies.

When we walked in every head turned, because it was the kind of place you just didn't go into unless you knew you were welcome. So when the guys saw me in my dress, bedraggled from walking through the downpour, mascara smeared from crying…well, those cops were a tight bunch. They took care of their own. One look at me, and they pulled the tables into a circle, sat me down, pulled a bottle of the finest scotch in the joint and poured me a double on the rocks. I'd grown up with these guys, you see. Their wives had babysat me when Dad worked a weekend or school night shift. They had come over in the middle of the night when Dad had to go interview a suspect. They had covered for me when I snuck out to make out with boys in high school. These cops had all been there for me my whole life.

I finished my first double scotch and listened to them discussing plans for Michael, and then waited while Detective Rolando poured me a second. I looked at them all in turn: Rolando, Vickers, Johnson, Dad, Benson, Ayers, Mickelson...Dad had obviously texted them to meet us here after I'd bolted from the wedding.

"No revenge, guys." I stared them down until they saw I was serious. "He's not worth it. He can have Tawny and she can have him. No revenge. Although, if you ever catch him speeding, don't let him off with a warning. I'm not going to waste another moment of my life on him, and neither should any of you."

I got a chorus of agreement. After finishing my second double scotch, I started taking the pins out of my hair and, once my hair was down, it was on.

I switched from scotch to bourbon, from doubles to shots chased by pints of local stout.

See, I'd learned to drink with the cops, too—and these boys could pound the liquor like nobody's business.

I could say I lost track then but, hell, I hadn't bothered counting in the first place.

At some point, Mickelson put breakup music on the bar's radio, and considering how drunk I was by that point I got into it. Really, really into it.

Dad and Ayers had left at some point to haul in some suspect they'd been chasing, so I was alone with Mickelson, Benson, and Rolando, Dad's closest friends on the force, men who were like uncles to me.

Mickelson was seated beside me, spouting drunken wisdom. "Can't let the bastard get you down, Dru. Gotta keep your head up, y'know? He's a bastard, and a punk, and he ain't worth your tears. So just forget him, right?"

"Right," I said, because that had been my plan all along, but they kept bringing Michael back into the conversation. Which, to my inebriated thinking, was counterproductive. "I gotta start over."

"Start over, that's a great plan. Scrap everything, and start new," Rolando agreed.

I stood up, wobbled dizzily across the bar to the grimy window. A plane getting ready to take off, taking advantage of a lull in the rain. "Been in Seattle my whole life. Never been anywhere else. Michael is…

everywhere I go in this whole damn city I'll see him. I was with him for four years. Four fucking years! How long was he cheating on me? Or was that, like, some kind of stupid last hurrah, instead of a bachelor party? Or wait, no, he had a bachelor party. And I'm pretty sure they went to a strip club. So…fuck, whatever. I just—" I wasn't really talking to anyone at this point. "I dunno if I can stay in Seattle anymore. I gotta…I gotta get out of here."

Rolando came up beside me, careful to stand a respectful distance away, but close enough to grab me should I pass out or start heaving. Either was possible. "Where would you go?"

I shrugged, which sent me off balance, and I put a hand on the bar to steady myself. "I don't know, 'Lando. Anywhere but here. Maybe I'll just…get on one of those planes and go where it goes."

Rolando patted my shoulder. "Your old man wouldn't know what to do with himself if you left, Dru. But I get your point."

"I've been here my whole life. I went to college here, got my first real job here, met Michael here. How can I start over in the same place I've always been?" I was starting to see double, but I felt the truth of my own words deep in my bones.

I had my purse on my shoulder, which contained all my ID and bank cards, as well as my cell phone and charger. I had no clothes, though, except the wedding dress I was still wearing.

But fuck it, right?

I couldn't stay here any more—I *had* to leave.

I stared out the window as a plane taxied onto the runway and took off.

What if…?

I straightened.

Another plane was visible in the distance, lights on, propellers spinning, waiting for the cue to leave. I didn't really even see it, just what it represented: freedom, a fresh start. I saw twin propellers spinning, wing lights blinking, saw it pivoting from the line of waiting small aircraft onto the runway.

I turned to Rolando and Mickelson. "I'm leaving."

They both frowned. "You're—what?"

I grabbed my purse off the back of the chair and slung it over my shoulder. "I can't stay here anymore. I need to get away."

"So where are you going?" Mickelson, who resembled a slightly smaller version of Fat Bastard from *Austin Powers*, stood up and hobbled after me. "You can't just leave, Dru. What about your dad?"

I lifted my phone out of my purse and waggled it at him. "I'll call him when I get wherever I end up. I'm not leaving forever, I just—I can't be here anymore."

I pushed out the door and jogged in my three-inch

heels across the parking lot—this was truly nothing but a postage-stamp airfield: no security, no fences, no one to stop me as I hauled ass through the grass to the runway

Rolando was hot on my heels. "You're drunk, Dru. You can't do this now, not like this."

"I have to. It's crazy, but it's what I have to do. It's happening. Tell Dad I love him and that I'll call him as soon as I can, okay?"

I slipped my heels off and held them in my hand, then took off running across the field toward the runway. The plane was taxiing toward the runway now, props whirling into a blur. I was wasted, but somehow I stayed upright until I reached the runway, held up my arms, and waved at the plane to stop.

The pilot flung open his door, props slowing. "What gives, lady? You can't just jump in front of a plane like that. You wanna get killed?"

I climbed up the side and opened the door, and hopped into the co-pilot seat. "I'm going with you!" I shouted.

He stared at me. "The hell you are."

I opened my wallet and pulled out all the cash I had—over a thousand dollars I'd been planning on spending on my honeymoon in Hawaii. "Here," I said, handing it to him. "Twelve hundred dollars to shut up and take me wherever it is you're going."

"I'm taking a load of supplies to—"

"I don't care, I don't want to know!" I said, interrupting him. "It doesn't matter. As long as it's far from here."

He stared at me for a long moment, then took the cash, stuffed it into the breast pocket of his short-sleeve button-down shirt; I thought I heard him mumble something like "Alaska here we come, then," under his breath, but I wasn't quite sure, because the last few shots had suddenly caught up to me, and we were taking off and I was dizzy and fighting nausea.

When I finally beat the urge to puke, I turned to the pilot. We were in the air now and climbing steeply, going up through the rain clouds into the night sky above them.

"Did you say Alaska?" I had to shout the question, because it was so loud in the cabin I couldn't hear myself speaking.

He handed me a pair of headphones with a microphone attached to it, and when I put it on, he glanced at me. "Thought you said you didn't want to know where we were going."

"It sounded like you said 'Alaska,' though."

He nodded. "Ketchikan, Alaska, sweetheart."

I went faint. "I thought—I was thinking somewhere more like…Portland, or San Francisco."

He chuckled. "Nope, we're going to Alaska.

Well, you are. When we land, I'm dropping off this load and picking up a load of fish and taking it inland. Won't be going back to Seattle."

Dizziness hit me again, and I bent over to put my head between my knees. "Alaska? *Jesus.*"

He eyed me warily. "You gonna puke? Because there're sick bags under your seat if you are."

I grabbed a sick bag, but instead of puking into it I used it to help me breathe.

"Alaska." I said it again, as if saying it again would make it more real.

"Ketchikan, to be exact. Nice place, lots of cruise ships go through there. Beautiful. A bit chilly, sometimes, but beautiful."

Another wave of nausea tossed through me. "Would it be horribly rude if I asked you to shut up?"

He just chuckled. "Fine by me."

And he did just that, shut up, fiddling with knobs and switches and tapping gauges, adjusting the controls.

Alaska?

What the hell had I gotten myself into?

# TWO

# Sebastian

WHERE ARE THE FUCKIN' CRUISE SHIPS WHEN YOU need 'em?

I wiped down the bar for the forty-seventh time in the last hour, staring out at my bar, which was dead as a doornail, deader than a graveyard and a ghost town put together. Not a damn soul in the bar and it was seven in the evening on a Saturday. There should be fuckin' *somebody* wanting a goddamn drink. But no, hadn't been one stinkin' customer since we'd opened at four. Usually the bar was hopping, or at least had a decent crowd, even on week nights or stormy days.

I'd blame it on the rain, but that didn't usually stop people from needing a drink or six. Shit, most of the time it made it busier, not deader.

I should just close. What was the harm? Wouldn't be anybody in anyway.

But I couldn't do that. Badd's Bar and Grill was struggling enough as it was, so if I had any hope of keeping Dad's bar alive, I couldn't afford to close early. Dad may be gone—three months in his grave—but no way I was going to let his bar go under, too. I'd been doing my damndest, but one guy to run a whole bar wasn't ideal, and meant I'd seen a decrease in business, simply because I couldn't keep up with the demand, so people went elsewhere.

I'd been raised in this damn bar. I learned to walk going from table three to four. Kissed my first girl in the alley behind the place, bedded the same girl in the storeroom in the attic, got in my first fistfight right out in that parking lot.

I wasn't going to let the place close. I'd struggle along somehow. Keep it afloat, even if it wasn't the hot spot it had once been. Maybe I just had to bite the bullet and hire somebody to help out. Hated the idea, since in all the years I'd been alive, we'd never hired a soul outside the family, and I hated the idea of breaking that tradition.

I'd been hoping there'd be some kind of windfall

after Dad died, you know? Like, an inheritance or something. I figured Dad had been doing okay all those years, figured he'd have money saved. Guess not. Don't know how he managed not to save anything, since he lived in the bar and rarely ever left it, and when my brothers and I were younger we all lived above it. Mom cooked the food, Dad served the drinks.

Then, when I was seventeen, Mom passed and I took over the food prep. I'd get home from school, tie on an apron and start slinging burgers and fries and chicken wings. It was my first job and now, ten years later, this bar was the only job I'd ever had. Dad let me help with the books when I was twenty, let me split the shifts with him—three days a week for him and four for me.

I knew the business had been struggling for a while, but in the last few months since Dad died things had really taken a nosedive.

I did my best to keep things afloat but it didn't help that I was the single employee. I cooked, bartended, bussed, mopped, swept, and worked open to close, four p.m. to two a.m. seven days a week.

The frustrating thing was that even though I had seven brothers to my name, not one was around to help.

That's right, there were eight of us. Mom and

Dad had raised eight boys in the three-bedroom apartment above this bar—four of us to a room in double bunk bed sets. When Mom died Zane had been fifteen, Brock thirteen, Baxter twelve, Caanan and Corin the identical twins ten, Lucian nine, and Xavier, the baby of the tribe, had been seven.

Ten years later, Zane was off being a Navy SEAL somewhere, Baxter was playing football in the CFL and was being scouted for the NFL, or so he claimed, Brock was a stunt pilot traveling the country doing airshows, Canaan and Corin were touring the world with their hard rock band, Bishop's Pawn, and Lucian was...well, I wasn't entirely sure. He'd left the day he turned eighteen and hadn't come back, hadn't so much as sent a damn postcard. I figured he'd taken the money he'd made working on fishing boats from the time he was fifteen and was just sort of bumming around the world like a damned vagabond. That was like him, brooding, lazy, and just inherently cool. Xavier had gotten a full ride to Stanford from soccer and academics, and there was talk of FIFA scouts watching him...on top of think tanks or some shit like that. Then there was me, Sebastian Badd, the eldest, stuck in goddamned Ketchikan tending a dead-ass bar, same as I'd been doing since I was seventeen.

All of my brothers were cool and good-looking and successful, and I was a fucking bartender.

Not that I was bitter, or anything. I mean shit, I was the best-looking of the lot, after all.

And, don't get me wrong, I loved the bar. It was home. It was my entire life. The hard part was that I'd never gotten a chance to do anything else. When Mom died it had been left up to me, as the oldest, to help Dad. I'd managed to get my high school diploma, but only barely. I'd been too busy cooking, bussing tables, and washing dishes to care about tests or homework. I worked so my brothers didn't have to—during the week at least.

Dad always gave me Saturdays off and made whoever was around help out. Usually that meant Zane, Baxter, and the twins, since Brock always had practice and Lucian and Xavier were too young to be of any help. Saturdays meant dates for me. I'd take my earnings from the week and cruise the town on my bike—a chopped Harley Dad and I worked on every Sunday—and go scouting for chicks. Didn't usually take long to find someone to kick it with for the evening, since I had Dad's size and looks and Mom's chill confidence and calm demeanor.

Well, most of Mom's calm demeanor; I had Dad's temper in there somewhere, and these days it wasn't hard to bring it out of me. I guess I was mad because I had to run this place on my own. Back then I'd been bored and full of anger over Mom's death and had been as ready to fight as I had been to fuck, and I've always been damn good at both.

Nowadays, the only fighting I did was to kick out the odd drunk. The fucking was a constant, since even though business hadn't been great, Badd's Bar and Grill still had a reputation for having a good-looking bartender who poured strong drinks and was always DTF if you were half-decent looking and had a nice rack—the good-looking bartender being me, obviously.

Ketchikan, being a popular destination for Alaskan cruises, almost always had a constant stream of tourists looking for a "local spot" to drink—which meant fine-looking honeys only in for a day or two. These easy hook-ups had a built-in escape clause: they knew they were leaving, I knew they were leaving, so there was no mess, no hurt feelings, no awkward morning-after chit-chat.

It was a good gig.

But it was the only gig I'd ever had. I had no idea what else I could do, what else I might be good at, what else I might want to do. I tended bar and fucked hot tourists, it's what I did.

It was *all* I did.

Today, I'd spent almost an hour daydreaming and being pissed at my brothers, and still no one had come in.

"Fuck it," I said, and poured myself a stiff scotch.

Stiff, meaning a rocks glass full to the brim with Johnny Walker Black Label.

I circled around the bar, sat down by the TV, and turned on ESPN, leaning the high-top chair back with my feet flat against the bar-front and sipped my scotch watching last night's replays and highlights.

Maybe two hours later, I was on my second glass, and still hadn't seen a soul.

Then the bell over the door chimed.

I hoped it was a pretty tourist, maybe a redhead with a nice set of tits, or a blonde with a fat, juicy ass.

What I got was Richard Ames Burroughs, the attorney in charge of executing Dad's will: three-piece suit, slim leather briefcase, oxford shoes, slicked, parted hair, glasses that could appropriately and not ironically be called "spectacles", and a tendency to literally look down his nose at me. He also had a tendency to act like the stools and bar top were infected surfaces, as if he might catch fuckin' crabs or something.

Trust me, bub, I wash that bar down enough that there ain't a single germ on the damn thing.

Richard Ames Burroughs stepped carefully across the floor—which was still clean from when I'd swept it before opening—and shuffled beside me. "Mr. Badd."

"Name's Sebastian," I growled.

"Sebastian, then." He pulled out the stool beside me, brushed it off with a napkin, and then set his briefcase on it. "I have your father's will."

I slugged my scotch. "He's been dead three months, Dick. Why are you bringing this to me now?"

"You can call me Richard, or Mr. Burroughs, if you please. And it was part of his will that it not be read for twelve weeks after his death. I do not know why, as he didn't choose to offer a reason." He paused, opened his briefcase. "I've sent copies to each of your brothers, or, at least, those for whom I could locate a physical address. But I'm getting ahead of myself. Your father was very specific that he wanted me to wait three months before reading the will, and that you were to be the last one to whom I read it."

I pushed the sleeves of my thermal Henley up past my elbows, baring forearms covered in the ends of my full-sleeve tattoos. "Okay, well, that's fuckin' weird. What's the damn thing say, then? Let me guess: I'm broke, he was broke, the bar is forfeit, and I owe a bunch of money I didn't know Dad owed."

"Lord knows that's exactly what one would expect, a filthy place like this," Richard said, plucking a folder from his briefcase. "But I think you'll be rather surprised."

I lowered my stool onto all fours, set my scotch down, and stood up to tower over the slimy pencil-dick lawyer. "Listen to me, pissant: you come in here talkin' shit about my fuckin' bar, I'll crush you like a goddamn cockroach." I crossed my arms and flexed to prove a point: my arms were thicker than his legs. "So how about you say what you came here to say and I won't knock your fuckin' Ivy League white teeth down your skinny little chicken neck."

I was coming across a little…aggressive, maybe, but he creeped me out and made me feel like he thought he was better than me, and that pissed me off.

He paled, stumbled backward a few steps. "No need for threats, Mr. Badd, I simply—this isn't—*ahem*. As you say, I'll get to the particulars of the will." He opened the folder, shuffled papers, adjusted his spectacles, read in silence for a few minutes, then replaced the papers in the folder but didn't close the folder. "Your father managed to save quite a large sum of money, if you don't mind my saying so."

I blinked at him. "He…what?"

"Your father owned this building outright and lived above it, so he had very little by way of bills except the overhead of the bar, which he kept to a minimum and, for many years, it seems this bar was quite successful. He was parsimonious, and used only small amounts of the profits. He spent remarkably little, as a matter of fact."

I nodded. "That makes sense. So how much did he leave, and who to?"

"To whom, you mean," Richard said.

"Don't correct my fuckin' grammar, you fuckin' dork," I snarled. "How much, and *to whom*?"

Richard blinked at me for a moment, and then he cleared his throat again. "*Ahem.* Um…he left a sum total of two hundred and ninety thousand dollars to be split even between the eight of you Badd brothers. Not a fortune, but a sizable sum. Plus the deed to the bar, but that's not part of the two-ninety being distributed per the will. As for the distribution itself, well, that's where it gets a little more complicated."

I growled. "Complicated? What's that mean? What's complicated about who Dad left his money to?"

"Well, usually in circumstances such as these, the monies are distributed equally amongst all parties, or in favor of one or another of the deceased's issue, which usually leads to arguments and lawsuits, but that's neither here nor there, in this case."

I twirled my hand in a circle. "Get on with it, Dick. What's the short version for us poor uneducated folks?"

He sighed. "It means your father left specific instructions which must be completed before any of the funds can be released."

"Instructions?"

Richard nodded. "Caveats is the legal term applicable here. It means neither you nor any of your brothers get any money from your father's estate until the terms are fulfilled."

"So? What are the terms?"

He quoted from the will: "'Before anyone gets a cent of my money, all seven of my wayward sons must return to Ketchikan, Alaska for a minimum of one calendar year, and spend that year living within reasonable proximity to Badd's Bar and Grill, and they must contribute a minimum of two thousand working hours in Badd's Bar and Grill during that time.'"

I had to sit down, then. "The fuck?"

"It means your brothers have to come back to Ketchikan to live and work here for one year. The two thousand hours figure is based on a forty-hour work week in a calendar year of fifty-two weeks."

I tried to get my brain going. "So...what else does it say?"

"It names each of your brothers and their likely locations of residence. It awards you sole ownership of the bar, upon signature of the deed, and awards you—and only you—ten thousand dollars. The rest of the money will be split evenly between the eight of you, which comes to...thirty-six thousand two hundred and fifty dollars each."

"So the ten grand to me…"

Richard consulted the will. "'To my oldest son Sebastian, I leave ten thousand dollars outside the parameters of the execution of the will's preceding terms, as a minor reward for his faithfulness over the years to me and to Badd's Bar and Grill.'"

I choked up. "Minor reward…*shit*." I blinked hard, went around behind the bar and poured more Johnny, slugged it down facing the grimy mirror behind the rows of bottles on the back wall. "Minor reward for my faithfulness. A fucking lifetime I've spent back here, and I get ten fuckin' grand." I had to laugh. "Jesus, Dad."

I leaned against the back counter, took another long hit of scotch, and cackled. To be honest, I felt a little unhinged. Ten thousand bucks?

I mean, thanks Dad, that's awesome. It'd keep the bar afloat for a while longer. But…shit. I kinda felt like maybe I deserved a little more by way of thanks. I was pissed, now. At Dad, for dying, and then for giving me a measly ten grand after all the hours I'd put into this place. Ten grand? Fuck. Felt like an insult. I'd have rathered it just go back into the pot to split up.

My brothers were going to flip the fuck out, though, that was a given—though whether they'd be more pissed that I got extra money or that they were being forced back here was anyone's guess. Zane hadn't been back in years, and I wasn't honestly sure he was even still alive. The twins were in Germany or something, last I heard, on that crazy world tour opening for some big name act.

I glanced at Richard. "Did the will say where Lucian is?"

He flipped through the papers. "Um…no. It says Lucian's last verified location was…Udon Thani, Thailand. That was as of six months ago, when your father created his will."

"Thailand? What's the little shit doing in Thailand?" I rubbed the back of my neck, feeling a tension headache coming on.

"I'm sure I have no idea, Sebastian. That wasn't my business to ask."

"Any idea how you're going to get hold of the rest of my brothers, then?" I asked. "Good luck with Lucian, by the way."

Richard closed the file, looking prim and satisfied. "Actually, I hired a private investigator to find your mysterious brother and, as of last month, my investigator was able to make contact with Lucian and inform him of the will. I don't know where he is or what he's doing, but he's been contacted and informed of the situation. I've already been in contact with the rest of your brothers. I've spoken on the phone with Xavier, Baxter, and Brock, and I exchanged emails with Zane and the twins, Canaan and Corin, all of this within the last month or so, and they all save Lucian have indicated that they will be returning as soon as their respective situations allow. Most of them should be arriving in Ketchikan within the next few days, I do believe."

I frowned. "You have Zane's email address?"

Richard seemed perplexed. "Well, yes, of course. It was included with your father's will."

"Didn't even know the bastard had email. Woulda been nice to know." I took a long sip of my drink. "'Course, it wouldn't do any good even if I did since I don't have one."

Richard coughed, which I suspected was meant to cover a laugh. "You were, honestly, the hardest to contact of all your brothers, with the exception of Lucian. There is no phone for the bar, you yourself do not have a cell phone, and this isn't the kind of scenario I could arrange via mail, thus necessitating my trip here from Anchorage."

"Yeah, I'm a caveman like that. I like to beat my prey over the head with a club before I eat it. Women too, as a matter of fact." I could tell Richard wasn't sure I was joking. "So. My asshole brothers are all coming back, then?"

"Zane is, I can say that for certain. He's making his way here from his most recent duty station, although I'm not sure where that is. The others said they would return as their respective schedules allowed. The twins are committed to the duration of their overseas tour last I heard, but they said they'll be back when it's over, or sooner if they could work it out. And, as I said, I was only recently able to locate Lucian, so his intentions are anyone's guess."

I rubbed my face with both hands. "My brothers all hate this place." I looked up at the lawyer. "Why would Dad do this, Dick? I don't get it."

"I would only be speculating, of course, since he didn't explain his reasoning to me. But if I were to venture a guess, I would say it was his final attempt to force you to reconcile with your brothers."

"There's nothing to reconcile. We've never had any beef between any of us...they just hate it here. All this bullshit does is saddle with me seven pissed off brothers who hate this bar and this city."

Richard shrugged. "I'm sorry, Sebastian. I'm only doing my job. There's nothing I can do to change this. You could challenge it, of course, but that would be a costly and lengthy legal endeavor, and I honestly do not believe any judge would be inclined to change or reverse your father's will for no good reason. The conditions are eminently reasonable, so it would stand, I'm certain."

"Awesome." I finished my scotch. "Well, that's

that, unless there're more fun surprises in that will of Dad's."

"No, that's everything." Richard set a stapled stack of papers on the bar. "This is a copy of the will, which you may keep. I've covered all the important factors. If you have any questions after reading it through, call me. I've attached my business card."

"Want a drink, Dick?" I asked.

He hesitated. "A glass of wine wouldn't go amiss."

I laughed. "Wine. You're funny, Dick. This ain't a wine bar, bub." I poured him a measure of scotch in a clean glass and slid it over to him. "We serve liquor and beer and scabies."

"Scabies…very funny." Clearly unwilling to come across as rude, Richard took a tentative sip of the scotch, swallowed, and coughed. "Well, that will certainly put hair on one's chest, won't it?"

I laughed. "You're a grown man, Dick, don't you already have hair on your chest?"

"It's…it's a matter of phrasing, Sebastian. I am not a hirsute person by nature, however, if you must know."

"Hirsute?" I ain't stupid, but I'm not the most well-read person ever. My vocabulary doesn't really extend to Ivy League sorts of words.

He took another sip and then indicated his

chest, his voice hoarse from the whisky burn. "Hairy. Covered in fur."

I struggled not to laugh as he tried gamely to finish the scotch without coughing, but it clearly wasn't his cup of tea. Or, cup of whisky, I should say. He finished it, though, I'll give him that.

I came around from behind the bar and slapped him on the back. "That's a man's drink, Dick. Want another? It's on the house."

Richard winced. "No, thank you. If you don't mind, I must be going. My flight back to Anchorage leaves shortly."

"Suit yourself." I shook his hand, and just because I was that kind of asshole, I put a little extra crush into my grip. "Thanks for coming, Dick."

"Yes, I...well, I can't truthfully say it was my pleasure, as my job is created via bereavement, but...I'm glad to have been of service. Call me if you have any further questions."

"Sure will, Dick, sure will."

He left shaking his hand and flexing his fingers. I may possibly have left handprints on his skin.

I spent the rest of the evening wondering which of my brothers would show up first, and how I'd react.

I was about to turn off the 'OPEN' sign and close up when the door opened, letting in late night rain and cold.

Instead of one of my brothers, though, an angel walked in.

A wet, bedraggled, hung over, pissed off angel in a sopping wet wedding dress.

But sweet mother of goddamn, she was the most beautiful girl I'd ever seen.

Five-eight, hourglass figure. Hair that would probably be somewhere between full-out Irish red and auburn, when it was dry. Creamy, flawless skin. Fuckin' *curves*, man. Like, Jesus. Whoever this fine-as-wine honey ditched at the altar was a sorry son of a bitch, or a complete jackass.

Those eyes though, bright blue, the kind of blue eyes you don't see on redheads that often. I don't know all the fancy words for different shades of blue, but if you've ever seen pictures of the ocean over by Greece, the kind of blue that's just so damn blue it seems impossible...that was the color of this girl's eyes. Did I mention curves? My cock went hard in my jeans just watching her stomp across the bar, watching the way the tight dress molded to her bell-curve hips and the way her silky, milky cleavage jiggled with each step.

That dress...Jesus goddamn. Skin-tight, obviously custom cut to fit her body, all drawn up into bunched wrinkles around her hips and waist, sleeveless top with heart-shaped bra cup things pushing up tits I'd love to drown myself in for hours on end.

And she was also the unhappiest looking person I'd seen in a long time.

I went back around behind the bar and leaned against it, gripping the edge so my forearms and biceps rippled; chicks seemed to dig the pose, so I used it to my advantage.

She plopped down in a chair, crossed her arms on the bar, and let her forehead thunk down hard. "Alcohol, *now*," she mumbled into her arms.

"Don't got any wine, princess, sorry."

She raised her head and gave me a glare so fierce and furious I felt it scorch the hairs on the back of my neck. "Fuck you, you goddamn orc." She thunked her head back down. "Scotch on the rocks. And leave the bottle."

Well. This could prove to be interesting.

# THREE

## Dru

I WAS IN NO MOOD FOR BULLSHIT. EVEN IF IT WAS COMING from the most intensely masculine man I'd ever laid eyes on. Intensely masculine, fucking gorgeous, in a tall, dark, rock-star gorgeous, badass, burly, tattooed sort of way. Six-four if he was an inch, arms that stretched the sleeves of a thermal Henley— what was it about those shirts that was so fucking sexy, anyway?—with tattoos covering his forearms and obviously extending up past his elbows. He had massive shoulders and a broad chest that tapered to a wedge, and I'd bet all the money I had left that his sexy V-cut lead down to a huge cock.

I blushed at the thought, because why was I thinking about his cock? I wasn't, not really.

I was too pissed off, too heartbroken, too lost, too hung over, and too hungry to think about a penis. Even if that penis was very likely a lovely, perfect organ the size of my forearm.

Stop—no more cock thoughts.

His hair was, put plainly, brown. But if I was going to be fair about his hair color, it was the kind of brown you'd see on a grizzly bear. Same texture, same color. He had it brushed backward in a casual, messy way that said he didn't really care because he knew he was damn sexy and didn't have to try. God, his hair. Plus the scruff on his jaw, a day or two of growth on a jawline Henry Cavill should be jealous of. And have I mentioned his arms? And his forearms? Fuck. They were absolutely perfect. The ink was professional artwork, not just biker or prison crap, it was actual artwork. I saw a raven in flight, some kind of twisted, dark angel, skulls done in the Mexican Day of the Dead style, Native American totems, plus more I couldn't make out.

But then he had to go and assume I wanted wine. Fucking wine.

But when I called him an orc, he just laughed, a deep, ursine rumble of amusement rather than take offense, and lifted a half-empty bottle of Johnny Walker Black Label off the bar where it had been sitting next to a rocks glass, as if he'd already been helping himself to his own wares. Although, considering the dearth of customers, I didn't really blame him.

He snagged a clean rocks glass from a stack by the service bar, tossed it into the air and caught it upright on the flat of his palm, poured what had to have been a triple, or even a quadruple. The man didn't fuck around with his pours, clearly. We might get along just fine if he keeps pouring the Johnny Black so liberally. When I had mine he poured a healthy measure into his own glass, and then held it out to me.

"To being so hung over tomorrow neither of us will remember why we're drinking tonight," he said, and god, even his voice reminded me of a bear, deep, feral, rumbling, with a hint of snarl.

I clinked my glass against his and took a long blissful drink before answering. "That's the best goddamn toast I've ever heard," I mumbled.

We drank in an oddly not-uncomfortable silence for a while, watching ESPN highlights, during which I finished my scotch, and the bartender poured more, another full glass.

I was in a foul mood, and the scotch helped a little, but only a little. A turbulent three and a half hour flight, followed by a rough landing, which had been on the sea itself rather than an airfield. In my drunken rush to get away from Seattle, I hadn't even noticed that the airplane I'd gotten into was a seaplane.

The length of the flight meant I'd gone from hammered to hung over, and then the pilot had taken my money and left me on the docks with my purse and wedding dress and not a damn thing else except a splitting headache and a broken heart. Well, the pilot actually wasn't that much of a dick: he'd given back six hundred of my cash, saying I looked so messed up he figured I needed it more than he did. But he still left me on the docks with nowhere to go, no one to talk to, in a rainstorm, alone...

Plus, I hadn't eaten since I couldn't remember when. Lunch? I'd left Seattle sometime around nine or ten, which meant it had to be nearing two in the morning now, if not past.

As if on cue, my stomach let out a vociferous snarl.

The gorgeous bartender's stupidly perfect Cupid's bow lips quirked. "Hungry?"

I shrugged and tipped back the rocks glass. "A bit, yeah." I was fucking starved, actually, but I'd be damned if I'd admit it to him.

"I could use a bite myself," he said, slugging back the rest of his scotch as if it was nothing, "so I'll rustle something up. Won't be fancy, but it'll fill ya."

He ducked under the service bar and went into the kitchen, flicking on lights as he went. From my angle, I could see most of the kitchen, which gave me an opportunity to watch him while I worked on my second big ol' glass of tasty scotch.

He turned on the grill, the kind with a flat metal top used in short order restaurants, turned on a deep fryer, pulled out a tray of hand-shaped burger patties and tossed four of them onto the grill, then opened a freezer and poured a few handfuls of French fries into the now-crackling deep fryer. He did all this with casual familiarity, moving with grace and ease around the kitchen. He set the handle-press thingy onto the patties to flatten them and make them cook faster, tossed two buns onto the grill to toast them, then set up two platters with tomatoes, onions, lettuce, and a side of mayo, all done expertly and neatly, with an eye for presentation. A few more minutes and the fries were done, so he lifted the basket out to drain, flipped the burgers, and then shook salt onto the fries, shaking the basket so the salt distributed evenly.

Next came a cardboard Miller High Life six-pack holder filled with silverware rolls, ketchup, mustard, vinegar, and A-1. There were no wasted motions, no idle moments spent just waiting for the food to cook. He laid a slice of cheddar on each burger, and then a slice of pepper-jack, and then slid his spatula beneath two patties at a time and set them in a top-down heater to melt the cheese, which only took a few seconds, then he laid two patties each on a bun bottom, set the top bun on them at an angle, and then shook half the fries onto one plate and half onto the other.

He shut off the grill and fryer, wiped down all the surfaces he'd used, and carried both plates in one hand and the condiments in the other, and even managed to shut off the kitchen lights with his elbow. He set one plate in front of me and the other next to me then, leaning over the bar from the customer side, poured us each a pint of some local amber beer.

Fifteen minutes after I'd said I was hungry, I'd finished my quadruple scotch and had a thick, juicy double cheeseburger in front of me, complete with still-steaming golden-brown fries and a pint of cold beer.

I liked this guy.

Just, you know…not *too* much.

And then, after a liberal slathering of mayo, I sank my teeth into the burger…

The man was a short order *god*, I tell you.

"Oh my god," I said, still chewing, "this burger is fucking amazing. I'm sorry I called you an orc."

He finished a bite of his own and grinned at me. "Hey, I've been called worse. Glad you like it."

I'm not sure I even paused to breathe, after that.

The burger was the most incredible thing I'd ever tasted, which may have partially been due to extreme hunger on top of being hung over and on my way toward getting re-buzzed. But it was also just a damn good cheeseburger. I knew I'd have to find a gym at some point to work off the calories, but right then I didn't even remotely give a shit. Not even half a shit.

If I can't indulge without guilt on what was supposed to be my wedding night, which had turned into the worst night of my life, then when can I?

When I finished the burger, I got busy on the fries and the beer, finally willing myself to slow down and take a breath. Embarrassingly, I noticed the gorgeous tatted-up bear-dude wasn't even halfway through his burger, yet.

I stared at him, silently daring him to say something about my table manners.

He just popped a fry into his mouth and washed it down with beer. "Hey, don't look at me like that. A chick who can dig into a cheeseburger like that is all right in my book. Plus, if you don't mind me saying so, you look like you're sporting a wicked hangover, and nothing cures that like good, greasy bar food."

"I'm not sure if I'm still drunk, or drunk again," I admitted. "Both, probably. And yeah, the food is doing wonders for my mother of all bitch hangover headaches."

"Finish the beer and I'll pour you another. No sense wavering between hung over or drunk, right?"

"As long as you know somewhere I can crash when I need to pass out, then keep pouring them."

"Gotcha covered, angel," he said, a sly look on his face.

I shot him a glare. "Angel?" Then the smirk on his lips registered, and I shot to my feet, knocking the stool over, and got in his handsome, rugged face. "Listen here, motherfucker, if you think you're getting me out of this dress just 'cause you make a decent cheeseburger, you'd better think again. You do *not* want any of this, and it's not on offer, so back the fuck off."

He raised his hands and eyebrows. "Whoa, lady, chill. Not what I meant." He tipped his head to one side, that smirk on his face again. "I mean, yeah, I ain't gonna lie, I'd love to see you out of that dress. But it's obvious that you're drinking to forget, and I may be an asshole, but I'm not *that* asshole. There are a couple of hotels not too far from here. I can drop you off, if you want. 'Course, it's tourist season, and even in this shitty weather, I'm guessing they'll be mostly booked by this point. And I've been drinking, so driving may not be the best option."

I sat down, knowing I'd blown up a little prematurely, but I was not about to apologize for it. "So what are my options then?"

He stuck a finger up at the ceiling. "Three bedrooms up there, and I'm only using one. They've all got sturdy locks and their own bathrooms. If you need to crash and sleep your hangover off, you're welcome to one."

"Alone?"

He nodded. "Like I said, I'm not *that* big of an asshole. But you only get one free night."

"Then you start charging?"

"Then I start hitting on you." He grinned widely. "You're welcome to stay free as long as you want."

"But I'll have to deal with your slimy advances?"

He toyed with a fry, and his deep chocolate brown eyes fixed on mine, and good fucking grief, those eyes were deep, vivid, full of life and promise and heat. "Angel, there won't be nothin' slimy about it. Trust me on that." And damn me, but I believed him. Which was a problem. "'Course, those bedrooms are gonna get awful crowded awful soon."

I scrunched my nose in confusion. "What's that mean?"

He sighed, and tapped a stack of papers on the bar. "Means my dead little bar is about to be drowning in Badd brothers."

"I'm still not following."

He indicated the hand-carved wooden sign over

the mirror on the rear wall: Badd's Bar and Grill. "I'm Sebastian Badd. This is my bar, and I've got seven brothers all about to converge on this place." He said this with a wince like he wasn't entirely overjoyed at the prospect.

I choked. There were seven more like him? "Your brothers…do they all look like you?" I couldn't help asking. I really couldn't.

He shot me the smirk again. "I'm the oldest, and the sexiest. The rest are ugly fucking trolls and orcs and ogres of the worst sort. You'll hate 'em. Especially Zane, the next oldest. He's *real* ugly."

"You don't like your brothers?"

"Nah, I love 'em." He lifted a shoulder. "It's just complicated. They're my brothers, and I love 'em, but let's just say they're not going to be happy to be here. We're all big dudes and this is a small space, so it's gonna get…interesting."

The odd thing about this whole conversation was the unspoken assumption that I'd be around to meet them.

I finished the last of my fries and washed them down with the last of my beer, and then stood up—somewhat unsteadily, it must be admitted. I fumbled for my purse, and then remembered I'd given the pilot half of my cash. Which left me with six hundred dollars…and credit cards that were all maxed out paying for the wedding and the honeymoon and my dress. Dad had helped, and Michael had put money in for the honeymoon too, and had paid for the catering, but I'd fronted the bulk of the bills. I had some savings, but it wouldn't last me forever.

Since I had limited cash, I dug out the only credit card I had that still had a little room left on it, and extended it to him. "Here, put it all on this."

He just eyed me, amused. "Not takin' your money, angel. It's on the house."

"I don't want your charity, and I'm not sleeping with you."

He stood up and moved to stand over me. God, he was tall. And those eyes of his bored into me, intense, fierce, primal. "It's not charity, and I'm not trying to get under that sexy fuckin' dress of yours."

"Kind of feels like you're trying," I said.

He sidled closer, so close I could feel his body heat, smell his masculine scent, so close I had to stare up at him, and my heart thundered in my chest at his proximity. "Honey, if I was tryin', you'd know, because you'd be naked and screaming my name. I'd have you on that bar, those creamy thighs of yours spread open and my tongue on your clit."

Well. Shit.

I squirmed, ached, and then remembered my anger.

"Fuck you, you goddamn orc." I turned away, shoving my credit card back into my purse and stomped out of the bar and into the rain.

I stumbled, my heel catching on something, sending me to the ground on my hands and knees. Mud splashed up, soaking my dress, my face, my hands. So much for a dramatic exit. I looked up and saw the rest of Ketchikan, mostly dark, with something huge and dark and bulky in the distance. Everything looked so far away, and I had no idea where any of the hotels were. I'd only found the bar because it was the only place with lights on close to where the pilot had dropped me off.

And now I was wetter than I'd ever been, drunk again, covered in mud, and fighting tears.

I sat down in the mud, tried to wipe it off my face with my hands, but my hands were covered in mud, and—

I'd promised myself the breakdown I'd had in the truck back in Seattle was the only one I'd allow myself, but apparently I'd lied to myself.

Because I was crying again.

Hard.

But now I was alone in the mud, sitting in the rain, with no Dad to comfort me.

Why had I run away?

What had I been thinking?

No job—I'd quit my job at the law firm I clerked at since they wouldn't give me enough time off for my honeymoon, and I'd had plenty of other offers in my field. I'd been confident I'd be able to find a new job when I got back, and had even sent out my resume to a few likely places. Except now I was in Ketchikan, Alaska with four maxed-out credit cards, limited savings, no job, no car, no family except Dad, no return flight available till who knew when, even if I could afford it and, oh yeah, my fiancé had been fucking my bridesmaid minutes before I was supposed to walk down the aisle to him.

I gave in and let myself sob.

And then I heard his footsteps in the mud, glanced over to see his massive boots squishing though the mud, faded jeans dappled by the rain, and then he was kneeling beside me, hair dampening with every passing second, but he seemed not to care. He reached out a big paw, wiped the mud off of my face and wiped it on his jeans. He wasn't smiling, but there was something awfully like compassion on his face, which only made me even more unreasonably angry.

"Leave me alone," I said. "I don't need your help."

"Too bad," he said, sliding his arms around me and lifting me effortlessly, "because you're getting it, like it or not, want it or not."

"Put me down, you orc."

He was too close, and I was full-on drunk again, and I hated him because he was fucking gorgeous and he could cook and he poured scotch with a heavy hand and he was gorgeous—did I already say that?—and he had tattoos and I'd always had a secret thing for tattoos, and he could pick me up easily, even though I'm not really dainty. I'm not, like, *big*, but I'm not small either.

He carried me easily across the muddy street, through a doorway, and up a set of stairs.

He kicked open a door, flicked on a light somehow, and then set me on my feet. We were in a bedroom, but that was all I could manage to make out through the onset of double vision.

"Can you manage from here?"

I nodded sloppily. "Sure, sure. No problem. Just gonna go to sleep."

He caught me before I fell over. "Angel, you're soaked, covered in mud, and wasted. You can't just go to sleep."

"Sure I can."

I wobbled, because with every passing second, the food, the scotch, the beer, and the exhaustion and the heartache were all catching up to me, and pulling me under. I couldn't stop it and I didn't care about anything but being warm and dry and horizontal, which were the direct opposites of everything I was at that moment.

"Goddamn it," I heard him murmur under his breath, and then I felt him guide me with his big hard warm hands on my waist toward the multiple darkened doorways spinning in kaleidoscope circles that I assumed was the bathroom.

The lights went on, and I heard a shower start. I was sleepy. So sleepy, and so drunk. And so heartbroken. It hurt, goddamn it...it *hurt*.

Then he was in front of me. "Hey, stay with me, angel."

"My name is *Dru*, handsome orc-man. Dru. D-R-U. Dru."

"Okay, got it. Dru." His face wove and spun in front of me. "You desperately need to shower. You're gonna catch a cold. But you're also completely shitfaced."

"Yes. Yes I am. I am very, very shitfaced. Thank you for that, by the way."

"No problem. Glad I could help." He held me by the shoulders to keep me upright. "But I need you to pay attention to me, okay?"

I nodded, sort of. "'Kay. What's up, buttercup?"

"I'm going to help you get undressed, and I'm going to help you shower, because there's nobody else."

"The fuck you are." I managed to work up a good glare. "You just want to get your sexy paws on me."

I caught his grin before my ability to focus on him went to shit. "Absolutely I do. When you're sober, and in your right frame of mind. Right now, I'm exercising my gentleman manners, which are pretty fuckin' rusty, I must admit. I won't be copping any feels, but I will be taking a few good looks as payment, all right?"

I tried to stare at him, to get his measure, but shit, I was absolutely plastered and couldn't even manage to make out one of him, let alone decide whether or not I was going to wake up with a sore pussy from being taken advantage of while drunk. Somehow, though, I didn't get that feeling from him. I was being stupid, and I knew it, but I was drunk enough not to care. If I was going to get taken advantage of while hammered, at least he was hot. Hopefully I'd remember some of it, and hopefully it'd be good.

"Whatever. Just make it good, okay?"

He moved around behind me without letting go of me and fumbled with the hidden zipper of my dress. "Make what good?"

"When you take advantage of my drunk ass."

He had my zipper open to mid-back, paused, and spun me around. Roughly, harshly, and good thing he had a strong grip on me because I would've gone down otherwise, and I don't mean on him, I mean to the floor—Dru go boom.

He was angry. "Listen, Dru. I know I'm just a

tatted-up bartender from the ass-end of nowhere, and I get I'm kinda rough lookin'. But I *have* never and *will* never take advantage of a drunk chick. Got it? You got nothin' to fear from me. Your virtue is safe as houses, all right?"

I cackled. "Virtue? That's rich. I lost my virtue to Jimmy Irvin in the back of his pickup after freshman prom." I saw, even through my drunken and spinning haze, that he wasn't amused. "Sorry. You said your name is Sebastian, right?"

He turned me back around—gently this time—and finished undoing my zipper. "Yeah, my name is Sebastian."

Now that I was unzipped all the way, I felt free, finally. "Jesus, that thing was tight." I experimented, taking deep lungfuls of oxygen, reveling in the freedom to fully expand my lungs for the first time in god knows how many hours. "Look, I'm sorry I offended you. But put yourself in my position for a second. *You* know you're a good dude who won't take advantage of sloppy drunk heartbroken should-have-been brides, but *I* don't know that."

He was watching me in the mirror, I could tell, and his eyes were glued to my tits with every breath I took. I wasn't wearing a bra. I was wearing panties, but they weren't much more than scraps of lace that could barely be called a thong.

My heart was pounding in my chest, and other parts of me were sitting up and taking notice of the fact that I was in a bathroom, my dress unzipped, tits one big breath from spilling free, and the man standing behind me was the drop-dead sexiest man I'd ever seen. And he was, even to my boozy, fatigued observational skills, attracted to me.

But I couldn't stand up straight without his help, couldn't even see straight. If he let go of me, I'd topple sideways, probably whack my head on the counter and would need stitches, and god only knew what kind of medical facilities they had in this town I was in, which, I suddenly remembered, I knew absolutely nothing about. I didn't even know, geographically, where in Alaska I was.

Sebastian's hands touched my shoulders. "Dru? You gonna puke?"

I shook my head. "No, no. Just…it's been a really long day and it's all sort of catching up to me."

"Gonna cry again? 'Cause I'm not sure how to handle that shit."

"No. I just…I need a shower." I met his eyes in the mirror, or tried to. All I managed was to look sort of in his general direction or, at least, in the direction of the two or three of him that were rotating in front of me.

"You got it?"

I pushed myself upright, kept one hand on the counter, and tried to wiggle out of the dress. But considering it had taken all three of my bridesmaids almost an hour to get me into it, my chances of getting out of it alone while wasted were…well…not great.

"Shit," I mumbled. "You're gonna have to help me. But if you touch my tits, I'll punch you. And Sebastian?" I glared in his direction best I could. "Trust me when I say you don't want me to punch you. I'm Irish, and I'm the daughter of a Marine Corps drill instructor. I can lay you out, okay?"

He seemed impressed, or at least, that's what my admittedly compromised ability to read facial expressions informed me. "I'll be on my best behavior, I swear."

This was a fucked up situation.

But I'd gotten myself into this mess, and Dad had taught me to always accept responsibility for my actions, and to just take what came best I could and deal with shit without flinching.

*Do what you gotta do, and deal with the emotions of it later*, Dad always said.

Do what I gotta do.

I put both hands on the counter, steadied myself, and looked at him in the mirror. "Help me out of this stupid dress, Sebastian."

# FOUR

## Sebastian

Fuck, fuck, fuck, fuck, fuck.

This was bad. I mean, it was goddamned amazing, but…it was bad. This girl was barely holding it together. I wasn't about to ask what had happened, but it hadn't been good. The way she'd just…broken down…out in the street—it put a fire in my belly, man. Pissed me the fuck off. Who could do something to a girl like that bad enough to make her break that way? She struck me as strong, tough, a take-no-shit sort of girl. She didn't break easy. But out there in the mud? She just shattered. Alone. Broken-hearted. And

I guess I was a sucker, because I couldn't leave her out there. It was obvious she was in no condition to be left alone, and I'd fed her the scotch, which meant she was my problem now.

And now here she was, sexy as fuck, covered in mud, obliterated, fighting another breakdown, so exhausted she had circles under her eyes, and fuck, so goddamn beautiful. Wet, muddy, straggly auburn-red hair sticking to her face and her bare shoulders, that sexy-as-sin wedding dress all splattered with mud and drooping under her big, lush, cream and ivory tits, her nipples and areolae playing peek-a-boo, hips like fuckin' magnets for my hands, and her ass—Jesus Christ, that ass. Round, full, juicy as a peach. But she was a fuckin' wreck. I couldn't do a damn thing. Couldn't touch. Couldn't put my lips to that creamy skin of hers, couldn't kiss away her heartbreak, couldn't fuck her so good, so hard, for so long she'd forget the name of whatever asshole had shredded her heart.

I had to be a gentleman.

And that wasn't me.

I drank, I fucked, and I tended bar. I didn't do the gentleman shit. The women who came through the bar were looking for one thing, just like me. A quick, simple, easy bang. No strings, no emotions, just bodily release and feeling good for a while. I didn't have to bother caring what they liked or thought or felt. I could read their body's reaction to what I was doing like a book, and I got them off, and they went back to their vacation, feeling dirty for having slummed it with the local bartender.

This chick wasn't like that.

She was class. The dress had to be worth a mint, just like the shoes she'd left on the floor of my bar and that purse on the floor of the bedroom. But it wasn't the money. She was no rich bitch; I could smell those, and I'd fucked plenty of 'em. She was just...*class*. She didn't fuck randoms. She didn't do hookups.

Whatthefuck was I thinking? I couldn't fuck this girl. No way, no how, never. She wasn't meant for me. I had to tame the beast in my pants, get her clean, and let her pass the hell out.

Internal scolding finished, I steeled myself, summoned all the self-control I possessed, and set to work helping the sexiest woman I'd ever seen out of her wedding dress...knowing I wouldn't be setting a finger on a single inch of her perfect fuckin' skin.

I had to tug pretty hard to get the gown down past her chest and, Jesus, every time I tugged, I bared more of her tits, which not only were big, but were all natural, bouncing like fuckin' Jell-O every time I tugged. I felt my cock hardening in my jeans, and did my best to ignore it. A few more tugs, and the dress was at her hips, and then past them, and then finally she was standing there in front of me in nothing but a white strip of lace around her hips. Bare-ass, the white string disappearing between those sweet, lush, juicy cheeks. I could see her in the mirror and—Christ, the thong didn't cover much in front either. I mean, for real, it didn't cover shit. Her pussy was straight up eating that skimpy little thong like a last meal, and if I didn't have a hard-on already, I sprung hard as goddamned steel at the sight of those plump pussy lips sticking to damp white silk. Yeah, she was wet. Not just from the rain and mud, either. She was staring at me in the mirror, those ridiculous blue eyes wobbling and focusing and wavering, but fixed on me with unreadable thoughts and emotions ripping across her features and blazing in her eyes.

Fuck me.

I had to let go of her, had to clench my hands into fists and close my eyes and think about that time a delivery truck hit a puppy.

Naked old nuns.

Naked old *priests*.

Cold, wriggling fish.

Worms in the dirt.

When I opened my eyes, she was still staring at me in the mirror. But now I was looking, and her tits were on full display in the mirror, big, round, high, perfect, with dark silver-dollar size areolae and thick, plump, erect pink nipples, and any work I'd done to push down my erection was totally undone.

And she was just *looking* at me, and I swear to fuck she was thinking she wouldn't mind if I copped a touch, if my self-control slipped a little.

"Quit fuckin' lookin' at me like that, Dru, swear to Christ." My growl was the deepest, snarliest sound I think I'd ever made.

"Like what?"

"I dunno. Whatever you're thinkin', lookin' at me like that, you best quit." I tugged aside the shower curtain, adjusted the water mix so it wasn't too hot or cold, and then grabbed her wrist in my hand. "Get in, angel."

She stepped in, fumbled for the knob to add more hot water, and then glanced at me, steadying herself against the wall. "I'm still wearing my underwear."

I ground my teeth, spoke through clenched molars, because now she was in my shower, all but naked, water sluicing down her skin, pasting her hair to her scalp and shoulders, and I was fighting every instinct I had, which was to climb in there with her and scrub her clean just so I could get her all dirty again.

I couldn't help the pissed off glare I gave her. "Well pardon me, but there's no way in fuckin' hell I'm taking that off you. This is taking all my self-control as it is. So you'll just have to shower in that fuckin' thong, because I ain't helping you out of it."

"Oh." She ducked her head back under the spray, rinsing her hair, then wiped her face and peered around the shower. "Shampoo?"

I snagged a bottle from under the sink and handed it to her.

She lathered her hair, occasionally steadying herself against the wall with one hand, or grabbing at me with the other. I was getting soaked by the spray, as was the floor but, fuck it, I didn't care. Not then. Watching her shower? God, I was the luckiest bastard in the whole fucking world, and the most cursed: treated to the sight of her nude body, all that perfect skin, all those goddamn perfect curves, watching droplets of water slide down her breasts and between her thighs...*fuck*—but I was cursed, because I couldn't touch.

And then she glanced at me, considering, thinking. She steadied herself with a hand on the wall, hooked her thumb into the lace of her thong, and worked it down around her hips, then slid her thighs together and wiggled her hips to shimmy it down to her knees, and then it was off and at her feet. She bent to grab it, went off balance, and I had to grab her shoulders to keep her upright, which meant I got blasted by the scalding hot water, and I had my hands on her naked wet skin, and now she was inches away from me, water running down her face and her eyes were wide and blue and frightened and aroused and full of sadness.

But she had her thong in her hand.

And, in that moment, her eyes on mine, her thoughts and feelings running clear as day across her face and in her eyes, her naked wet body pressed up against mine...

She set her soaked thong on top of my head, and giggled.

It dripped hot water into my hair and down my face and onto the back of my neck. I snagged it off my head, wrung it out, and backed away from her. I had to.

That giggle.

Motherfucker, that giggle.

Sweet, innocent, playful, sexy, breathy.

If I could make her giggle like that in bed, tickle her, tease her with my tongue until those erotic little giggles turned to moans, which would turn to begging, which would turn to screams of orgasm as I swept my tongue against her clit, tasting the sugar of her pussy...

I started for her, reached for her, fully intending to toss her onto the bed and make her beg for my cock in that musical voice of hers...

I got so far as to rest my palm on her hip, and then my fingers curled against her skin, and her eyes fixed on mine, and she wavered, fell back against the shower wall, breathing hard, tits rising and falling with each gasping breath, and fuck, fuck, *fuck*, her thighs were shaking, and I swear to Christ I could smell the desire from her pussy through the steam of the scorching hot water, and she was reaching for me too, but she still had one hand on the wall to keep herself from toppling over, and—

Shit.

You're a fucking bastard, Sebastian Badd.

I spun away from her before I did anything we'd both regret, but I was so pissed at myself, at her, at the asshole who'd broken her heart...so fucking pissed. Adrenaline coursed through me as I ripped myself away from her.

I lashed out, smashed my fist against the door frame as hard as I could, splintering it so thoroughly chunks of molding split off and hit the floor.

"Jesus, Sebastian! What the fuck!" She was shocked, scared.

I kept my eyes off her, grabbed a towel from under the sink and set it on the counter. "I can't do this. Sorry. Try not to pass out and break your fuckin' head open."

I left the bathroom, closed the bedroom door

behind me, and then put my back to it, clutching at my hair with both hands. My fist throbbed like a bitch, but I didn't care.

I listened to the shower going for so long I thought she'd for sure passed out in there, but eventually the water shut off and then I heard the bed springs squeak as she hit the bed.

"Sebastian?" I heard her voice beyond the door, muzzy, slurred.

"Yeah."

"Need a trashcan. In case I puke."

"Got it." I fetched a trashcan from one of the other bathrooms, and then knocked on her door. "You covered?"

"Mostly."

I opened the door and moved beside the bed. She was diagonal across the mattress, facing the foot end, and by 'mostly' covered, she meant she had the towel wrapped around her waist to cover most of her ass, and she was lying on her stomach with her head over the side of the bed.

"The dress is all you got with you, I'm guessing?"

She nodded. "Yep. And a pair of heels. And my purse, and my broken heart. But no clothes."

"I'll get you a shirt to sleep in, then."

I brought one of my old, faded Badd's Bar and Grill shirts, from back when Badd's was a relatively high-draw tourist attraction rather than a run-down one-man operation. It was soft, the logo so faded you could barely read it. I touched her shoulder gently, and then sat down near her head.

"Can you sit up?"

She shook her head sloppily. "Nope. No can do, Mister Sebastian sir. I'm all drunked out. All done. Bye-bye."

"Awesome. Well, work with me, here. I'm gonna get this shirt on you, okay?"

"Okay."

I held her by the shoulders, helped her roll onto her back, then lifted her to a sitting position, and somehow managed to make sure the towel stayed in place over her chest in the process. I tugged it over her head, and tried to help her get her arms through, but she got lost or confused or something, and I couldn't figure out which arm I had and she couldn't figure out where it was going, and she got all tangled up, her head halfway through the opening, one arm in the wrong sleeve, the other fumbling behind her.

"Waitwaitwait." She whacked at me with both hands. "Stop, you stupid gorgeous orc man. I can do it."

I let go of her, trying not to laugh and failing badly.

"Stop laughing at me!"

"I'm sorry, it's just funny. You're funny, but it's a cute funny."

She finally got the shirt sorted out and got it down in place, and then gave me a sad, sorrowful look. "I'm not supposed to be *cute*. I'm supposed to be *sexy*," she said, her voice plaintive and mournful. "I'm supposed to be *married*. I'm supposed to be *married* right now! It was supposed to be Michael taking my dress off. I should have his cock inside me right now, but instead I'm here, drunk out of my mind, heart-broken, and wishing it was you with your cock inside me instead, and I don't even *care*, because Michael is an ASSHOLE!" She shouted the last word so loudly I flinched.

I had to force myself to ignore the one phrase out of everything she said that really registered…take a wild guess which. I palmed her cheek gently. "You are sexy, Dru. And I'm sorry your fuckhead ex-fiancé broke your heart. He's the worst kind of asshole in the whole world, and you're better off without him."

She giggled at me again. "Wanna know why Michael is an asshole?"

"He stood you up?"

She shook her head side to side in a sloppy, wide, exaggerated gesture. "Noooooope. He was fucking my bridesmaid right before the goddamn wedding. And her name was *Tawny*! Who the fuck names their kid Tawny? Did her parents *want* her to be a slut? Because that's how you get a slut. And she's a slut. I mean, I'm sure there are nice, normal, non-slutty girls out there named sorry—I mean...Tawny—shit. What I meant was, sorry to all the non-slut girls named Tawny in the world for assuming they're all sluts. But *she's* a slut. She fucked my fiancé on *my* wedding day! Who does that? Tawny does that, because she's a slut! Fuck you, Tawny, you fucking slut."

She stared at me, eyes swimming dizzily, and then grinned as if there was a joke I'd missed. "Did you hear what else I said? I said I wanted your cock inside me, and not Michael's. I bet you have a *huuuuuuuuge* cock, the hugest, the biggest, most beautiful cock ever, right? You do, I just know you do. And if I wasn't totally wasted and supposed to be *married* RIGHT NOW, I'd be fucking you so hard you don't even know. You—don't—even—*know*!" She jabbed her index finger into my chest. "Did you get all that?"

I sighed, struggling with myself. "Yes, Dru, I got all that."

"Well?"

I frowned. "Well what?"

"Do you?"

"Do I what?"

She pointed at my crotch. "Have the hugest cock I've ever seen."

I wanted so fucking bad to show her what I had, because despite the situation, I was so hard it hurt. "Never had any complaints. But for now, I think you need to go to sleep."

"Alone."

I nodded. "Yes, alone."

"Good." She flopped backward onto the pillows, and I tugged the blankets out from beneath her and covered her with them. I was on my way toward the door when her sweet, sleepy voice stopped me. "Know what sucks, Sebastian?"

"What's that?"

"You'll remember this whole thing tomorrow, and I won't." She tried to point at me, but missed, and hit the bed beside her instead. "Or, at least, I hope I don't remember this tomorrow. I hope you don't either, 'cause I'm a fucking mess. I hope I wake up with amnesia. Can you give me amnesia?"

"No. And even if I could, I wouldn't."

"Why not? I don't wanna remember this. None of it."

"Because forgetting is a cop-out, angel, and you're stronger than that."

"How do you know?"

I flicked off the lights, hearing her fading. "I can just tell. Now sleep. You're safe here."

"That's cause you're an orc, and nobody fucks

with orcs. Except you're a sexy orc. A damn sexy orc."

Shit was getting seriously interesting.

I left her snoring, a trashcan on the floor near to hand, and went to my bedroom.

I locked my door. Locked my bathroom door, stripped naked, turned on the shower, and told myself to stop thinking about her.

But it was futile.

I got into the shower and fought it as I washed my hair. I fought it as I scrubbed soap over my skin.

She was all I could see. All I could smell. All I could feel. I could picture every inch of her naked, wet body, and I could almost feel her pussy tight and wet and warm sliding around my cock as I pushed into her, could almost hear that sexy playful giggle as I teased her—shit, *shit*...she'd be so wet for me, she'd feel like—god, like nothing I had ever felt before. I just *knew* fucking her would feel like nothing I'd ever felt before. The way she'd move under me, on top of me, the way she'd whimper and moan and beg for me to fuck her harder...

My cock throbbed in my fist as I jerked myself thinking about Dru, picturing her wet skin against mine, her slick pussy swallowing every inch of my cock, which I knew for a fact would be the longest, thickest, hardest cock she'd ever had inside her, and I'd fuck her until we both went crazy with it—

I came so hard I thought I'd go blind, emptying my balls in gush after gush, until I went limp and had to brace against the far wall to stay upright.

I was a fucking bastard.

Because I knew I'd jerk off to Dru again, and frequently.

I just couldn't touch her.

You don't fuck the heartbroken ones: they cling, and I don't do clingy.

Not ever, but especially not with my seven brothers about to descend upon me.

Which raised one very pressing question: Where the *hell* were all eight of us going to sleep? We hadn't really fit four to a room back when we were kids; we were all big men who took up a lot of space now, and these rooms, while not tiny, were definitely *not* going to fit eight grown men, even if I *did* give up having a room to myself, which I wasn't super excited about. Shit, none of us would be.

What the *fuck*, Dad? I'd have help at the bar, sure…but still. What the fuck?

# FIVE

## Dru

I WOKE UP TO A POUNDING HEADACHE AND A MOUTH SO parched I thought I'd swallowed sand.

What the fuck—where was I? What happened?

I couldn't remember anything, at first. Which was a mercy, of sorts.

I tried to fall back asleep, but, as a rule, once I was awake I was up for good, no matter how exhausted or still drunk or hung over I was.

The bed underneath me didn't feel right—it wasn't *my* bed. It was too firm, and the sheets felt wrong, and the blankets smelled wrong, and the pillow was too thick and it smelled wrong. I wrenched my eyes open, stared at the ceiling for a few minutes, which was a mistake, since it was further evidence I wasn't at home. This ceiling was flat white drywall with no molding to hide the corners. My ceiling at home in Seattle was much higher and was industrial chic, black painted metal rafters meeting exposed brick walls.

I turned over to the side, and saw two minor miracles: a litre bottle of water, and two aspirin. Also, there was a note.

Masculine handwriting, sloppily and quickly scrawled, but legible:

*Dru,*

*Bet you're feeling like shit about now. Drink the whole bottle of water and take the aspirin, and then come downstairs. I'll make you some breakfast.*

*Just so you know, one of my brothers is here, and he's the ugliest motherfucker you've ever seen, so be warned. He's also a major douche-tard, so don't expect manners from him, as he's spent the last few years pretending he's a badass. His name is Zane, and if you ignore him long enough, he'll go away. Unlike me.*

*Couple other quick things: I have a buddy in town who owns a dry-cleaning business, so he's got your dress to see if he can work some magic on those mud stains. Second, I have another friend who owns a second-hand clothing shop, so she brought you some clothes. I got no fucking clue what size you are, so I told her what size your dress is and she guessed from there. Hope they fit.*

*Lastly, I seem to have developed an odd case of amnesia regarding last night. Too much Johnny, probably. So don't feel weird, since neither of us remembers shit about shit.*

*Sebastian*

*PS: you're fucking adorable when you sleep. You snore.*

Fuck.

*Fuck.*

FUCK.

***FUCK!***

I remembered everything. All at once, like a freight train of heartache and embarrassment.

The video on Eric's phone of Michael drilling Tawny from behind in the dressing room, minutes before he was supposed to say "I do" to me.

Getting obliterated with Dad's cop buddies.

Literally jumping on the first airplane going anywhere, and offering the pilot all my cash to take me wherever he was going.

Which turned out to be somewhere called Ketchikan, Alaska.

Stumbling half-drunk, half hung over, and all

pissed off into some shitty dive bar on the docks, and getting wasted all over again with the sexiest mother-fucker I'd ever laid eyes on.

Who had poured me scotch.

Fed me delicious food.

Carried me out of the mud.

Undressed me.

Put me in the shower.

Put me in bed.

And hadn't taken advantage of me.

Even though I had told him, I was pretty sure, that he probably had the hugest cock and that I wanted it inside me.

And then—*and then*…he'd left me water and aspirin and a cute note.

And gotten my dress dry-cleaned.

And provided real clothing for me.

And was going to make me breakfast.

It was probably the hangover, but I could have cried at the thoughtfulness and care he'd shown me.

I worked on sitting up, which took a few minutes because moving was hard, and being awake was hard, and being alive was hard and *everything* hurt like hell, but most especially my head and my heart ached in different but equally excruciating ways. I twisted the top off the water, took four huge slugs of the still-cold water, and then chased the aspirin down with more water. Then finally took a good look around me. The room was spare, sparse. The bed I was on was nothing but a mattress and box spring on a frame, no headboard or footboard. Plain white sheets and a thick gray quilt. There really wasn't anything else in the room except a side table on my left, which had the water on it, the note, and my phone, with my charger cord connected to a wall plug. He'd even plugged in my phone.

There was a window, so I gingerly stood up and walked stiffly across the small room and looked out.

Jesus.

Ketchikan was *gorgeous*. The view from the window showed docks extending along the shoreline with boats of all kinds moored to them, and then the sea rippling with whitecaps and dotted with sails and fishing boats and a massive cruise liner off in the distance approaching the shore. Then farther to the left side of my view the hills were carpeted in green trees, a leaden gray sky above, and colorful houses climbing up into the hills, and a mountain off in the distance, white-capped.

I'd picked a beautiful spot to run away to, that was for sure.

I turned away from the view and noticed a pile of clothing on the foot of the bed: a pair of jeans, a pair of black yoga pants, two V-neck T-shirts—one black and one white—a hooded sweatshirt, a thick ca-ble-knit sweater, an unopened three-pack of plain cotton underwear, a sports bra, two pair of thick wool socks, and a used but expensive-looking pair of hiking boots.

My throat felt thick and hot, for some stupid reason.

It was just clothing.

But...he'd thought of *everything*. Even a bra and underwear, and had made sure the underwear weren't second-hand. The bra, too, still had the tag on it, which had been scribbled over with a sharpie and a second-hand price handwritten on the back. I put on the underwear and the bra, both of which fit, although the bra was a little small. The jeans were exactly my size, so I put on those along with a T-shirt and the hoodie and, let me just say, being dressed in warm, clean clothing felt like a luxury after the events of the day before.

My hair was a disaster, though. I discovered that after peeking into the bathroom. I finger combed it out as best I could, which didn't do much for the tangles, but at least now it was *kind of* less fucked. I turned to leave the bathroom, and that was when I saw the damaged doorframe, and had a mental flashback.

He'd reached for me, as if his self-control had finally fizzled out, had his hand on my naked hip, and

I remembered feeling his hand being so warm and strong, cupping the generous curve of my hip like his hand was made to mold to my curves, and then he'd spun around and punched the doorframe so hard the molding had splintered, his fist leaving a crushed indent in the wood and plaster.

Shit, the man could hit *hard*.

I was delaying, I realized.

I had to leave the relative sanctuary of this room, had to go downstairs and face Sebastian and his supposedly ugly douchetard brother.

Enough of the sissy shit. It was time to woman up.

So I tugged the hood over my head, pocketed my phone, twisted open the doorknob, and left the room. There were two other bedrooms in the hallway, both doors closed, the hallway opening into an expansive great room. The kitchen area was separated from the living room by an island counter with stools on the living room side, and the sitting area featured two overstuffed armchairs, a mismatched leather couch and loveseat, a battered coffee table, and a small flat screen TV mounted on the wall opposite the couch. Windows let in natural light, and revealed breathtaking views of the harbor and the green hills.

Nothing expensive, nothing fancy, but comfortable, cozy, homey.

At the other end of the hallway from the great room was a doorway, which I assumed led downstairs. The great room was empty, so I assumed Sebastian and his brother were downstairs. Heart thudding, I descended the narrow staircase, pushed through the door at the bottom, emerged inside the bar next to the kitchen—

And into a tense, frozen tableau.

Sebastian was wearing a pair of faded, ripped blue jeans and a plain white V-neck T-shirt, which was in no way equal to the task of containing his muscular bulk or hiding his tattoos. I could actually see a lot more of the tats now that he was wearing a short-sleeved shirt, the sleeves of which stopped just above the bulge of his biceps and looked to be so stretched I was worried the stitching was going to pop. It was also stretched across his shoulders and chest, high-lighting the breadth and width of his torso, and then draped down to cling to his slim waist.

He was also barefoot and, holy mother of fuck, what was it about a man who was barefoot in blue jeans? So cliché, I know, but shit, it was *so* goddamn hot.

The tats, though. I actually licked my lips, look-ing at them. Each image was distinct yet bled and merged with the others on each arm, extending across the back of his shoulders and down each arm. There were a lot of totems, animals, skulls, playing cards, pop culture images twisted somehow into a whole menagerie of images with their own stories.

Facing Sebastian was another man, this one a little shorter than Sebastian by maybe three or four inches, making him about six feet to Sebastian's six-four, but *Jeeeeesus* and holy hell, the man was *built*. I mean Sebastian was ripped, but this man...god, he was on a whole other level of massive. He had the same essential build—broad shoulders, a wide chest, tapered waist—but this other man took the image and ran wild with it. Arms thicker even than Sebastian's, nearly as thick as my thighs, a chest you could use as an anvil, the man was just...*insanely* muscled. Yet it still wasn't bodybuilder bulk...he was lean, hard. Everything about him just screamed *DANGER*. His head was shaved to the scalp on the sides and had only a thin scruff of brown fuzz on top. He had only one tattoo that I could see, a screaming eagle on his left biceps, the eagle clutching a trident in one talon and a flintlock pistol in the other, with an anchor super-imposed in front of it. I recognized the logo, but it took me a minute to put it together; Sebastian's note had said his brother Zane had spent the last few years "pretending to be a badass." The logo was that of the US Navy SEALs.

Damn. Probably not "pretending" to be a badass

then, I'd guess.

Sebastian had also said Zane would be the "ugliest motherfucker" I'd ever seen, yet, powerhouse warrior's physique aside, Zane was every bit as sexy as Sebastian. Craggy cliff-side jawline, deep-set dark eyes, high cheekbones, a wide expressive mouth... Yeah, Zane Badd was fucking hot as hell. But where Sebastian was hard, gruff, and rough looking yet with an intoxicating patina of warmth and charisma, Zane just looked...scary. His eyes were cold, dark, wild. Sebastian had that same wildness in his gaze, but Zane's eyes were just flat out *icy*. The man had seen and done some truly hellish things in his life, and it bled into his overall aura.

Neither man had seen me yet. They were standing face to face in the middle of the bar, a few scant inches between their massive chests, eyes blazing, fists clenched; they were both *pissed*. Close to blows, it looked like, to me.

"I had no fuckin' clue Dad was gonna put any of that shit in his will, Zane! How the fuck could I? I didn't even know he *had* a goddamn will, much less that he'd been having heart trouble. He just up and died, in the middle of a shift. He was dead before he hit the fuckin' floor, and I didn't hear shit about the will until yesterday. So don't come barging in here acting like I knew something you didn't."

"That rat of a lawyer faxed me a copy of the will, Bast. You got ten grand none of us got. Explain that shit, then."

Sebastian seemed to be seconds from blowing his top and attacking his brother. Who, from the looks of it, was every bit as close to going in after Sebastian in turn. And given the absurd size and power of both men, I wasn't sure this bar would survive if they started fighting.

But what was I going to do? I was half their size, didn't know either of them, and was intruding on a clearly personal argument.

"If you saw the will, and if you saw I got that ten grand—which I haven't seen a fuckin' dime of, by the way—then you saw what Dad said in his will. Because I was always the one to step in around here. I took over the kitchen when Mom died. I took over the paperwork so Dad could semi-retire. *I* ran this place, Zane. *Me.* All of you guys ran off to chase your dreams and I stayed here to run the bar with Dad. Nobody even asked if that's what I wanted. So then Dad gave me a few extra bucks as a *minor reward* or some shit, and you've got the balls to act jealous? Fuck...*you.*"

Sebastian punctuated the last word with a hard shove, sending his brother stepping backward a couple steps.

And Zane? Well...he didn't take it well. Obviously.

His fist flew, cracked against Sebastian's jaw and twisted him sideways.

And then it was on, both men rushing at each other, spitting curses and swinging fists.

I had to stop it.

It wasn't even a conscious thing, honestly, I just reacted. From the time I was two years old, Dad had taught me martial arts. Every morning before dawn we ran through the katas, and once a week I went with Dad to his gym to spar. I never really cared about belts or anything, because I did it for Dad more than anything, but I'd passed the second-degree black belt test, on Dad's insistence.

So I knew I could handle myself, and jumping in to stop a fight was just second nature. I had the skills, so I was obliged to use them when necessary in the defense of others—another lesson Dad had impressed on me, growing up.

So when the fists started flying, I went in.

I blocked Sebastian's right cross and redirected his momentum aside, sending him stumbling, and then spun to face Zane, who already had his own punch rocketing toward where Sebastian had been— and where I now was. I twisted to dodge it, stepped inside Zane's reach, caught his off-hand and twisted against the joint in a wrist-lock.

The plan had been to spin him around and shove

him away to separate the brothers, but I underestimated the snake-fast speed of Zane's instinctive reaction to the wrist-lock. The man was a Navy SEAL for fuck's sake...what had I expected? He simply accepted the pain of the wrist-lock and slammed the heel of his palm into my chest, right against my diaphragm. Knocked the wind out of me, sent me stumbling, gasping for breath. It wasn't a hard hit, and had been instinctive, the result of hundreds of hours of practice.

Before I could react, he had his fingers around my throat, cutting off my breath and lifting me clear off the floor a solid inch. "Who the fuck is this bitch, Bast?"

Of course, my training had obviously covered how to counter a hand around the throat, and I wasn't about to be choked out or intimidated, SEAL or not. I grabbed his hand in both of mine, twisted to break his grip, wrenched his arm around behind his back, spinning him in place, and then brought my knee up between his legs as hard as I could.

Which dropped his big soldier ass to the floor, post-haste.

I crouched beside Zane, who was writhing on the floor in agony. "My name is Dru Connolly. And if you ever call me a bitch again, I'll rip your fucking balls off, do you understand me?"

He nodded, cupping his balls with both hands, struggling for breath.

I felt two hands grab my shoulders and pull me away. My first instinct was to start breaking bones, but then I realized it was Sebastian, so I let him pull me a few feet backward.

I twisted in place and stared up at him. "You said your brother was ugly, not that he was a complete asshole."

Sebastian's lips quirked. "I think I also said not to expect much by way of manners from him."

"True." I noticed then that Sebastian's lip was split, and he was trickling blood from his nose. "You're hurt. Come here."

Another instinctive reaction, happening without conscious thought. I pulled him over to the bar and sat him down in a chair. There was a clean white towel sitting on the bar, folded in quarters; I grabbed it, stuffed some ice from the service bar into it, and touched it to the puffy, swollen, split open lump on Sebastian's lip, and then used one of the dangling corners to dab at his nose. I wasn't sure what came over me, honestly. Even as I was doing it, it felt odd. Unlike me. Yet also oddly…right. And familiar.

Which freaked me the fuck out.

I don't have much of a nurturing instinct, and never have. Or, at least, I never thought I did. Michael sliced open his finger cutting bell peppers once, and my idea of nurturing him then had been to toss him a roll of paper towels and tell him not to bleed on the peppers. That cut had required four stitches, and the man had been my fiancé. Now, a man I'd met the night before got into a fistfight with his own brother and got a split lip and bloody nose for the trouble, and I was wifing on him so hard my ovaries were wondering if it was baby time.

I blinked up at him as I realized what I was doing, and that he was staring down at me with those wild warm intense brown bear eyes, exuding heat and sexuality.

I stepped back abruptly. "Thanks. For the clothes, I mean. And...for—for last night. You were a true gentleman, and I—yeah. Thanks." I turned away, moved past the still gasping and writhing Zane for the exit.

I made it to the door, had my hand on the knob.

"Wait." Sebastian's voice halted me. It was a growled order, rumbling so low and so powerfully I had no chance of resisting.

I couldn't move. I felt him come up behind me, felt him grab me and spin me around. "Why'd you do that?"

"Do what?"

"Jump in like that."

I shrugged. "Instinct. I told you already, my dad

is a cop and a former Marine, and I'm his only kid, so he taught me everything he knows and then some."

Sebastian was too close. "You kicked my brother's ass, and he's a Navy SEAL."

"I wouldn't say I kicked his ass, but even Navy SEALs are still men with sensitive balls."

"He didn't mean it. The choking or the bitch comment."

"Felt like it, in both cases. And I don't take being called a bitch any better than I do having a man put his hands on me against my wishes."

"You wrist-locked me." This was from Zane, behind us both. "It was muscle-memory instinct."

I stepped past Sebastian. "Yeah, and what about calling me a bitch?"

He was on his feet, albeit gingerly, and limped over to me. "That was uncalled for, and I apologize. I was pissed off, and you got in the way of it." He held his hand out for me to shake. "Can we start over? I'm Zane Badd."

I shook his hand. "Dru Connolly."

Zane glanced past me to Sebastian. "Since when you do you do girlfriends, Bast?"

"I'm not his girlfriend," I said, before Sebastian could answer.

"Not yet," Sebastian murmured under his breath, just loud enough for me to hear.

"Not *ever*," I said, shame and embarrassment over my behavior last night blasting through me. "I need to find a flight back to Seattle."

Sebastian frowned down at me. "Why?"

"Because nobody knows where I am. I sort of ran away on the spur of the moment, and I—"

Zane spoke up, then. "Sorry, sweetheart, but you're not going anywhere."

I whirled on him, ready to get pissed all over again if he was trying to order me around. "And why not?"

He leaned past me and pulled open the door, revealing a torrential downpour, and then let the door close. "My flight here landed just barely ahead of this storm, and I heard the pilots saying all flights were going to be canceled for at least the rest of the day, if not longer. This storm is huge, and nasty."

"Shit." I turned away from both men and moved to sit at the bar. "I've got to call Dad at the very least. "

Sebastian pushed Zane toward the door to the upper level. "Come on, we'll talk upstairs."

When they were gone, I pulled out my phone and unlocked it. Sixteen missed calls, nine voicemails, and forty-seven texts.

Fourteen of the calls, seven of the voicemails, and forty-two of the texts were from Dad, everything else from Michael.

Really? He had the balls to try and get hold of me after what he did? Dumbass.

I was tempted to delete everything from Michael unheard and unread, but I didn't—I couldn't. I'd been with him for four years, and couldn't just dismiss him that easily, as much as I wanted to. I was still in shock, I think, still mentally and emotionally processing what had happened, what I'd seen.

Yet another reason to keep my distance from a man like Sebastian Badd. I knew the old adage about the best way to get over someone was to get under somebody else, but I didn't roll that way. It wouldn't work. No amount of casual fucking could erase four years of my life with Michael. No matter how spectacularly Sebastian might fuck me, it wouldn't fix my broken heart.

It *would* be fucking spectacular, though…or, should I say spectacular fucking.

Shit. I was not supposed to be thinking about how good Sebastian would be in bed.

Bad Dru. I wasn't fucking him. I was going to go back home and deal with the mess that was my life.

The problem was, I didn't want to go back home. I didn't want to walk the Seattle streets and see our favorite restaurants and bars. I'd have to go back to my condo. I'd smell him on my sheets, and I'd have his toothbrush in my bathroom, and his pubes in my shower drain, and his size medium condoms in my bedside table, and his clothes in the drawer I'd given him. He was woven into every facet of my entire fucking life, and I didn't have the slightest clue how to unravel it all.

Against my own will, my thumb tapped the messages app, and brought up the text message thread with Michael.

**Dru, it wasnt what you think., please call me!!!!**

**She meant nothing to me baby i swear. It was a moment of stupidity please please please forgive me! Ill do anythng!**

There were three more texts in the same vein, each more desperately misspelled and unpunctuated than the last. I didn't respond to any of them, but I knew he'd get the 'read' receipts. He'd know I saw them, which meant I'd be hearing from him at some point. No way I was ready for that, so I pulled up the voicemails and listened to the ones from Michael first.

In the first one he sounded frantic, desperate, a little crazy. "Baby, baby—you gotta call me back. I know what you saw, and it's not like you think. It was just that once. We can fix this, Dru, I know we can. I love you."

Delete.

"Dru, baby. I'm so sorry." He sounded calmer in

this one, and honestly close to tears. "I screwed up. I know I did. I just—I wish you'd give me a chance to explain."

Explain your cock in Tawny's blown-out pussy, asshole.

Delete.

When I finally drummed up the courage to open Michael's last voicemail, it wasn't what I was expecting. "I'm guessing you won't listen to this, and if you do, you won't call me back. I get it. I was an asshole. Nobody has any clue where you are and we're all worried. It's not like you to just vanish. At least call your dad so he stops panicking. I think if you don't let him know where you are soon, he's gonna make me disappear, and I'm not entirely sure that's a joke." He sounded lucid, but drunk. "There's so much I could say, but I've been drinking and I'm not gonna say it in a voicemail. I just—I know I messed up, but—*fuck*. Your dad's calling again. Hopefully somebody will hear from you at some point, Dru. We're all worried. So...bye, I guess."

I didn't delete that one. Not sure why, honestly. I just...couldn't.

Something wet dripped from the end of my nose onto the bar top.

What the fuck? I refused to cry about that bastard again. Not anymore.

He wasn't worth wasting any more time or thought or energy on. Nobody was ever going to be faithful; Mom left Dad and me when I was eleven, cleaned out the bank account and split with some dude on a Harley. I remember it. She had a backpack, a too-big helmet, and walked out of the house, climbed onto the back of a rumbling Harley, wrapped her arms around the rider, a big, burly, hairy beast of a man, and they left, just like that. Dad stood beside me on the front porch, watching, utterly shell-shocked.

It had come totally out of left field. Dad had joined the Marines at eighteen, had spent twenty years in the Corps, and had finally retired. He hadn't been sure what he was going to do, and had been at loose ends. Money wasn't tight, but we weren't flush, either. We'd had a nice house, a decent car, food to eat, enough extra cash to go to the movies now and then, out to eat maybe. I remember Dad being home a lot, and Mom working at a diner to put a little more cushion in the bank until Dad figured out his next career.

And then, without a word, without a reason, without so much as a single argument or blowout, Mom just…left.

It had scarred both Dad and me for life. Dad never dated again, and I'd always found it impossible to trust anyone except Dad. I never really had many friends, never really dated all that much. I got into lots of trouble in high school, of the drinking and smoking pot and fucking boys in the back of cars variety, but that was because I was angry and confused. I didn't have a mom to show me how to be a woman, and Dad had his career as a cop by then, so there wasn't anyone to tell me no. None of the boys I ever fucked meant anything. It was what troublemakers did, and it was—believe me when I say I get how fucking cliché this is—a cry for attention.

I met Michael my junior year of college. He was a few years older than me, cool, laid-back, good-looking, had an intact nuclear family, mom, dad, brother, sister. He wasn't exactly close to his siblings, but he *had* them and saw them regularly. His dad was an asshole and his mom was a drunk, but he *had* them, both together in the same house, still married. It was odd, for me. We'd go over to his house, the same one he grew up in his whole life—unlike me, a Corps brat who'd been to six different elementary schools between kindergarten and fifth grade—and we'd sit around the dinner table with his whole family, and they'd argue and bicker and drink too much and sometimes Michael and his brother would nearly come to blows after too much red wine, but they'd always hug before Michael and I left, and he'd hug his mom and dad and sister too, and it was just...so weird. It made no sense to me. They were dysfunctional, sure, but in a *normal* way.

My mom had abandoned me. I'd been more independent at twelve than most college kids. I made my own breakfast, packed my own lunch, and usually made dinner for Dad, too. I did my homework without being told, and most of the housework. I could take a bus from home to the precinct, and did so regularly. I'd routinely accept rides to and from school or to the station from Dad's cop buddies, which meant climbing into the passenger seat and playing with the radio and turning on the siren if they got a call.

I could shoot a gun better than most rookies, knew a dozen different ways to break someone's wrist, and owned my own Taser. Which I'd once used on a guy on a bus who was trying to cop a feel on fourteen-year-old me.

My dad was big, gruff, cynical, tough, intimidating. He once arrested a boy I'd been fooling around with—the kid had wanted me to blow him and I'd said no, and he'd gotten a little handsy in his teenage displeasure. Unfortunately for Billy Price we'd been in his car outside my house, and Dad had been watching. Honestly, Billy had been lucky Dad hadn't pepper sprayed him. He'd been cuffed, booked for assault, and had spent the night in the holding cell with the drunks before Dad let him out. I hadn't needed Dad's intervention, but I hadn't been upset about it either.

Then along came Michael and his normal family and his affectionate-but-not-clingy ways, his not-impressive-but-decent cock, his not-impressive-but-decent ability to last for more than five seconds in bed, and the fact that he'd claimed to love me. He'd pick me up from work at the law firm, take me to dinner, buy me roses, take me to the movies or a concert, and we'd have sex and wake up and have breakfast, and he'd go to work in the marketing division of Amazon and I'd go to work in the small but intense firm where I was a law clerk, and that was life. He seemed happy. I'd thought I was happy.

He proposed over dinner at a swanky restaurant, and we planned the wedding. We'd planned it to be small, just his family and closest friends. Dad and I didn't really have anyone except Dad's cop buddies since we didn't give a shit about Mom's family, and Dad was the only child of long-dead parents.

I never questioned Michael. He didn't stay late at work, didn't keep his phone under his pillow or text at odd hours or take secretive phone calls. There was no lipstick on his collars, no perfume I didn't recognize on his body.

The lipstick on the collar thing, though—does that actually happen? How do you get lipstick on a guy's collar? Are you kissing his shirt?

Point is, there weren't any warning signs.

We had regular sex. He never acted weird. He wasn't super possessive or jealous, never obviously checked out other chicks...

Then...on our wedding day, he fucked Tawny Howard in his dressing room.

If I hadn't caught him, would he have married me? Taken me to bed on our honeymoon with Tawny's pussy juice all over his dick?

I shuddered, since now I had no clue what else he'd been up to—or, rather, *who* else he'd been up *in*. We never had sex without protection, since I wasn't on birth control—I had regular, not-very heavy periods and hated the way birth control messed with my hormones. I was glad for that, now, because it meant I was clean even if he was a cheating bastard whore.

I felt another tear trickle down my cheek, and then another. He'd probably been cheating on me the whole time, I'd just been too stupid to see it. I'd made the conscious effort to trust him after he'd told me he loved me. He'd said it first, without any pressure from me. It hadn't even felt forced, or unnatural, or fake. I'd *believed* him. And I'd let myself feel like I was in love with him, too. I'd put blind faith in him, which had gone against every instinct I'd ever had. I hadn't *wanted* to trust him, hadn't *wanted* to fall in love with him. But I'd made myself trust him because, as I told myself, if I didn't choose to trust someone eventually, I'd go through life alone, like Dad. Who was sad, lonely, and difficult, except where I was concerned.

Speaking of Dad…I opened our iMessage thread and started reading through the backlog.

**Dru? Where the shit are you, girl?**

**Seriously. Call me. NOW.**

**WHErE THE fUCk DID YOU GO?!**

**DRU EMMALINE CONNOLLY CALL YOUR FATHER FUCKING PRONTO!**

The texts got increasingly angry and frightened, until the last few were nearly unintelligible. The voicemails were worse. He sounded absolutely terrified, and for a guy who'd done a tour in Iraq and patrolled the worst parts of Seattle every night, that said something.

Shit.

SHITSHITSHIT.

I'd fucked up.

Mom had left him for no reason, and now I had, too, or at least I was assuming it must have felt like that. I mean, I'd told Rolando to tell him I'd call him, but for someone who'd already had his wife abandon him, it had to have felt like a betrayal. Like a knife to the heart.

I wiped my eyes, tried to swallow the lump in my throat, and hit Dad's speed dial in my phone, and he picked up before it finished the first ring.

He sounded groggy, scratchy. "Dru?"

"Yeah, Daddy. It's me."

"Where the motherfucking goddamned hell did you fucking go?" Only a Marine Corps DI could swear like that.

"I'm in Ketchikan, Dad."

"Alaska?"

"Apparently."

A moment of silence, then the sounds of the burr grinder and the faucet as Dad made coffee. "Explain."

"I—I'm sorry, Dad. I'm *so* sorry. I didn't think about how it'd make you feel, I just…I had to go. I couldn't stay in Seattle another second. It was a crazy spur of the moment thing and I was drunk…but it was the right thing to do for me. I'm just sorry I worried you."

"*Worried* me? Worried is what I'd be if you got in a fender bender or some shit. I heard from Rolando that you jumped in front of a seaplane during take-off and climbed into the plane drunk and still in your wedding dress, and took off in it? That's not worry, that's a heart attack. I tore 'Lando a new asshole for letting you do that. He should've cuffed you before letting you get on that fucking airplane."

"I wouldn't have let him. I wasn't thinking straight. I was panicked, I was—wait, you didn't have an actual heart attack, did you?"

"No, no. Thought I was having one, and even went in to see Doc Roberts, but he said it was called panic, not angina. I'm healthy as a horse, just worried about you. You're all I've got, baby-cakes."

"Everything in Seattle is stained by Michael. I'll come back, I just don't know when."

"So you're in Alaska?"

"It's where the plane was going. It's nice here."

"You need anything?"

"A new heart?"

This got me a sad laugh. "You and me both, babe."

"I just need time."

"Are you somewhere safe, at least? You need money or anything?"

"I've got savings. I'm…" Was I safe? I mean, sort of. For Dad's purposes, I decided, yes, I was safe. "I'm okay. I mean, I'm not okay, but I'm somewhere safe. I'll be fine."

"You want me and the boys to put the hurt on that ex asshole of yours?" He paused a moment. "Wait, he is *ex*, right? You're not taking him back, are you?"

"No, don't hurt him, he's not worth it. And *hell* the *fuck* no I'm not taking him back. I'll probably let him try to explain himself, at some point, but I'm *not* taking him back. I got my ability to forgive from you, after all."

"Yeah, I don't got that ability."

"My point exactly, Dad."

He chuckled. "Ah. Right." He was quiet for another moment. "Sure you're okay, baby-cakes? I got an old buddy from the Corps in Spokane who has a plane. I can send him to come get you."

I should. I should have Dad's Corps buddy come get me and bring me home. There was nothing in Ketchikan for me.

Except a certain tattooed bartender...

Nope.

NOPE.

No way. Bad plan. Super bad horrible terrible no good very very terribly stupid plan, having anything to do with Sebastian. Or his beefcake asshole Navy SEAL brother.

But I couldn't bring myself to do it. I didn't have any good reason, and lots of good reasons not to, but I wanted to stay. I wasn't sure where I'd go, or what I'd do, but as long as I was in Ketchikan—a long, *long* way from that stupid cheating motherfucking dickhead bastard cock-face shit-eating son of a bitch Michael—I might as well stay here and figure things out, like I'd originally planned...albeit *planned* might be the wrong word, but I was going with it.

You don't grow up a DI's daughter without learning how to string swear words together.

Had nothing to do with Sebastian.

I just needed a change of scenery, somewhere new and unfamiliar to put my thoughts in order, to sort out my feelings, to just…let myself be hurt and learn to get over it. Plus, the storm wasn't letting up, so I was stuck here for another day or so anyway.

"Dru?" Dad's voice shook me out of my thoughts. "Are you still there?"

I blinked, cleared my throat. "Sorry, Dad, I got lost in my head for a second. No, I'll be okay for now. But keep that buddy on the hook, because I might need a ride out of here when I'm ready."

"You got it, honey." I heard the sound of coffee pouring. "Well, I'm gonna let you go, then. I love you, Dru. And I'm sorry you're going through this."

"Thanks. I love you too, Dad. And I'm sorry I freaked you out."

"Now that I know you're alive and okay and where you want to be, I'm okay. Take whatever time you need. I'll be here when you get back, and if you need anything, *anything*, just call me. All right, honey?"

"You got it, Dad. Love you, bye." That stupid lump in my throat wouldn't go away.

"Bye."

I set the phone on the bar and spun it in circles.

At least I'd always have Dad.

I headed upstairs in search of Sebastian to remind him about the breakfast he'd promised me.

# SIX

## Sebastian

"WHAT WERE WE SUPPOSED TO DO, BAST? FORGET everything any of us ever dreamed of doing with our lives? We all hated it here. We wanted more. You always seemed content to run the bar with Dad." Zane was sitting on one of the stools, flipping idly through a magazine while I rustled up breakfast in the upstairs kitchen.

"Nobody ever asked me what I wanted, Zane. That's all I'm saying. You all just assumed. What if I wasn't content here? You left, then Brock…" I stirred the scrambled eggs a little more forcefully than I needed to. "One after another, everyone just left. It was just Lucian and me for the last few months, after Xavier got that ride to Stanford, but Lucian...you know how he is. He was working Clint's fishing boat more than he was home, saving his bank. Then he just fuckin' vanished. Packed a bag, boarded a cargo ship headed east, and I ain't heard a word from his ass since."

"Last I checked in, he was in the Philippines."

"Lawyer said Thailand."

"That was six months ago. I had a buddy in Intelligence ping him for me a few weeks ago, and got him tracked down to Manila."

"Nobody ever tells me this shit," I groused.

"That's 'cause your caveman ass don't have a fucking computer or cell phone."

"I have a computer."

Zane laughed. "Dude, that's not a computer, it's a dinosaur. I'm pretty sure my first cell phone had more computing power than that old piece of shit."

It really was an ancient piece of shit. I think Dad got it in like '96 to keep his receipts and inventory more organized, or something. I mainly used it to play solitaire on boring evenings. Sometimes it was Minesweeper, but I didn't really understand that one. Inventory happened on a clipboard, and receipts got filed in a filing cabinet. No internet, no email, and I wasn't sure it even had a CD-ROM player, or whatever it was called. The most technologically advanced piece of equipment in the bar aside from the twenty-year-old register was a radio connected to four little speakers I'd installed up on the ceiling. The radio got three stations clearly: country, rock, and pop; it stayed tuned to rock.

"Whatever," I said. I didn't want to get into the real reason I didn't replace the damn thing.

Zane, however, was a perceptive bastard. "I get that it was Dad's, but he's not in the computer, Bast. He's gone. You won't be replacing him if you get a new computer and an internet connection."

"Fuck you," I snarled. "What the fuck do you know?"

Zane had done that ninja thing he could do, where he'd moved so quickly and silently I didn't even know he was right behind me until I felt his hand on my shoulder.

"Dude, look, I get it, okay?"

I spun on him, shoved him. I knew it was stupid to physically provoke him, since he really was a deadly motherfucker, but I couldn't help it. "You don't get a goddamn thing, Zane! You...weren't...*here*."

He growled, and his hand latched around my throat. Four inches shorter than me, but the motherfucker was strong as hell. He had me shoved up on my tip-toes and seeing stars. "Because I was in fucking Afghanistan killing terrorists, you asshole! I was crawling through the dirt dodging RPGs when Dad died. I went off the rez when I found out, but I was in-country. What was I supposed to do? Go AWOL? Fuck you too, Sebastian. You're not the only one who lost him." He let me go, turned away with a sigh. "Shit."

I followed his gaze and saw Dru standing in the entrance watching us.

"I—I'm sorry. I'm obviously interrupting." She turned around to leave.

"Stop, Dru, wait." Zane's voice stopped her. "You're getting a bad impression. Don't go. We're not usually like this."

"I don't need to be around your family arguments," she said, opening the door to the stairs. "I've got drama of my own—I don't need yours, too." She was down the stairs then, her footsteps slow but steady.

I pushed past Zane. "Plate the eggs for three, and finish the bacon," I told him.

He frowned at me. "Like I can cook?"

"Do your best," I said. "If you can HALO jump, you can manage bacon."

I scrambled down the stairs after Dru, not really sure why, apart from a gut feeling that I didn't want her to leave yet.

I just wanted my dick inside her, part of me argued, and I knew she didn't need that from me.

Didn't stop my dick from wanting her, though. Or my feet from going after her, but I wasn't sure if my feet were acting in service of my dick or the strange feeling in my gut that wanted her to stay. Of course, "gut feelings" usually happened somewhere other than my heart, but I was going with gut feeling since it seemed simpler and easier to explain.

I caught up to her at the front door of the bar.

My hands wrapped around her waist, spun her around, pressed her back up against the door. She stared up at me, blue eyes sad and angry and shocked and confused and…sparking with lust as fierce as my own.

I kissed her.

It wasn't a rough, demanding kiss, but it wasn't some slow sappy wet thing, either. I kissed her like she was mine, like I had all the time in the world to kiss her thoroughly, like I'd spent a thousand nights and thousand days kissing her like this, my hands on her waist, pulling her against me now and pushing my body against hers.

God, she was soft.

Pliable.

Her tits were firm lumps squashed against my

chest, her lips warm and damp on mine. She was perfect. She just *fit*. A moment of frozen disbelief, and then some other part of her took over, a part of her that wanted this kiss as bad as I did. Her mouth moved, then, her lips sliding on mine, tilting, gliding, wet on wet, and then I probed the seam of her mouth with my tongue and she opened for me, accepted my tongue and slashed hers against mine. I pulled her closer, and I knew there was no way she was missing the iron staff of my erection wedged between us. I tasted her tongue, and then felt her moan, heard it, tasted it. God, that moan. It sent fire into my veins.

Made my already pulsing cock throb all the harder.

Her hands drifted up as we kissed, one settling on my arm to stroke my biceps, tracing my ink, the other buried in my hair above my ear and gliding down to trace the outside of my ear—and *Jesus* fuck me that touch, the softest, gentlest, questing brush of her fingertips over my ear…what was it about it that made me so crazy? It drove me wild, made my chest buzz and my heart hammer and my cock pound and my throat emit a snarl as I scooped her up, carving my hands over her round, juicy ass and lifting her up, pulling her hard against me, shoving my zipper into the tight wedge of her thighs. I slammed her up against the door, and thank god it was locked, otherwise we would have gone toppling outside.

The kiss went wild, then.

As if she were starving. As if this kiss could sate some deep need inside her, as if she'd never been kissed like this. Which had to be a joke, because how could any man have a woman like this in his hands and not go wild? I felt like an animal, my libido gone primal, demanding I paw her clothes off and ravage her senseless, fuck her boneless, make her mine, leave my mark on her pale cream skin. I couldn't stop. I was ravenous, monstrous, feral. My fingers clawed into her ass and my tongue slashed and tangled against hers and my hips drove against her core. She was whimpering, gasping against my mouth, moaning into my kiss, groaning into my lips.

I spun in place, walked three steps forward, and laid her down on a table, kicking chairs aside, my mouth never leaving hers. Her legs hooked around my waist, keeping me in place, firm against her denim-covered core. Didn't stop me from grinding, from moving as if I were fucking her, as if I could feel her tight hot wet pussy through the denim. Much more of this, and I would be. I was hard enough to drive nails at that point, and grinding against her so hard I was in danger of spooging in my shorts like a damn teenager, but fuck if I cared. I needed her, needed more, couldn't stop. Didn't even try.

She was sober, and she wasn't stopping me.

Hell, she was begging for more. Her mouth was wild on mine, kissing me back just as fiercely as I was kissing her.

I *needed* to fuck this woman.

My hands took over, took my train of thought and ran with it.

My hands left her ass and slid up her hips, pushed the cotton of her sweatshirt up to bare her belly, and then the sports bra. I broke the kiss, slid down her body to flick my tongue in her belly button, then kissed her stomach down toward the waist of the jeans, then back up to her diaphragm. Across her ribs just beneath the lower edge of the sports bra.

Fuck.

No way I could restrain myself, not now that I had my lips on her, not now that I'd gotten a double handful of that sweet ass of hers, and especially not now that I had her prone beneath me, her legs around my waist, her tits inches from my lips, just a bit of fabric between my mouth and her nipples.

A pull and upward tug, and her boobs slid free of the sports bra, and—god, I was just done, then. The sight of those fine-as-fuck tits was nearly too much. I had to clench my muscles and force my come to behave. Big, round, real, just a bit more than a full handful each...the most lush, beautiful tits I'd ever laid eyes on.

"Jesus, Dru." I heard my mouth saying what my cock was thinking. "You are so fuckin' sexy."

"Sebastian—" Her voice was breathy, erotic music to my ears.

I answered by sucking her nipple into my mouth, and they tasted just as fucking divine as I'd imagined last night as I watched the shower water trickle over them, and when I'd jerked off to the image of them last night and again this morning. And if I didn't get off now, I'd be making a trip to the bathroom to jerk off thinking about her again.

She writhed up off the table, pressing herself against me, moaning, cupping my head in both hands, and then I slid my mouth to her other breast and sampled the salty skin flavor of that one, palming the damp, puckered nipple of the one I'd just had in my mouth, and she whimpered again, and the sound went straight to my throbbing cock.

I flicked my tongue against her nipple, one after the other, thumbing and twisting whichever one I didn't have my mouth on. But she had other lips I wanted to taste, and I'd seen those too, just as plump and damp as the ones on her mouth, and I betted they tasted like sugar. I cupped her breast with one hand and flicked her other nipple with my tongue and brought my free hand to the fly of her jeans, ripped open the button and slid the zipper down, shoved my hand beneath her ass and grasped denim and cotton underwear elastic and jerked them down in one rough yank, baring her pussy.

She squealed, but the squeal ended in a whimper as I brushed my lips across her pussy, breathing out as I did so, and she smelled amazing, like good, clean pussy. Recently waxed, soft as silk. Seeping desire. Fuck, I could see the juices dripping down her labia. I licked them away, and she writhed, gasping, and then groaning long and low and fierce as I slathered my tongue against her clit. I dove right in, no fucking around, no teasing, just went straight for eating her pussy like a starving man.

She was twisting under my mouth in no time, bucking, writhing so hard I had to press my forearm across her hips to keep her where I wanted her. Which only drove her crazier.

"Sebastian! Fuck! God, your mouth, it's—*fuck*!"

"Come for me, Dru." I slipped two fingers inside her tight wet pussy, explored her channel, slid them out, back in, faster, faster, mimicking what I'd do to her with my cock the second I got the chance. "Let me feel this tight fuckin' cunt squeeze around my fingers."

I curled my fingers inside her, felt her shudder, felt her thighs clench around my hand with bruising, crushing force as she bucked up off the table to smash her clit against my mouth. I sucked her clit between my teeth and then flicked it with my tongue and fucked her with my fingers. I pinched her nipples, one then the other, sucked, licked, flicked, and fingered her to pulsating, clenching, spasming, teeth-gnashing orgasm.

Inside—Jesus Christ…I needed to be inside her.

"Fuck, fuck, fuck—Sebastian, oh my god, oh my god—" Dru panted, the words nearly lost in the grinding of her teeth and the hoarse whimpers.

Then, mid-orgasm, she completely lost her goddamn mind.

"STOP! STOP! Jesus Christ, what the fuck am I doing?" She kicked me away, fighting her orgasm, trying to stand up, to get away from me, trying, it sort of seemed, to even get away from herself, from the pleasure rushing through her.

She lunged off the table, and I let her. At least, until I realized she wasn't capable of even standing up straight, yet. I caught her, pulled her against my chest and held her as she shivered and shuddered through the last waves of her climax, and then crouched without letting go of her and snagged her jeans to drag them up her body. Got them to just beneath her butt cheeks and then slid her underwear up, tracing a finger around the circumference of the waistband to make sure they were up all the way around her body, then tugged her jeans into place, zipped and snapped them. Tugged her bra down over her tits—a sad thing, to have to put away such sweet tits—and lastly let her shirt fall into place so she was dressed.

She shoved away from me, stumbling backward, wiping at her mouth and staring at me in disbelief. "I can't believe myself. Fuck—*fuck*." She leaned against the table I'd just laid her down across. "I cannot believe I just—goddammit—"

"Dru, what's the problem? I thought you wanted that. It felt like you were into it, babe." I moved closer to her, mainly because I couldn't help it.

The woman was fucking magnetic. I was drawn to her helplessly. I had to be closer, had to get my hands on her again, in any capacity I could.

She skittered away, putting out her hands as if to fend me off. "Stop, don't, Sebastian—don't touch me."

I stopped, hands up in surrender. "Okay, okay, hands off, but I gotta admit I'm a little confused." I watched her carefully, watching a river of emotions flicker across her features too fast for me to read any of them.

She shook her head. "That wasn't supposed to happen. I shouldn't have done that. Not with you, not now. Not at *all*. Jesus, I'm just so fucking mixed up, and I—" She seemed like she was close to panicking, like last night, but this time she was sober, which meant it would be worse, because it wouldn't be sloppy drunk girl cute, but sober emotional woman messy. "I can't—I can't—"

"Whoa, okay—just take a breath, all right? Why don't you sit down?" I pulled out a chair at the bar for her, and she sort of automatically sat down, breathing hard and scrubbing at her face. I went around behind the bar and pulled her a beer, because if I know anything it's when someone needs a beer. "Drink, Dru."

"I don't want a drink," she said, her hands over her face.

"Yes, you do."

She peered at me, then glanced down at the beer I'd pulled—a lightly hopped local ale. "Maybe I do. God, I'm a mess."

"It's allowed," I said, leaning on the bar closer to her, just so I could smell her intoxicating scent, if nothing else.

She took a drink, sighed. "You mentioned breakfast? I don't know if I can handle anything else on an empty stomach."

I strode over to the stairs, opened the door and yelled up. "Zane! Where the fuck is the food?"

"What, I'm supposed to serve your ass too?" Zane shouted back, but I heard his feet on the stairs.

He came down precariously balancing three plates in his hands. He handed me two of them, paused in the doorway as he caught sight of Dru hunched over the bar, curled around her beer and struggling to calm down...at ten o'clock in the morning.

He quirked an eyebrow at me. "That's all you, bro."

"Thanks," I said, rolling my eyes at him as he tiptoed dramatically back up the stairs. "Sissy."

"Hey, give me a tango with an AK over a weepy female any day of the week." He shut the door at the top of the stairs, and then I was alone with Dru.

Who was, yes, crying into her beer.

God help me.

Zane might have been on to something. What was I supposed to do now? I had no clue. I wasn't even sure what the fuck had just happened to make Dru freak out on me like that. All I knew for sure was she tasted like heaven on my tongue and felt like perfection in my hands and I was still so fucking hard in my jeans it was hard to walk.

I brought the plates over to the bar, pulled myself a beer—because, fuck it, why not?—set a plate in front of Dru and sat beside her with mine. She didn't openly flinch away from my presence—we were close enough that our shoulders were brushing. She picked up her fork, poked at the eggs a few times, and then dug in eagerly. I followed suit, but spent as much time watching her as I did eating.

"Not bad," I commented. "He overcooked the bacon and undercooked the eggs a little, but not bad."

She ignored me, focusing on the food, washing down every few bites with beer. When she was finished, she pushed the plate back a few inches, curled her hands around the pint glass, and stared down into the golden bubbling liquid.

I waited, sensing that she'd start talking when she was ready.

"I caught my fiancé cheating on me with a bridesmaid on our wedding day. Yesterday, I guess. Feels like a whole other life, in a funny way. Like…the naive girl who thought she was getting married to a man she loved. I was that girl just yesterday, but today I feel like someone else."

"Was the bridesmaid one of your friends?" I asked.

Dru shook her head. "No. I don't really have any female friends, to be honest. No sisters, cousins, aunts, nothing. Just me and my dad. The bridesmaids were all my—they were all Michael's friends' girlfriends. And the one he was fucking, Tawny, she was a friend of one of the other bridesmaids. There were three groomsmen—Michael's three best friends—and Michael felt we needed a third bridesmaid, so Lisa asked her friend. I'd met Tawny like, twice? Maybe? We'd all get together for drinks, and Tawny was there a couple times. I never liked her. I always thought she came across as kind of slutty. Turns out I was right, apparently."

"Apparently," I agreed. "Think that was a one-and-done sort of thing? Like, he cheated on you just the once?"

"That's what I can't figure out. I can't come up with any warning signs I missed along the way. So, from that aspect I want to say, yes, it was the one time. But then that doesn't make any sense, does it? Why on our wedding day? It makes literally zero sense. On our wedding day, in his dressing room, in the same building as me. I was literally around the corner and down the hall, getting myself ready." She sniffed. "I was…I was having jitters, you know? Like, am I doing the right thing? So I put on my dad's coat over my dress so Michael wouldn't see me in my dress before the wedding, and went to see Michael. I thought he would calm me down, remind me why we were getting married."

"And you walked in on him fuckin' a bridesmaid."

"Not quite. I didn't actually go in." She took a drink, swirled the dregs. "His friends, the groomsmen and the bridesmaids, they were all sitting outside his dressing room watching something on one of their phones, laughing like crazy. I was like 'hey, what's so funny?' and they went quiet, like oh it's nothing. Just a stupid video going around. Then I heard him. I know the sounds he makes when he's fucking, and that's what I heard, which made me wonder why they were all so weird about that video. So I made them show me. And it was him, in that dressing room, fucking Tawny."

"They *recorded* it?" I asked, incredulous.

Who the hell would do that?

She nodded. "Through the cracked-open door. The funny part was that he had his tux pants around his ankles, right? And he was going at her like crazy, got a little too into it and tripped over his pants and fell backward onto his ass. His dick went flopping all over the place and Tawny was left wiggling her stupid little hips like he was still fucking her, but he was on the floor with his dick out and his pants around his ankles.

"They were watching this over and over again, cackling, while he was still going at it inside the room, fucking Tawny on our wedding day." She heaved a sigh. "I just don't get it. He couldn't wait till, like, after our honeymoon to cheat on me? He couldn't even make it through the actual wedding day? Like what the fuck? And me, like…what the hell is wrong with me that he'd claim to love me, that he'd propose to me, plan a wedding with me, and then cheat on me? And that I had no idea? What have I been missing?"

"He's an idiot," I said.

"Yeah. That's a given." She shook her head in disbelief. "But it calls so much into question. About *me*. Like...why am I not good enough? Why was I not enough for him? It's not like we never had sex, you know? We did. Pretty frequently. Not every day, but a lot. And I—I always thought it was pretty good between us. But I guess it wasn't. If he had to go to someone else, on our *fucking wedding day*, then obviously I'm missing something. There's something I didn't give him that he needed."

"Now that's bullshit," I said. I grabbed her knees and spun her to face me. "This ain't on you. *He's* the cheating bastard. One hundred percent of the blame falls on him. Even if you guys had been having trouble, like things weren't great and the sex wasn't on point all the time or whatever so he wasn't getting it from you—that doesn't give him reason to go fuckin' around with other girls."

"But that's my point. Sex was good. We both got off, or at least he did every time. I didn't always, but he did. He got it from me, and he still cheated on me, and god knows who else while we were together. I mean, there *had* to have been others in the four years we were together."

I felt a little unhinged, thinking about some other asshole with his ungrateful hands on this goddess. He'd had her sweet, sexy body all to himself whenever he wanted it…I couldn't imagine not making sure she went to bed so glutted on orgasms she couldn't stay awake any longer, so thoroughly fucked she couldn't walk the next day. I couldn't imagine not doing anything and everything to please her. God, I'd only made her come once, and she'd freaked out halfway through, but I knew watching her come would be its own reward every single time. Making her come, feeling her come apart, watching that beautiful face twist as she came, feeling that goddamned incredible body buck and writhe, her sweat under my hands, her pussy under my mouth, her cunt squeezing my fingers—Jesus, she squeezed *hard*, too. I could only imagine how hard she'd squeeze around my cock.

The asshole didn't deserve her.

He didn't deserve to fucking live if he had this woman, had the opportunity to make her his forever…and then wasted it.

He gave real men a bad name.

I was a player, sure. I fucked a lot of different women on a regular basis. There'd been threesomes, and foursomes, and two girls in the same night at different times. The most I'd ever had in one night, but not in my bed at the same time, was four girls and, god, I'd barely been able to walk the next day, but it had been fucking worth it. But I'd never made any promises to anyone. I'd always been up front about how shit was. I made it clear we were gonna fuck and she was gonna go her way. No cuddling, no pillow talk, no seconds. I'd only broken that rule once, for one woman. She'd been a cougar, and had taught me a few tricks; the sex had honestly been good enough that I'd been the one to want seconds when she'd been ready to leave after the first round.

But Dru?

I hadn't even had her once, and I wanted thirds, and fourths.

And the stupid bastard had given that up?

Dru glanced at me, and I realized I'd been spacing out, thinking. "What's that look on your face for?"

I shook my head. "You probably don't wanna know."

She tossed back the last of her beer and glared at me. "Don't tell me what I don't wanna know."

I finished my own beer and pushed the glass aside. Took her knees in my hands, slid a little closer to her. "Fine. I was thinking that I've never had it good enough with any one girl that I've ever wanted to bang anyone more than once. That's the truth. But you? Dru, if I got you into my bed, I'd never let you out." I stood up off the stool and crowded her space, stared down into her eyes, let her see the truth in mine.

"The sex wouldn't be *pretty good*. It'd be the best goddamn sex either of us ever had, every single time. I'd make you come so hard so many fuckin' times you'd be beggin' me to quit just so you could catch your breath. I'd fuck that tight, wet, sugar-sweet cunt of yours every single night and every single day so hard for so long you'd be walkin' bowlegged. And no matter how much we fucked, Dru, I wouldn't ever get enough. And I damn sure wouldn't so much as think about another woman for as long as I had you. Shit, all I've gotten is one little taste of that pussy, and I can't think of anything else."

She blinked up at me, eyes wide, chest heaving, fingers clenched into fists on her lap. Her mouth opened, but no words came out.

I cupped the back of her neck and leaned in, brushed my lips across hers. "*That* is what I was thinkin'."

"Oh," she breathed.

I moved my lips on hers, not quite kissing her, more teasing her with the promise of the kiss. "Yeah," I whispered back. "Oh."

She gazed up at me, torn. She wanted the kiss. Hell, she wanted everything I'd just promised her. It was a promise, too, and not an idle one. But she was still fighting whatever hang-up she had about letting go, and giving in to this thing between us.

She was quivering, shaking, barely breathing. Her lips trembled against mine, and her hands stole up to rest on my chest.

Bingo.

I pressed my lips against hers, traced her mouth with my tongue. She slid off the stool, pressed her body against me. God, those curves crushed against me, it drove me nuts. I'd sort of gotten my hard-on to go away, and now she was staring up at me with those absurdly blue eyes again and her tits were squishy against my chest and her hips were in my hands and her lips on mine were soft and warm and wet—

"God*dammit*, Sebastian!" She wrenched herself out of my hands, knocking over a stool in her quest to escape. "Stop *doing* that to me."

"Doing what?"

She backed away from me. "Kissing me like that. Touching me like that."

I followed her. "See, your mouth says 'don't do that,' but your body and your eyes say 'do it again. Do it again and don't fuckin' stop.'"

She bumped against the front door. "I don't want to use you as a rebound."

"I don't mind."

"*I* mind," she snapped. "Yeah, I want you. That's

obvious. But I'm not in a mental or emotional place to be wanting anyone."

"I can make you feel good, Dru." I pressed her up against the door, palmed her hip, touched my forehead to hers. "You deserve to feel good."

"It's too much. It's too soon." Her hands were fumbling behind her back.

"Not enough, and not soon enough. Let me erase it all, Dru."

"I don't want to forget it all."

"Not what you said last night."

"I was drunk. I made a fool of myself. I said a lot of stupid untrue shit."

"See, I think what you were sayin' last night was the truth. Embarrassing? Nah. And not stupid, either. Just the truth." I was rocking a monster erection, and I ground it against her core. "You feel that? It can be inside you. Making you feel incredible. Making all the bullshit go away. You want it. It doesn't have to be complicated, Dru. It can be simple, and real, and good. As long as you want it."

She closed her eyes, squeezed them shut, and shook her head. "Goddamn you, Sebastian. You're so bad. So bad for me."

"Spell it with two Ds and you've got it right, honey."

She huffed, because that was a pretty cheesy-ass

line, but it was so bad it was good. Or…so Badd it was good.

Thank you, thank you, I'll be here all night.

She shoved open the door she'd unlocked while I was running my mouth, and ducked out into the storm.

I followed her out. "DRU!" I shouted, over the hammering rain and crashing thunder.

She stopped a few feet way, already soaked to the bone. "What?"

I pointed at a small sailboat docked a few slips away. "That's mine. Hang out there until you're ready to come back."

She nodded, and jogged toward my boat, hopped onto the deck and vanished into the cabin.

I let her go.

She'd be back.

I hoped.

# SEVEN

# Dru

GOOD GODDAMN AND HOLY MOTHERFUCKING HELL, that man was *potent.*

Once he closed in, once he got those big strong hands on me...I was just lost. The way he kissed me, those soft lips brushing against mine, teasing me with the kiss, drawing it out of me, making me crazy. I couldn't handle him once he got close. And if he put his hands on me? Shit...I was gone. And his mouth? God, god, god. I'd never in my life felt anything like how Sebastian made me feel, spread out for him on that table.

I'd never been taken like that, just...*claimed.* He sensed that I wanted him, sensed that I'd been willing, and he just took me. No apologies, no requests for permission or *is this okay?* He just made me his, and made me feel fucking incredible, brought me to orgasm within seconds. Michael could make me come, but it took a lot of work, took a lot of direction and *no, slow down, not there, don't stop don't stop, goddamn it I said don't stop!* And then he'd usually stop, or slow down or speed up just when I was getting close, which would ruin it. And yes, sometimes I'd fake it just so I could give myself an O later, my way, no fumbling. Other times he'd get it right and we'd both get our Os, and it would be great. We'd feel close and in love and it was...nice.

Sebastian set me on *fire.*

There was not a single second of hesitation or fumbling. He knew exactly how to make me come, found my G-spot with unerring accuracy, slid those thick strong fingers inside me and licked my clit and tweaked my nipples—and *god*, the way he'd jerked my pants down was *so* fucking hot.

It wasn't *nice* with Sebastian. It was...nuclear intense.

He made me come like it was his only mission.

I remembered how hard and how thick his cock had felt behind his zipper, both when he'd pressed me up against the door the first time, and then again just before I'd escaped. He'd probably been fighting the hard-on the whole time, the poor guy.

He made me come without expecting anything in return.

I mean, obviously he wanted more. But when I'd freaked out, he'd backed off. He'd talked me down, fed me, comforted me. And then he'd gotten me all worked up and whispered those dirty, beautiful promises in my ear, and I'd run out on him again, leaving him with what had to be another aching erection.

And last night? He hadn't trusted himself not to touch me when I was wasted, so he'd left the bathroom rather than risk taking advantage of me. And I'd been completely naked and had toyed with him, taking off my panties in front of him, talking about his cock—

Which I'd been right about, as a matter of fact: the thing was *huge*.

I took a second to examine my surroundings. The cabin of the sailboat was tiny. Barely enough room for me to stand up in, and I was several inches shorter than Sebastian. But it was cozy. Blond wood accents, chrome, all-weather carpeting, a table with a booth for two, a galley, a door leading to a small bedroom, another leading to a bathroom. Not much, but it was warm and dry and comfortable.

Problem was, I felt terrible about running out on Sebastian.

He'd made me feel incredible, and then he'd handled my freakout with grace.

Goddammit.

I couldn't stay here in this little boat. I wanted to hide from him, wanted to pretend nothing had happened. I wanted to sit here in this cabin and nurse my aching heart.

God, it hurt.

Now that there was a little time between me and The Betrayal, as I thought of it, I realized Michael's infidelity and the way I'd discovered it was deeply, intensely painful. Way more so than I'd even estimated. It cut me deep, past the bone to the very essence of my soul. Eradicated everything I thought I knew, everything I thought I wanted in life. Undermined my ability to trust anyone, and that was already pretty well fucked by Mom's betrayal.

It hurt so bad.

Why, Michael? WHY?

There was no easy or obvious answer.

The only thing that was obvious was how crazily I was attracted to Sebastian. Which made no sense, and I didn't know what to do about it, because I wanted him more than I'd ever wanted anything, but my heart fucking hurt so goddamn bad I didn't dare trust myself with it, much less a guy I barely knew.

My libido had an opinion, obviously:

It doesn't have to involve my heart, just my pussy.

And my tits.

And my mouth.

And my hands.

And my ass.

And every inch of my flesh, which I was sure he'd kiss. Carefully, and thoroughly.

And fucking hell did I want that.

*"You feel that? It can be inside you. Making you feel incredible. Making all the bullshit go away. You want it. It doesn't have to be complicated, Dru. It can be simple, and real, and good. As long as you want it."* He'd actually said that to me, out loud. And it had nearly worked. Because I *did* want that. I wanted all the bullshit to go away. I wanted to forget everything, and I knew as surely as I knew my own name that Sebastian could make good on that promise. He could drown everything out.

If I let him.

But I shouldn't.

It would be reckless. I'd get invested. I'd want more from him. And even if he was capable of more, of putting real emotions on the line, I wasn't sure *I* was capable of that, not after what Michael had done. Plus, this was *his* home, not mine. I'd have to go back to Seattle at some point, right? My life was there. Dad was there.

Michael was there—but shit, that was an argument for the other column.

I was going in circles, and I knew it.

*"I can make you feel good, Dru. You deserve to feel good."*

*"Let me erase it all."*

I could let him erase it all. I could go back across the street and let Sebastian make me feel good for a while. And then, when I'd gotten enough, when I felt strong enough again to face Seattle and the prospect of starting all over without Michael...I'd go back. A few days, max.

Spend a few days fucking Sebastian, letting him make me feel good, and then I'd go back to Seattle.

Forget Michael.

Forget Tawny.

Forget the botched wedding and my maxed-out credit cards and the fact that I'd quit my job and that the lease on my apartment was up at the end of the month and I had nowhere to go.

But none of that mattered, did it? Not right now. I was in Ketchikan, Alaska, far from all that bullshit, and I had a sexy as hell man across the street who wanted me and who could give me a few days worth of the best orgasms of my life.

*Fuck it*, I thought.

I wasn't typically a "fuck it" kind of girl. I thought things through. I did the right thing. I paid attention to the details and formulated plans, and made decisions logically. My lease was ending and I was getting married, thus I hadn't lined up a new apartment because I'd be moving in with Michael. I'd been offered a couple of law clerk positions out of college, and had taken the one I liked best, which had turned out to be a mistake because they weren't intending to actually move me up or use me to the fullest of my abilities, so I put out some feelers and knew I'd be able to get a new position at a bigger, better firm. Thus, when my boss told me I couldn't take any time off for my honeymoon, I'd put in my two weeks notice. Michael made good money, I made good money, thus I had no problem maxing out my credit cards to pay for the wedding, especially since Dad wasn't really in a place to pay for it all, and god knew Michael's parents wouldn't.

But looking back, those had all been serious mistakes. Well, I mean, I could still get a job if I went back to Seattle. That much, at least, didn't depend on Michael and the wedding.

*If?*

No…that was crazy talk. Of course I was going back.

Just…not yet.

The cabin of the sailboat was nice and warm and cozy and dry, and most of all, private. I could chill here. Relax alone, no fucked-up situations to navigate.

I stripped off my clothes and laid them out to dry, went into the bedroom and climbed into the bed, pulled the covers up to my chin…and promptly fell asleep.

When I woke up again, my phone told me I'd slept four more hours, and I was still tired. So I unlocked my phone, pulled up the Kindle app, and read for a few hours, finishing one book and starting another. I read until my eyes dragged again, and then set my phone aside and let my eyes close, letting myself float back under the surface of consciousness. The next time I breached awareness, it was dark outside and the rain had stopped. My phone read just past ten at night, and I was wired. I dressed in my mostly dry clothes, remade the bed, left the boat and jogged across the street to Badd's.

The bar was middling busy, with every seat at the bar and most of the tables full, but it wasn't quite standing room only. Zane was behind the bar, and looked like he was holding his own, popping the top on a beer, then pouring a little too much vodka into a highball…he was no Sebastian behind the bar.

I angled up to the bar and got Zane's attention.

"Where is he?"

Zane shrugged as he added tonic to the vodka, a wedge of lime, and a straw. "Not sure. Out back, maybe? Thought I saw him head out that way. He couldn't have gone far, because it's so busy. If it gets any busier around here, I'll have to fire myself."

"Thanks," I said, and wandered through the kitchen, to the back door, which was propped open by a big jug of frying oil.

I heard voices, one of them definitely Sebastian's. I peered through the opening and saw Sebastian leaning against a wall, hands in his hip pockets, a frown on his face. There was a woman facing him. Scantily clad would be an overstatement. Miniskirt so short it barely covered her ass and nothing but a bralette on up top. Five-inch heels, teased-out hair. And she had her hands all over Sebastian. He wasn't touching her back, but he wasn't stopping her either. They were in profile to me, so I could see everything.

"It was good between us, wasn't it, Sebastian?" Her voice was wheedling, trying to be seductive. "I made you feel good. You remember what I can do with my mouth, don't you?"

"Allie...god, stop. We're not doing this." He shifted, so he wasn't quite as close to her, pulling away subtly. "*I'm* not doing this. You should go."

She just laughed. "I'm not asking you to date me,

I'm just…looking for a good time. That's what you're best at, right? A quick and easy good time? That's all I'm looking for."

"Allie, you're not hearin' me."

She sank to her knees, her hands going to his fly. "Oh come on, Sebastian. You know you want this. You know how good I can suck your cock, don't you? I can suck your cock and make it last for hours, Sebastian." She was stroking his length over his underwear, getting ready to take him out and blow him. "That feels good, doesn't it? You're so hard it aches. I can fix that for you, baby."

I felt betrayed. Stupid, but I couldn't un-feel it. He owed me nothing. He was nothing to me. But there it was, raw and real and undeniable, sitting like a ton of jagged-edge bricks on top of the already raw wound of Michael's betrayal. I couldn't handle this, too.

I turned to leave and my foot hit something that clattered; I heard Sebastian's voice shouting my name, but I wasn't about to stop and listen to him.

No point.

I ran pell-mell through the kitchen, back across the bar, ignoring Zane's curious expression.

Outside it was raining again, not a torrential downpour but a steady rain. Enough to soak me through in the few steps I made it out of the door before I felt a hand grasp my shoulder.

Not a smart move. I couldn't have helped my re-action even if I'd wanted to, and I didn't want to. I grabbed his wrist, pivoted to put my shoulder in his armpit and used my momentum and shorter stature to haul him over my body in a brutal throw. He land-ed on his back in the street, gasping and blinking up at me.

"Do not EVER put your hands on me like that, asshole. Not ever. Thought you'd have learned that already, but I guess not." I turned away from him and started walking down the street.

He was still gasping for breath, but managed to make it to his feet, haltingly, painfully. "Wait—" He coughed, sucked in a deep breath, and tried again. "Dru, please. Please wait."

"Why? You've got your ex waiting for a redo. Why would you want me?" He stumbled around in front of me, put his hands up placatingly, but he didn't touch me. His jeans were still open and unzipped, I noticed.

"I didn't let that desperate slut touch me, Dru. I kicked her ass to the curb before I even knew you'd seen anything. The second she tried to put her hand on my cock I stopped her. I told her to leave, and I wasn't nice about it. She's not an ex, okay? She's just some chick I boned once and she was sniffing around, hoping for seconds."

"And that's supposed to reassure me?" I crossed my arms over my chest and shot a look at his fly.

He glanced down, realized he was still open, and zipped and buttoned his jeans. "No, I just—"

"Because that's all I'll be too, eventually, right? Some desperate bitch showing up hoping for a pity fuck from the almighty Sebastian?"

"That's not what I meant." He sounded a little irritated.

And I knew I wasn't being rational. He didn't owe me anything. I had no right to treat him this way. If he wanted to fuck someone else he could, and there was nothing I could say. If he wanted to let some chick blow him in the alley behind his bar, he had every right to that, and he owed me zero explanations.

And honestly, the fact that I felt like he *did* owe me that, that I wanted it from him...bothered me. I shouldn't want that.

At that moment, I saw Zane poke his head out the door of the bar. "Yo, Bast. Need your help, brother. Gettin' a little hairy in here."

Sebastian growled in frustration. "I gotta go. But please, don't leave. I didn't touch her, didn't let her touch me. She means nothing to me, Dru, and that's the truth whether you believe it or not. I don't normally go around explaining my shit to anyone, but for some reason the thought of letting you just leave without—I don't know. I don't know. I just know—"

"SEBASTIAN!" Zane's voice was powerful and irritated, now. "Got pissed-off customers, man. Let's go. This can happen later."

"Go, Sebastian," I said. "Your brother needs you."

He growled again. "Please don't leave. This ain't over, honey. Not by a long shot."

And then he was trotting back into the bar, and I was alone in the street, in the rain, completely clueless as to what I was even supposed to think or feel, much less what to do next. So I went back to the sailboat. Felt at odd ends, loose, adrift, with nothing to do.

I didn't want to leave. I wanted more with Sebastian. I wanted *him*, full stop. It was foolish, probably. I'd only end up being hurt worse than ever, left to crawl back to Daddy in Seattle and try to rebuild the shattered ruins of my fucked-up life. Staying was a risk. And for what? A few minutes of feeling good in Sebastian Badd's strong arms?

Fuck yes. *Exactly* for that. Because those few minutes promised to be…shit, better than anything I'd ever experienced. I just *knew* that's what it would be. Life-changing, earth-shattering sex. And goddammit, but I wanted that. I wanted it bad.

But was I really willing to risk getting all attached to Sebastian because of how good the fucking was, only to have him send me packing once he'd had his fill of me? Because if what I'd had with Michael hadn't been good enough for *him* to stay faithful, then what were the chances a man like Sebastian would find me satisfying? I mean, he was a god. Beyond gorgeous, tough, rough, dominant, skilled at sex, ran his own bar, had women so desperate for a second round with his cock that they were willing to do anything to get it, even blow him in the alley just for a chance to have more with him. And here was me, who couldn't even get a boring regular old Joe like Michael to remain faithful.

Yeah, good luck. But something inside me insisted I give him a shot. Because it *would* be that good. It would be worth the risk.

I tried to put it out of my mind for a while.

I read, scrolled through social media on my phone, checked the news apps, read some more. Managed to crash again, even though I'd slept most of the day already.

I woke up with dim gray light filtering in though the windows. My phone was dead, so I had no idea what time it was, but my guess would have been around seven or eight in the morning.

And my first thought was Sebastian.

I wanted him. I knew it was likely to end badly, but some crazy, impulsive drive inside me was telling me to go for it. That I couldn't let Michael wreck my life, or force me to put up even higher walls than I already had. I couldn't let Michael's betrayal turn me into a coward, into someone too scared to go after what she wanted. And I wanted Sebastian. I had no clue what it would look like, how it would go, how it would end, or if my heart would survive the experience, but I was willing to take a chance. I *had* to.

Fuck it.

I shoved open the door of the cabin, ducked out, slammed the door behind me, and jogged through the downpour back across the street. I opened the door to the bar, but found it empty. The lights were all off, and the door to the stairs leading up to the apartment was open, so I figured he must be up there, probably sleeping since it was still early morning.

I found Zane crashed on the couch looking sleepy but watching the news on TV. He blinked at me, and then jerked a thumb at the hallway. "His room's the one at the very end."

Sebastian's door was closed but not latched, so I went in. He had a king size bed with a simple metal railing headboard and footboard, with messy flannel sheets and a thick fleece blanket. A dresser with six drawers, one of them open, a T-shirt hanging half out, a dish on top containing a handful of change, a Leatherman multitool, and an old silver watch. Underwear on the floor, a pair of jeans. An old, battered Taylor acoustic guitar in the corner sitting on the wide bottom, a pick in the strings on the neck. A pair of Timberland boots, well worn. A wool pea coat hanging off the open door of the closet, looking like it had been hanging there on the open door since the end of last winter. Nothing on the walls, no alarm clock, no phone cord or radio or anything, nothing electronic at all, as a matter of fact. The only things on the nightstand table next to the bed were a litre bottle of water and a small framed black and white photo of a woman, who I assumed was his mother, standing next to a man who I assumed was his father.

No Sebastian, though.

The bathroom door was slightly ajar, and I peeked in, got a glimpse in the mirror of Sebastian standing facing the toilet.

Legs spread wide apart, head ducked, shoulders heaving. Jeans tugged down around his thighs to bare a taut, muscular ass with a dusting of dark hair. One of his hands was braced on the wall in front of his face, his arm straightened to hold up his weight, and the other was in front of his body. He was rigid, his ass flexed forward. His arm was moving back and forth slowly.

"Fuck…" he groaned, his voice low and snarling.

And unexpected. I jumped when he growled that curse word, caught spying on him. Watching him masturbate.

"Dru...*fuck*—" he rumbled.

He was jerking off thinking about me? My heart hammered, my gut twisted, my hands shook, and my core heated.

I couldn't look away. Absolutely could not.

I moved slightly, adjusting my angle so now instead of seeing just his back, I could see more of his profile in the mirror. His fist sliding up and down his huge, hard length. And I do mean *huge* and *hard*.

I watched as he stroked himself, and felt heat billow through me, felt wetness seep into my panties. He didn't hurry, just stroked himself slowly and leisurely, taking his time. After a couple minutes of slow stroking, his hips started to flex back and forth, and his breath started to huff past gritted teeth, and his fist started to move a little faster.

He hadn't seen me; his eyes were shut tight, his jaw clenched as his fist flew faster and faster.

And then he stopped. His eyes flicked open, and he reached out, pumped a handful of lotion into his palm, smeared it on his cock, and began stroking again, starting slowly and working quickly back up to speed.

"Dru...god, *Dru*..."

My heart hammered every time he said my name, and my core dripped desire at the sight of his big hand sliding up and down his huge, hard cock. I pictured my own hand on him, stroking him…I'd need both hands, and could probably only fit a little bit into my mouth.

But then he glanced in the mirror, and saw me.

"See something you like, Dru?" he said, his voice a growling bass murmur.

"Yes," I heard myself say. "Don't stop."

He resumed stroking his cock, but didn't take his eyes off mine in the mirror. "Come in here." I pushed open the door enough to slip through, and then closed it behind me. Sebastian used his free hand to shove aside the shower curtain. "Sit."

I sat on the edge of the tub, trembling, inches away from him. Inches away from his thick cock. I stared up at him, trying to look more daring than I felt.

"Why're you here, Dru?" he asked, his fist not stopping, still sliding slowly along his shaft.

"I—I want to forget, Sebastian. I just—I just want to forget. Like you said. Feel good for awhile."

"Gonna freak out on me again?"

I shrugged. "Probably."

He smirked. "Fair enough." He glanced down at himself, and we both watched him stroking his dick. "You like to watch?"

"I've never watched—this, before. Never watched

anyone do this."

"Never had anybody watch before either."

I licked my lips, glanced from his eyes to his cock. "Keep going."

So he did.

His fist slid up and down, slowly, leisurely, the lotion squelching wetly with each stroke. Then he started to jerk, going faster, and his jaw clenched, and his molars began to flex and pulse as he ground his cock into his flying fist.

I ached.

My hands, folded on my lap, twitched to touch him.

His eyes closed momentarily, then flew back open and pinned me. "Touch me, Dru. Help me finish. It's your fault I'm this hard."

I reached out, hesitated with my fingers a hair's breadth from his shaft, and then I closed my hand around him. God, so thick, so soft, yet so iron-hard. I glided my hand up to the head and all the way down, my fist sliding slickly over the lotion. We both had a hand on his cock, now, his below mine. We stroked him together, faster and faster.

"Fuck—Dru, your hand feels so good around my cock."

"Your cock is amazing, Sebastian." I grinned up at him. "I guess I was right the other night, huh?"

"Guess so," he grunted, and his hips began to thrust.

I worked him faster, and his hand fell away, so it was only mine on his flesh. I cupped his ass with my other hand, and set a quick fluttering rhythm of strokes on his throbbing cock. Harder, faster.

God, how long could he hold out?

He started grunting, low under his breath. Glanced at me. "Gonna come, Dru."

His beautiful cock pushed into my fist and his eyes pinned me and his abs tensed and flexed. I watched, rapt, as my small pale hand slid up and down his tan flesh, and then he froze, hips thrust forward.

"Fuck...*fuck*, I'm coming, Dru. Watch me come."

I tilted away from his body, cupped my palm under the tip of his cock and kept stroking him. He snarled, thrust his hips once more, and then he came with a low growl. His dick pulsed in my fist and come spurted out of him and into my palm, overflowing to drip down into the toilet, and then he grunted and thrust into my fist and came again, filling and over-filling my palm, again, and again, and I kept stroking him until he finally stopped growling and grunting and coming into my hand.

"Jesus, you come a lot," I said, marveling at the unbelievable amount of come in my hand, dripping down between my fingers into the water below, coating my palm in wet hot white stickiness.

"You got no fuckin' idea," he growled. "Wash your hands and get those clothes off."

I shivered at the fierce potency in his voice. "Are you always this bossy?"

He growled at me again. "Just had your hand on my cock, Dru. I need to eat your sweet cunt until you come on my tongue, and then when I'm hard again, I'm gonna fuck you six ways to Sunday. So if you don't do what I tell you, I'll do it for you."

I stared at him, taking in the blaze of his brown eyes, the heaving of his chest, the droop of his dick. He stepped out of his jeans and underwear, peeled off his shirt, tossed them both on the floor, and stood naked in front of me. And holy shit, the man was *ripped*. Chiseled abs, bulging pecs, rippling biceps, and all that incredible ink stretching from wrist to wrist and shoulder to shoulder. The V, god yes, the V-cut. And his cock, even going limp—only momentarily, it seemed—was impressive. Fully erect it had been the hugest thing I'd ever seen, thicker and longer than any cock in my experience, and just perfectly straight and so beautiful...and so big he'd stretch me to burning, I was sure.

I shivered at the thought.

And apparently I didn't move fast enough for him, because Sebastian snagged my wrist, turned on the faucet, rinsed his come off my hand, dried it with a towel, and then jerked open the bathroom door and hauled me out into his bedroom. Kicked that door closed, then spun around to face me with his hand on the lock.

"You wanna leave? Now's the time, sweet thing. I'm gonna lock this door, and I'm not letting you out until you beg for mercy."

I lifted my chin. "I don't want to leave."

I didn't, really I didn't. But the look in his eyes was feral. I was starting to wonder if my idea of getting a few orgasms out of this guy and then going back to Seattle unscathed had just maybe been a *little* unrealistic. He looked ravenous, as if he were seconds from pouncing on me and devouring me.

I'd never been devoured before. Hell, I'd never even been looked at like that before.

He grabbed a handful of my sweatshirt, tugged the hood over my head, and then yanked the hoodie off. Tossed it aside. Jerked my T-shirt off, and then my bra. Ruthlessly, efficiently. Then he ripped open my jeans and shoved them down along with my underwear, and when I stepped out of them, I was naked. The whole process had taken less than thirty seconds.

He wrapped his hands around my waist, and for a moment he was soft and tender, staring down at me with those big brown grizzly bear eyes gone affectionate and appreciative. It lasted for as long as he was staring into my eyes, and then his gaze flicked downward, took in my breasts, my belly, my core…

And his grip on my waist tightened.

"Not a sound, Dru. Yeah?"

I nodded, and that was when the world as I knew it ended.

He lifted me up by my waist and tossed me backward onto his bed, a casual, easy movement that sent me flying across the room to bounce once, and then he caught me in his arms on the second bounce and was all over me, skin pressed to skin, his mouth on my neck, lips kissing and sucking, teeth nipping, tongue licking. He moved his way down to my breasts, and he lapped at them, suckled my rigid, sensitive nipple into his mouth and sawed his teeth across it, eliciting a moan from me. I didn't have time to even process how I'd gotten on the bed yet, and he was flicking my nipples and biting them just a little too hard, and then he was grazing his mouth down my belly, flicking his tongue into my belly button in a way that had me fighting the urge to squeal, and then he was off of me, off the bed. He wrapped his hands around my ankles and yanked me to the edge of the bed, shoved my legs open, and dove in.

"Jesus, Sebastian, slow down!" I gasped.

"No." He growled the one-word answer.

"But I—oh fuck. Oh fuck. Ohhhhhh—*fffffuuuuuck!*" A shock of utter bliss drew the word out of me, elongated each consonant, each vowel, each syllable, his mouth closing around my clit, tongue flicking madly, lips creating suction, and then he slid two fingers into my slit and I couldn't help a gasp from leaving my lips as he scissored his fingers and then curled them inside me to find my G-spot as if he had some kind of radar or divining rod for finding that spot inside me.

Two licks, two fingers, and I was gone.

I spasmed off the bed, biting down on my lip to keep silent, and then he swirled his tongue around my clit and I lost it, bucked under him, coming within a record short amount of time.

"God, Dru, you come so easy," Sebastian breathed, his voice buzzing against my slit. "Gimme another one. Let me feel this pussy squeeze me again."

He added a third finger, and his mouth went back to my pussy and circled my clit, and I'd never in my life come more than once in a single session even on my own, much less before penetration had even occurred, yet there I was hovering on the edge of a second one already.

"Pinch your nipples. Make it hurt."

I *had* to obey. I couldn't explain it, the effect his commands had on me. I wasn't a take-orders-easily girl, but something about the way Sebastian growled his orders hit some instinctual nerve inside me and had me obeying him automatically. Had me wanting—no, *needing*—to obey him.

I squeezed both nipples, rolled the erect buttons between fingers and thumbs until heat seared through me at the exquisite sensation.

"Harder," he snarled. "I said make it *hurt*."

So I pinched my nipples hard enough that a whimper left my lips, but the pain turned instantly into something else as his thick fingers worked in and out of me and his tongue and lips scoured my clit and labia.

And then I felt a sharp sting just outside my outer labia, in the crease where pussy met thigh, and my eyes flicked open to see Sebastian moving back to licking my clit. I leaned forward, pulled at the skin, and saw that he'd left a big, dark love bite there.

"You...gave me a...a hickey—" I demanded, between barely-suppressed gasps of pleasure, "on my *pussy?*"

He glanced up at me across my body, and his smile wasn't sweet or kind or affectionate, but wild and fierce. He bent closer to my core, pulled my thigh aside and pressed his lips to the same spot on the opposite side, and I felt the nip of his teeth and the suction of his tongue and lips in a sharp sting, and then he pulled away, leaving another hickey.

"Mine." His tone brooked no disagreement, and his hands on my body left no room for argument.

His? Fuck, there was no way I'd survive that.

But then thoughts were eradicated as he went back to driving my orgasm out of me.

Didn't take him long.

I felt it boiling, and this time I didn't need his command for my fingers to find my nipples and pinch them *hard*, and then heat and tension were blasting through me and washing over me, and I was seeing stars, darkness rippling across my vision as I arched up off the bed. His hands were under my ass, lifting me off the bed, holding me against his mouth as he licked and sucked me through the orgasm, and then set me down and his tongue kept going, wet and warm and insistent and hungry, sliding down my slit to lick at the seeping juices of my desire.

When he'd lapped me clean, he finally crawled up my body and onto the bed, hauled me to the pillows, once again manhandling me as if I weighed nothing, as if I was his to do with as he wished.

And I was, wasn't I? I'd put myself in his hands, let him lock the door behind us, and now I was naked, flush with two intense orgasms, and not even remotely sated.

I expected him to demand I return the favor, suck

him to hardness again, but instead he lay against the pillows on his side, pulled me to him and wrapped me up in his arms. Both arms went around me like steel bands, crushing me against his body. I smelled him, felt him, felt his heat and the softness of his skin...

And then he cupped my face and tilted my mouth to his and kissed me.

Slowly.

Deeply.

Thoroughly.

He fucked me with his mouth as intimately and deliriously as he was going to fuck my pussy. I moaned, because how could I not? His tongue was plundering the cavity of my mouth, tangling with my tongue and tracing my teeth, and I was safe and warm locked in his powerful arms. He had one hand on my cheek, fingers brushing past my ear and his thumb under my jaw, directing the kiss, and his other arm was tucked under the hollow where my hip dipped in to my waist, and his hand was splayed across my ass, fingers dimpling the flesh, clutching, pawing, kneading, exploring the expanse and curve of each globe in turn. And god, why was that simple touch so fucking erotic? All he was doing was caressing my ass, but it sent thrills through me, made my hips push against his body, forced my thighs to open and accept his leg between them in a poor excuse for what I really wanted: his cock, erect and inside me.

But he was in no hurry.

He kissed me with artistry and passion, cupping my face and exploring my ass at the same time. How long did we lay there, on his bed, wrapped up in each other, just kissing? I had no idea. Forever. All day. All night. Or maybe just a few minutes. Not long enough, surely. His kiss was intoxicating, his touch like fire on my skin.

And then I felt his cock thickening against my hip and belly. I brought my hand to his face, caressed his rough stubble and put all of myself into the kiss, gave back, tasted his tongue, sucked his breath into my lungs. I had to. I couldn't not. You don't get kissed like that and not give it back. It leaves you delirious, wild. There was a tumult deep inside me, a crazy rush of emotions I didn't dare examine, so I shoved them all deep down and focused on the taste of his lips and the feel of his stubble under my palm, and then I wedged my other hand between our bodies and found his cock.

He hissed between his teeth as I fondled him, feeling him hardening in my hand. "Your touch is like magic, Dru. I don't know what it is you do to me, but just your hand on my cock makes me crazy."

"Fuck me, Sebastian." I whispered this against his lips. "I need your cock inside me so fucking bad."

# EIGHT

## Sebastian

HOLY SHIT, HER VOICE AS SHE BEGGED ME FOR MY COCK? Her eyes? She was trembling, shivering, her thighs quaking around my leg. I've always been blessed with a refractory period as short as my cock is big, but something about Dru had me hard as steel faster than ever, and now she was begging me for it?

"Yeah?" I rolled away from her, tugged open my nightstand drawer and ripped a condom free from the string. "How bad?"

She snatched the condom from me, shoved me to my back, and tore the packet open, tossed it aside with the rubber in one hand. She fiddled with it for a second, figuring out which way it rolled, then gripped my cock at the base and rolled the condom onto me in a hand-over-hand movement, which had me stifling a groan.

"So fucking bad I'm crazy with it, Sebastian. *Please.*" She said this as she slid her thigh over my hips and sat astride me. "You promised you could make me forget. So I'm begging you, please, take it all away."

She braced her hands on my chest, and her loose auburn-red hair draped around my face and onto my shoulders, and her weight was an arousing promise of what was about to happen. I reached between us, gripped my cock with one hand and fingered her opening with the other. I guided the head of my cock to her slit.

Nudged almost but not quite in, so the head was splitting her pussy open but it wasn't quite inside her. I let go, caught her hips to keep her from sliding down on me before I was ready. She leaned forward, the tips of her tits brushing my chest, and her eyes were the hottest wild blue. I needed to be inside her as badly as she needed me inside her, but I wanted to savor this. Burn the memory into my mind. Sear it into hers.

"Like this?" I teased.

"No," she murmured. "Deeper."

I let go of her hips. Cupped her tits and leaned

up to bite her lower lip, drew it out and let go. Her eyes flared open as I pinched her nipples, then went heavy-lidded as I flexed my hips to tease my cock a little deeper.

"Yeah…" she whimpered. "Like that. Deeper."

I gripped her hips again and guided her to flutter up and down shallowly on the head of my dick. Teasing us both. Making myself absolutely crazy with it. I could feel her, feel that sweet cunt wrapped tight around my cock, and it wasn't enough, I needed deeper, needed to fill her, needed to claim her pussy as mine, *mine*, needed to slam deep and feel her thighs quake around me as she came.

She was quivering, gasping, needing to impale herself on me. "Please, Sebastian. *Please.*" She was desperate, now.

I was, too. I was done with this cruel game I was playing.

I let go of her hips. "Show me how deep you want me, Dru."

"Oh *fuck*—finally." She pressed her forehead to mine and kept her eyes on mine, hesitating a split second, hips writhing helplessly, and then she sank down around my shaft. Slowly, deliberately, her eyes going wide as I stretched that tight perfect pussy open. "Jesus *Christ*, Sebastian. I can't—oh god, I can't take it all."

"Yes, you can," I growled. "Slow. Back up. Go slow."

"I'm trying, but you're so fucking huge, I just—" Her eyes were wide, glimmering and gleaming with delirious awe, and a little pain as I stretched her apart. She lifted her hips to draw me out, hovered there for a moment, catching her breath, and then sank down again, taking me deeper. "God, Sebastian. So—fucking—*good*."

I couldn't breathe. Legit, I was breathless, shaking all over. Being inside Dru...it erased every moment that had ever gone before. It was...perfection. I wasn't even all the way in yet, and I was fighting the urge to pin her to the bed and fuck her like a savage beast. Equally, I needed to just hold her like this, cup the beautiful swell of her lush hips and let her ride me to completion and just soak in her incredible beauty, just drink in the angles of her face, the fall of her thick red hair around her shoulders, the way her heavy tits trembled as she lowered herself on me. I just wanted to *feel* this, to drown in the feel of being inside this woman.

I didn't want it to ever end.

I wanted to savor each individual second of this.

She gasped as she slid down my cock again, her fingers digging into my pecs, sharp strong claws piercing me to cling hard. The pain only reminded me that this was real, that I was really here with her, feeling this, filling her, splitting her open. It wasn't a dream, wasn't my imagination. It was better than I'd fantasized while jerking off. Infinitely better. Her body was so goddamn glorious, I didn't dare even blink, because I didn't want to miss a single second of the way she looked on top of me.

Before she'd even taken half of my length, she backed away again until just the tip was inside her, and she hesitated there, as if preparing to feel me fill her all over again. I felt my heartbeat hammer wild and staccato as she hovered there, waiting, waiting, and I was crazy from not knowing when she'd slide me back in, or how deep, or how slowly. It took everything I had to hold still, to let her get used to me in her own time, her own way.

She sucked in a sharp breath, dug her fingernails even deeper into my skin, nearly breaking it now, and then slowly lowered down onto me. And god, fuck— she was so tight I felt every millimeter as I pushed into her, felt her pussy squeezing around me like a vise, gripping me, sliding wet and slick and hot—it was…it felt like going home, sliding into her. Filling her.

She took almost all of me, gasping breathlessly as she withdrew again, hesitated, forehead to mine, breathing hard. Then, in the same agonizingly slow, wet, torturous slide, she impaled herself on me all over again. Groaning the whole time, her voice low and hoarse and primal, like a lioness. Almost all the way out, hovering at the apex of the withdrawal, and then this time instead of sinking down on me, she fluttered her hips, rolled them to fuck the top few inches of my cock into her pussy. She was teasing me and teasing herself, groaning low in her throat in a sound so fucking insanely erotic it had my balls clenching, had my cock throbbing, had me clawing my fingers into her ass, holding on for dear life.

God, I needed to move, needed to thrust. Needed to fuck. But I couldn't. Wouldn't. Not until she was ready.

Without warning, she slapped her ass down onto me, took all of my cock in a single hard crushing thrust, taking a mouthful of my shoulder and biting down to stifle her cry. I growled at the stinging ache of her teeth in my flesh and the sudden dizzying onslaught of ecstasy as I felt her pussy swallowing my cock, filling her tight cunt so completely I couldn't possibly keep quiet because of the raw heady bliss of the way she felt.

"Fuck—" I breathed, my lips brushing her ear. "Dru, you feel like—Jesus, I didn't know it could feel like this."

She was sobbing, gasping, her ass flush against my hips, her cunt squeezing around me as if she was already orgasming. "So much, Sebastian. So fucking much."

"Look at me, Dru," I growled. Her gaze met mine, and wetness glazed her bluest blue eyes. "Those good tears, darlin'?"

Her fingers clawed into the meat of my chest, hair loose and wild around our faces, her knees squeezing my hips as she straddled me, she could only nod at first, teeth catching her lower lip. Then she spoke, through gritted teeth. "The best. Too good."

"Can you take me now?" I asked.

She nodded again, her breath catching and stuttering as she began to roll her hips, and then buried her face in the base of my throat.

I wrapped her thick auburn hair around my fist and hauled her face back up so she was forced to look at me. "Need your voice, Dru. I need to move. Can you take all of me now? Say it."

She inhaled raggedly. "I can take you, Sebastian. Give me all you've got. Give me everything."

I clutched her tight against me and rolled to pin her spine to the bed. "Don't close your eyes. Don't miss a second of this, Dru."

"I won't."

I pushed my hips harder against her, pushed my cock as deep as it would go. Then, slowly, I pulled back, and she whimpered as if to mourn the loss of me inside her. Gently, then, I slid back in. My arms were braced on either side of her face, her thighs framing my hips, feet planted in the mattress near my knees. Her hands were clutching my shoulders, and as I pushed in, her fingernails became claws all over again, and she gasped when I filled her. Again, and again, and every time I thrust into her she clawed her fingers deeper into my flesh, and I relished the desperation of the way she clung to me, the ferocity in her fingers and the erotic breathy gasping of her voice.

But I was still going slow. Taking her measure, more than anything. Just getting started. Not wanting to overwhelm her or frighten her off with my full power.

But she sensed it. Scraped her hands through my hair and down my back to grip my ass. Her palms smoothed over my buttocks and then she traced them with her fingertips, and then she slammed her hips up against mine and dug her fingers rough and fierce into my ass and yanked me against her to deepen the thrust.

"*More*, Sebastian. I said I can take you. Give it to me." She lifted her face to mine, kissed the corner of my mouth, teasing me with a kiss, and then bit my earlobe. "I'll take all you have and beg you for more."

I reared back and started moving more earnestly, staring down at her. "I like it when you beg, sweet thing."

She smiled, a pleased, amused little grin. "Yeah?"

"Yeah."

She pulled me against her with one hand on my ass, and wrapped the other hand around the back of my neck and tugged my ear to her lips. "Fuck me, Sebastian. *Please*...please fuck me." She whispered into my ear, writhing her sweet, tight, wet pussy around my throbbing, aching cock. "I need you to fuck me so hard I can't breathe. Fuck me senseless."

I leaned back, got my knees underneath me, lifted her thighs and pushed them up against her belly, stretching her out, splitting her open, letting me in deeper. I slid closer to her, seating my cock as deep as I could go. Withdrew, pushed back in. Slow at first, testing her depth. She groaned as I pushed deep, tangled her fingers in her hair and arched her spine off the bed.

"Yeah, just like that," she groaned.

I thrust harder then, slowly letting myself unleash the beast I felt snarling inside me, raging to get loose. "Like this?"

She nodded, spine arched completely off the bed, one hand diving between her thighs, the other going to her nipples. "Yeah, Sebastian, just like that. So good. So fucking good. God, please don't stop."

I grinned down at her, adrenaline bashing

through me as I realized how voracious she was, that she could take all I had and still demand more, just like she'd said she would. "I'm just getting started, baby. I need to feel you come around my cock."

Her eyes went blank for a second, and she froze, eyes going cold and hard and pain-filled. "Don't call me that. Don't ever call me 'baby.'"

I faltered. "Okay. Sorry?"

She sucked in a deep breath, closed her eyes and just breathed for a few seconds. When her eyes opened again, there was remorse in them. "I'm sorry, Sebastian. I just—"

I set her legs down and wrapped my arm under her neck, moved to my side and hauled her tight against me, cupped her ass as I thrust deep. One hand tangled in her hair, the other on her ass, our legs woven under and over each other's.

"Hey, you don't like it, that's all that matters, darlin'. Don't gotta explain shit to me, okay?" I moved into her, slow and sinuous. "Just you and me here, sweet thing. Nothing else matters. You feel me?"

She clung to me, just breathing, and then nodded after a moment. "I feel you."

"All right now?"

Her eyes opened and met mine, and her fingers skated through my hair. "I'm good. More than good. I'm sorry, I just—"

I shut her up with a searing kiss, thrusting my tongue in and out of her mouth to mimic the action of my cock. "No apologies. Don't want it, don't need it."

I nipped her lower lip, and then she tilted her head back to give me access to her throat. I kissed and bit my way down the ivory column of her throat to her breasts, and then found her nipples, licking and sucking and biting them until she was gasping.

"That's what I need, Dru. Those sounds you make." I rolled her to her back again, leaning away to leave room for her hand between our bodies. I guided her fingers down between her thighs to her clit. "Get yourself there, honey. Let me feel you come apart beneath me."

She started out tentatively, all ferocity subsumed beneath whatever my use of the word 'baby' had brought up for her. I wanted her back, that fierce unrelenting lioness. But I had to go slow, had to coax it out of her.

I moved gently, slowly, shallowly as she closed her eyes, pressed her fingertips to her clit and began slowly circling. I bent over her, kissed her tits, flicked her nipples with my tongue. Braced my weight with one arm and pressed my palm to her free hand, tangled our fingers. Not sure why I did that, honestly. It just felt right. Felt like what she needed in the moment. Once our hands were joined, though... something shifted. Inside me. In her. I felt it within us both, as if the press of her palm to mine broke open some connection between us and now that the link was created it blasted everything apart for us both. She gasped, her eyes flicking open and meeting mine, and that need was back, the hunger, the raging desperation. Her eyes went wide and glistened wet, and I loved that, seeing her near tears from the intensity of this. I felt it too. I couldn't deny how fucking intense this was.

Her fingers moved faster, and I started sliding deeper as her touch went wild, blurring faster and faster until her hips left the bed and pressed her pussy against me in a silent demand for more. Her lip was caught between her teeth and her eyes watered and her ass bucked and writhed, and her hand crushed mine.

"Oh—oh fuck, oh fuck yes, fuck yes..." she groaned. "Sebastian, god, I'm—I'm gonna come, Sebastian."

I let myself move a little harder, then, and she whimpered, groaned, squeezed my hand in hers so hard I thought my fingers were going to break, but I loved it and gave her the pressure back just as hard. I felt her pussy clench around mine, and her hips went wild, bucking against me as she detonated, eyes sliding shut.

"FUCK! Oh shit oh fuck oh god, Sebastian! God, I'm coming so fucking hard it hurts—"

"Look at me, Dru, darlin'. Look at me while you come."

She wrenched her eyes open wide, fingers flying in a blur around her clit as I fucked her slow and deep. "I need you to come, Sebastian."

"I will," I said. "I will. I promise. But I'm not done with you yet."

# NINE

# Dru

NOT DONE WITH ME YET? I'D JUST COME HARDER THAN I ever had in my life, and he wasn't done yet?

He waited until I was shaking with the aftershocks of my orgasm, still gasping, still sobbing, and then he moved back to sit on his heels, his shins against the mattress, pulling me up with him so I was sitting on his thighs. I was shaky and weak and trembling, so I clung to his neck with both arms and curled my legs around his waist. He flexed his hips to push into me, and I couldn't help another gasp. Just like that, then, for the space of maybe a minute, Sebastian just lazily flexing his hips to thrust into me, until I started feeling greedy for more, started feeling the need build up within me all over again.

I pressed my mouth to his ear. "More, Sebastian. *More.*"

"Thank fuck," he growled. "Thought you'd never ask."

I pulled back to meet his eyes. "You don't seem the type to wait to be asked."

"I'm not," he said, rising up onto his knees, "but you had a moment. Didn't want to push you too fast."

"You're sweet." I latched more tightly around his waist with my legs and used my arms to lift up, then sank down. "But I'm over my moment."

"You sure?"

I dug my fingers into his shoulders; he seemed to like that, and god knew I couldn't help it, not when his teeth nipped the side of my neck and his cock was filling me to bursting. "Totally."

"'Cause I thought I lost you there for a second."

"You did. But I'm back."

He cupped my ass and lifted me up and drew himself out of me. "I got the wild thing back?"

I clawed his back and sank down on him, feeling his hard sweaty muscular back stutter under my fingernails, bit the round of his shoulder so hard he growled in pain, and his hips pistoned almost on instinct, thrusting his thick, hot, iron shaft into me so hard I lost my breath. "You tell me," I gasped, moving with him, writhing on him, tearing at his back with my nails and biting him as hard as I dared. "This wild enough for you?"

"No," he snarled. "Not even fuckin' close."

He threw me off of him, my pussy throbbing and aching with his absence. His cock slapped against his belly, and his gaze was primal, the brown gone nearly black, his broad chest heaving, his hard, chiseled abs tensing with each breath.

He slid off the bed to stand at the foot, just staring at me and gasping for breath. I was left panting, empty, desperate, confused. On my back, legs splayed open, pussy drenched and on display, tits swaying in rhythm with my breathing.

He grabbed me by the ankles and jerked me down the bed, wedging his hips between my thighs. "I ain't usually one to ask, but I need you on the same page as me, so I'm gonna ask, just this once." He gripped his cock in one hand and fed it into me, buried himself deep, then cupped his hands under my ass, lifted me off the bed and toward him so only my upper back was on the mattress, then just held me there. "How hard can I fuck you, wild thing?"

I writhed in his grip, undulating, secure in his hold on me, knowing he wouldn't let me fall. I met his gaze and pinched my nipples with one hand, hooked my heels around his ass, and fingered my clit with my other hand. "As hard as you want," I breathed. "Wreck me."

"'Wreck me' she says," Sebastian grunted. "You sure?"

"Too much talking, not enough fucking."

He growled wordlessly, then. Tightening his grip on my hips until I knew I'd have bruises where his fingers dug into my flesh, but god, I craved that ferocity in him. I needed to feel him lose control, needed to feel like I had that power over him, that I could push him past his limits and break him, the way he'd broken me. I'd gladly and proudly take the bruises as tokens, reminders of what we had together.

I writhed against him, and then I felt the shift in him. Felt him swell, both inside me and above me. He pulled away, drew out, and then slammed back in, jerking me against him, and the slap of our bodies meeting was loud. I clenched my teeth on the deep groan his thrust ripped out of me, and I wasn't even finished groaning when he pulled back and thrust deep again, tearing another groan from me.

Faster, then.

Harder.

Each thrust went deeper, each thrust slammed harder into me.

"Fuck, you feel so good, Dru," he murmured, "so fuckin' good."

"Your cock is the most incredible thing I've ever felt, Sebastian."

He watched as my pussy swallowed his cock, watched himself disappear inside me. "The way you take me—shit, it's like you were custom made to take my cock."

"I think—" I had to gasp for breath as he ramped up his speed, truly and wildly fucking me now. "I think I was. Oh my fucking *god*, Sebastian, yes...*yes*, just like that. Oh god, fuck me so good—fuck me harder, *harder!*"

"Jesus, woman..." Sebastian snarled. "You're a fucking animal."

I met his thrusts with my own, fingered my clit as he slammed into me. "Only for you...oh my *fuck*—yes, just like that. Harder, Sebastian. Never stop, god, never stop fucking me just like this." I'd lost myself, by then. I was someone else, some crazed, animal version of Dru that had never seen the light of day until Sebastian got his hands on me and his cock inside me.

This Dru was insatiable, powerful. She was fully me, the best me. Truly, deeply *me*. And he was bringing her out of me.

His fucking reached a climax then, his hips relentlessly pounding against mine, his cock slamming into me so hard and fast I lost track of where one thrust ended and the next began, and everything was narrowed down to this, to Sebastian's hands on my ass jerking me into his thrusts, his cock inside me, his eyes on mine.

I couldn't keep quiet. Not anymore. I cried out, another orgasm ripping through me, this one the most blinding yet, making me spasm and arch and writhe in his grip, but I couldn't match his slamming, pounding speed, could only cry out and take his fucking.

"Come for me, Sebastian! Let me feel it. Let me have it."

"I am, god, I am. Right now." He breathed this, and his thrusts faltered. He set me down on the edge of the bed and bent over me and pushed into me, leaned close and claimed my mouth as he came, grunting against my lips.

"Yes, Sebastian, fuck, you feel so good. Come for me. Keep fucking me."

His thrusts resumed, but his mouth never left mine. I dug my nails into his back and dragged them down his flesh, his orgasm spurring another of my own, his cock sliding against me just right, the tip digging into my G-spot, his release driving my own. He snarled and grunted as he fucked me; I felt him spasm inside me and came with him, clawing at him all the harder.

"Look at me, Sebastian," I breathed. "Look at me while you come."

He met my gaze with his, crawled up onto the bed and knelt between my thighs and cupped my hips to pull me closer as he pounded into me through his orgasm, and his eyes never left mine, widening as he came, brows lowering, jaw clenching.

"Fuck, oh fuck—Dru…Jesus," he gasped, "I didn't—I didn't know—"

He fucked me deep and stayed there, flexing to dig deeper, words cutting off into another primal growl. I felt him fill the condom, thrust deep, and then when he was done he thrust again through the aftershocks, burying his face in my breasts. I cupped the back of his head and writhed with his fluttering pulsing shallow thrusts.

"What didn't you know, Sebastian?" I asked.

"That anything could feel that way." His voice was muffled against my tits. "That fucking could—" He stopped, seeming unsure of how to put it.

"Feel like so much more than just fucking?" I finished for him.

He grunted. "Yeah. Exactly."

He wasn't looking at me anymore, I realized. I wiggled out from underneath him, reaching between us to make sure the condom stayed on him. I sat on my heels and stared down at him as he lay on his belly, face buried in his arm.

"Hey, Sebastian."

He rolled to his back and threw his forearm across his forehead, chest heaving, eyes closed. "Yeah, sweet thing."

"What happened to 'wild thing'?" I asked. "I liked that better."

He smirked. "Gimme a few minutes to recuperate, and I'll show you."

"Look at me," I demanded.

His eyes opened, and I saw the distance in them. "What?"

"Now *I'm* losing *you*," I said.

"How do you mean?"

I lay down on the bed beside him, rolled on my side to face him. "That was intense, yeah?"

He grunted an affirmative. "Pretty fuckin' intense, yeah."

"So why are you acting like this?"

"Like what?" His eyes were on mine, but the mask was still in place.

"Like this was a hook-up and you're just waiting for me to leave."

"Well, what're you expecting? Cuddles?"

That stung. I felt my eyes water. I rolled away from him, sliding off the bed. I snagged his white T-shirt off the floor and tugged it on, gathered my sodden clothes and opened his door, pausing in his open doorway.

"Something like that, yeah," I said, trying to hide the hurt.

I stepped as quietly as I could out of his room, hoping to escape Zane's notice.

Which I should've known was futile. He was behind the counter in the kitchen, rummaging in the fridge. He straightened when he saw me, and his gaze raked over my body, covered in nothing but Sebastian's too-big T-shirt. Then up to my face.

"He ain't the 'something like that' type, sweetheart." Zane twisted the top off a bottle of beer. "Sorry to be the one to break it to ya."

"How the fuck would you know?" I asked, shoving open the door to the room I'd slept in the night before.

"Because none of us are, and we all learned from him."

"Well fuck me," I said.

"Noooope," Zane drawled. "Bast already did. Makes you a no-fly zone for the rest of us."

I growled in irritation. Shut the door to my temporary room behind me, tossed my wet clothes onto the floor and sank onto the bed, fighting tears.

What had I expected? Either from him or myself? I'd known going in that I wouldn't be able to just fuck him and not get emotional about it. I was an emotional wreck, after all. I'd just been cheated on, rejected. I'd wasted fifteen thousand dollars I'd never get back on a wedding that never happened. No wedding. No husband. No honeymoon.

And now I was in Ketchikan fucking Alaska half in the bag for a sexy, tattooed bartender I barely knew, a man I'd just met, fucked once, and was totally ruined over.

How could I ever fuck any other man ever again and not compare him to the way Sebastian had just fucked me? He'd set an impossible to beat standard, and then had just shut down, shut me out.

Rejected me all over again.

Why?

Because it had started smacking of *involvement*.

Fucking pussy.

I should have known better. I should have known *myself* better than to allow me to talk myself into rebound sex with a perfect stranger less than forty-eight hours after the second-worst day of my life. And I should have known better than to expect more than one fuck from a player like Sebastian, especially when it started feeling like something real, something more than fucking. So much more.

Because it had been, hadn't it?

I'd felt a *connection*.

Real, powerful, potent, and undeniable. And completely unlike anything I'd ever felt before, with anyone.

I peeled Sebastian's T-shirt off, because I couldn't handle his scent any longer.

Except his scent wasn't just on the T-shirt, it was on me. On my skin. In my hair. I spread my legs and pulled the skin of my thighs apart to look at the stark black love bites he'd left on either side of my pussy. He'd *marked* me. Claimed me. For a few handfuls of minutes, I'd felt so utterly perfect, beautiful, powerful, desired, *needed*.

And then he'd just slammed a wall down, and that was that.

So much for never letting me leave his bed.

I had to get his scent off me so I jumped in the shower and rinsed off, scrubbed my skin a little too angrily, and then got out, dried off, and dressed all over again in the other change of clothes. Outside, the rain had slackened off a bit, it seemed, so if I was going to get out of this bar and away from Sebastian, now was the time.

I ignored Zane completely as I left the room and rushed down the stairs, purse in hand. Ridiculous, that all I had was a white clutch purse meant to match my wedding dress, but whatever. It had my wallet and phone in it, which was all I really needed.

There was a series of coat hooks at the bottom of the stairs, just inside the stairwell, and hanging from one hook was drab green raincoat with a deep hood. I slipped it on, zipped it up over my purse, and left the bar.

I was tempted to go back to Sebastian's sailboat, but I wasn't ready to be found yet—assuming he would even go looking for me.

So…I just walked.

And tried desperately to talk myself out of feeling hurt and rejected by Sebastian. It didn't work, of course, but I had to try. It was better than just wallowing in it, right?

I was so fucking stupid.

It was true, and I knew it. There wasn't even any point in arguing with myself over my own stupidity. Stupider yet, I'd known going in that this would happen.

Double dumb.

# TEN

# Sebastian

I HEARD THE APARTMENT DOOR OPEN AND CLOSE, AND knew Dru had left. Whether for good or just to think, I wasn't sure, and tried to tell myself I didn't care.

I pulled on a pair of jeans commando and left my room, found Zane lounging on the couch with a beer, watching some action flick on cable TV.

There was half a bottle of Jack in the cabinet above the fridge, and despite the hour, I needed it. Not even noon and I was already a mess over that woman. I dug out the bottle, a block of cheese from the fridge and a knife from the block, and sat down beside Zane on the couch, cutting myself a thick slice of Colby Jack and shoving it into my mouth.

Zane watched me twist the top off the Jack, just sort of staring at me oddly. I got the bottle to my lips, tipped it back, and then his hand flashed out and snatched the bottle from me, spilling whiskey all over my bare chest.

"What the fuck, dude?" I demanded.

He snatched the cap from me before I could react, twisted it back on, and tossed the bottle across the room. "The fuck are you doing, dumbass?"

"Drinking? Because I'm an adult and I can?" I pushed up off the couch, but Zane's fist slammed into my chest and knocked me back onto the couch.

"No, you're not. You're a fucking dumbass. The dumbest dumbass I've ever met, and that includes the first-day washouts at SEAL training. You let that girl walk out the door and don't go after her, you might as well cut off your teeny-weeny little boy balls, because you sure as fuck don't deserve 'em." He indicated the bottle of Jack with an angry wave of his hand. "And instead of manning the fuck up, you're gonna hide in the bottom of a bottle like some wet behind the ear yellow-belly pussy? You're a pussy. Fuck you, pussy-boy."

I stood up, rage rising inside me. Who the fuck

did he think he was?

I stomped across the room, snatched the bottle, and moved toward the kitchen. I'd planned to put it away, but Zane must've interpreted my action as intent to drink anyway.

He was across the room and in my face in a flash. "I can kick your ass, Bast, and you'd better not fucking forget it." He took the bottle from me and set it far too gently on the counter, then returned to stand an inch in front of my face, his voice deadly quiet. "Thought Dad raised us better than to pussy out of the hard shit, especially by drinking."

I let my anger show, then. "Do *not* bring Dad into this, you bastard."

The door opened, and both of us turned to see who it was.

Baxter was standing in the doorway with Brock behind him. Both were damp from the rain and looking a little shocked. Zane and I quarrelled almost as much as Canaan and Corin did, but for us to show true anger at each other was very rare. Mostly we just bickered, since Zane was every bit as alpha male as I was and thought he was the more mature and responsible one most of the time, as if he was the oldest rather than me, which caused us to butt heads over pretty much everything.

The problem was Zane usually *was* the more

mature and responsible of the two of us. He was by far the most serious of all of us, which was to be expected given his calling in life. He'd seen and done shit I didn't really want to know too much about, stuff that had scarred him deeply, left permanent marks on his soul. It left him with little tact and no tolerance for bullshit, which meant he'd call me out and not spare my feelings in the process.

Like now.

Thus my anger: I knew he was right, and it pissed me off. And I was pissing myself off by being a stupid pussy, and Dru was pissing me off by being her amazing too-good-for-me self and making me feel like a fucking pussy, and the looks Brock and Baxter were giving me were pissing me off, just because they were my little brothers.

Needless to say, I was a lot of different kinds of pissed off.

"The fuck are you two knuckleheads looking at?" I snarled.

At six-two, Baxter was between Zane and me in height but closer to Zane in terms of raw bulk. Whereas Zane's body was that of a warrior—lean, hard, and conditioned to handle the most gruelling of circumstances—Baxter, being a semi-pro football player, was overall thicker. He carried a little more body fat over his muscles, was conditioned for raw power and to absorb the brutal impacts of tackles. His hair was, like most of us Badd brothers, a deep, rich brown, thick and wavy, clipped close on the sides and left long and messy on top. Same dark brown eyes as all of us, but his reflected an easy-going, lackadaisical, party-boy personality.

He took his football career intensely seriously, though, and on the field Bax was an absolute monster, faster than his size belied and yet strong enough to break the hardest tackles with ease. I'd seen him shrug off hits from guys that stood six-eight and weighed four hundred pounds. He'd just brush their worst damage off like an irritation, and then take off like a rocket to nail the QB with the crushing force of a runaway semi.

Off the field, though, he took just about nothing seriously. He was a natural ladies man, every bit the player I was. He had an easy way of picking up chicks—and an easier way of ditching them. He drank like a fish, trained like a beast, and generally gave off an air of not giving a shit about much of anything except football, women, and booze. Which was true...mostly. He had his demons, like all of us, he just kept his buried deep and didn't bother trying to sort 'em out, preferring instead to drink and fuck and bench press them away.

Baxter sidled over to me, a weird look on his face.

He lifted both hands and curled his fingers into claws, pressed them to my chest, and slid them down a few inches.

Shit, shit, shit. Forgot about that—should've put a shirt on.

He moved around behind me then, and let out a chuckle. "Holy hell, brother," he said, laughing outright, now, "either you tangled with a mountain lion, or you've got a prime piece of tail stashed around here somewhere."

Another laugh, and his fingers were tracing what I assumed were Dru's fingernail marks on my back. From the extent of his touch and the disbelieving laughter from him and the rest of my brothers—all crowded behind me, now—I realized the marks she'd left had to be pretty extensive.

"I mean...*damn*, dude," Baxter said, awe in his voice. "She tore you the fuck *up*."

Zane, of course, had to get his two cents in. "Yeah, and he let her leave, too."

Bax spun me around, gaping at me like the bull-neck moron he was. "You *what*?"

"Like any of you assholes know shit about it," I snapped. "You haven't met her, and none of you fuckers have ever kicked it with a chick more than once, no more than I have. So I don't wanna hear dick about it from any of you."

Brock eyed me. "Was she good?"

I sighed and rubbed my face with both hands. "Most fucking incredible thing I've ever experienced."

"Which, of course, means you should bail on her pronto, right?" Brock quirked an eyebrow, a gesture I hated; it was a Dad gesture, that lifted eyebrow.

Brock looked the most like Dad. Just slightly shorter than Bax at six-one, he was leaner, rangier, more inclined to spend his time in the cockpit of his stunt plane than in the gym. Same brown hair and eyes, but Brock kept his hair neatly cut and swept off to one side like a GQ model, a few strands left to dangle near his left eye. Being my own brother, I had no problem admitting he was a pretty sonofabitch. It was annoying, honestly. He had a dry sense of humor, a sharp insight, and a tendency to ask the hard questions, usually at the worst times, too. Like now.

I slugged his shoulder. "Shut up, Brock."

He just laughed, and glanced at Zane. "He's got it bad, doesn't he?"

Zane jerked a thumb at the Jack. "That was his idea of dealing with it."

Brock clapped me on the back. "Good idea, big brother: drink her away. Makes perfect sense. That's clearly the most logical way of dealing with those pesky emotions. Works every time!"

"Smartass," I growled.

I should have known better, because the second the words left my mouth, all three of my brothers spoke in unison:

"Better than being a dumbass!"

That was Dad's favorite phrase to use, and hearing it from them all at once only pissed me off all the more.

"Fuck all'a you motherfuckers. I don't need this shit." I stalked back to my room, shrugged into a shirt, stuffed my bare feet into my boots, and then pushed past my idiot brothers to the stairs.

"Where're you going, dickwad?" Baxter asked.

"Hell if I know. Wherever you bastards *aren't*," I said, stomping down the stairs.

Brock was the one to follow me; I ignored him for the moment, but of all the present brothers, he was the most level-headed and thus likely to actually get through to me. The only other brother I'd ever really listen to when I was pissed off was Lucian, simply because he was the strong silent type. He rarely spoke more than a handful of syllables at a time, but when he did, he tended to cut to the marrow of things with well-chosen, hard-hitting words.

My raincoat was gone, which I assumed—hoped—meant Dru had borrowed it and was out there somewhere.

Fuck it. Just a little rain, not gonna hurt anything.

I was just going for a walk to cool off, I tried to tell myself. I was *not* looking for Dru.

"So, where d'you think she went?" Brock asked.

"I don't know."

"You don't know? You don't know where she'd have gone after you pussed out on her?"

"I just met her, Brock. Literally, the night before last. Nothing to puss out on."

"And yet you're already this hung up on her?"

"I'm not hung up on her, asshole." I didn't have to be looking at him to see the quirked eyebrow. "Put that fuckin' eyebrow down before I knock it off your pretty boy face."

"Super hung up, then."

"Shut *up*, Brock."

"What's her name?"

"Dru."

"She pretty?"

"Stop you in your tracks hot, man."

He kept pace with me as I stomped up the docks. "And the sex...you said it was the best ever?"

"I think my heart actually stopped for a second, near the end there."

"See, you say your heart stopped, but I think you're just out of touch with your feelings. You're mistaking your physical heart stopping for your *metaphysical* heart reaching out for her."

I stopped in my tracks and stared at Brock. "Where the *fuck* do you get this shit?"

He shrugged. "Books." A sly glance at me. "Tell me I'm wrong, though."

I knew better than to bullshit this particular brother. "Shut *up*, Brock."

He just laughed. "See? Super hung up on a girl you just met last night. A girl who also happens to be able to stop you in your tracks just by existing, gave you the best sex of your life and clawed you all to shit it was so good…and then you bailed on her. And now you're wandering the Ketchikan docks refusing to admit you're looking for her, and I'm guessing you don't have the first clue about what to say even if you actually found her."

"Shut the *fuck UP*, Brock!"

Goddammit, but he was right. I hated it when my brothers were smarter than me…which was most of the time.

He caught all that, and didn't even know the circumstances about why she was in Ketchikan in the first place. He'd really rip into me if he knew that.

I shuddered at the thought.

And, of course, Brock saw me chewing on things. "What aren't you saying?"

I glared at him. "God fuckin' dammit, Brock, why can't you just leave it alone?"

"Because you don't want me to. You'd have tossed me back into the bar if you didn't actually want to hear what I have to say."

He was right, as usual, so I just grunted. "Asshole. When'd you get so fuckin' smart?"

"Problem isn't your intelligence, Sebastian. It's that you've never had a chance to grow up emotionally."

I stopped in my tracks and whirled on him. "You'd better explain that shit *real* fuckin' fast, Brock."

Despite being three inches shorter, thirty pounds lighter, and four years younger, Brock didn't seem intimidated by my anger. He just clapped me on the back and kept walking along the docks, the water on our left, Ketchikan on our right.

"You were what, seventeen when Mom died? That messed all of us up in some way, but I think it fucked you up the most. You had to take her place in the bar, yeah, but Dad was so depressed for so long you had to be a surrogate parent to most of us."

"I didn't do shit," I grumbled, a heavy, uncomfortable feeling rolling through me.

Brock shot an irritated look at me. "Maybe we have different memories of those years, then. I seem to remember you making lunches for us. Helping us with homework you barely understood yourself—don't hit me! You know it's true and no fault of your own." He held up both hands to fend off my instinctively thrown fist. "You got us up in the morning. Made sure Bax had a ride home from football practice. Got me to flight lessons."

I tried to find some way of responding, but I had nothing. I *had* done all that, but it hadn't seemed like I'd had a choice. Dad slept late a lot after Mom died, and I'd just blamed it on having to close the bar every night, being up till three or four. Of course, I'd closed with him and still got up to go to school, and then after I graduated I made sure the rest of the boys did, too. It had to be done, and I was the oldest, which made it my job. Looking back, I saw that Mom's death had decimated Dad worse than I think any of us really realized and, perhaps unfairly, put a lot of pressure on me. More than I probably understood.

I shrugged, and stuffed my hands in my hip pockets. "Did what had to be done. Didn't mean shit."

"That's where you're wrong, you macho fuck-stick. It *did* mean something. You stepped up. None of us have ever forgotten that. We're all living our dreams, at least partially because you stepped up when Dad couldn't. And none of us hold that against Dad, but it sucked. For all of us, but it put a huge burden on you, especially." He punched my shoulder, and it hurt a lot more than I'd expected it to. "So when I say you never got to grow up emotionally, I just mean that you were so preoccupied with taking care of us, you didn't have a chance to let yourself sort through your own emotions. You're out of touch. You didn't get to mourn Mom, and you sure as hell haven't mourned Dad. You're all sorts of a mess inside, and then some girl comes along and challenges that status quo you've been hanging onto, and it fucks with your carefully insulated emotions, and you don't know how to handle it." He shrugged. "So you bail."

I sighed, a deep gusting growl. "And then you assholes come along and tell me everything I'm doing wrong."

"Only because we care."

"Yeah, yeah, yeah. So much caring going on I'm feeling all mushy inside. Jesus."

Brock raised his hands and shook them. "Oh no! *Feelings!* You'd better go punch a wall so you don't turn into a girl."

"Maybe I'll punch your stupid face instead of a wall. Make you a little uglier. God knows you could use it, pretty boy."

"You're just jealous."

"Jealous? Of *you*? For what?" I stopped walking and glared at him.

He was baiting me, of course, and I'd just fallen for it. "Oh, I don't know...maybe that I can use three-syllable words and form complete sentences without cursing?"

I charged at him. "You fuckin' twerp. Let's see you complete sentences after I knock your fuckin' teeth in!"

He caught my charge and somehow deflected it, redirecting my momentum aside so neatly I nearly toppled off the dock. Zane knew that Judo bullshit too and I'd roughhoused with him enough to learn to expect those dirty tricks and how to deal with them. Case in point? Pretend to be more off balance than I was, and then when he moved in to do some kind of fancy bullshit throw, slug him in the gut. Hard to redirect my chi or whatever the fuck if you can't breathe.

He took it like a man, though, and came at me with a blazing right hook that took me completely by surprise, mainly due to its complete lack of sophistication, which wasn't much like Brock, for the most part. It clocked me on the jaw, sent stars flashing behind my eyes, and left me dizzy.

Not dizzy enough that I didn't return the favor in kind, though, and I was satisfied to note *my* right hook sent Brock to the ground. Of course, I was dumb enough to stay within reach of him while he was on the ground. His legs shot out, scissored around mine, and threw me to the ground so fast I didn't know what hit me until my head was ringing and his legs were clamped around my throat. I rolled toward him, got my hands around his neck…and started squeezing. Now it was just a matter of who could go the longest without breathing before tapping out.

He tapped me, speaking hoarsely past my chokehold. "Wait—wait!" His legs released me, and he pointed down the docks. "Isn't that your raincoat?"

I let him go and followed his outstretched finger. Sure enough, there was a figure a few hundred feet away wearing an olive green raincoat several sizes too big, standing in front of a seaplane gesticulating somewhat angrily at the pilot.

Dru.

It was her.

And from the looks of it, she was trying to wrangle a ride out of here with my raincoat.

…And my heart.

Or some sappy emotional bullshit like that. All I knew for sure was that the thought of Dru getting on that plane and flying out of Ketchikan never to return felt a lot like wrong and scary and shitty—and something I really needed to prevent.

Like…*now.*

Brock sat up and quirked that damn eyebrow at me. "Well? *Go*, you macho fuckstick!"

I went and even managed to be mature enough to ignore the barb he'd sent my way. Well…mostly ignored. Except a middle finger or two flashed at him as I jogged down the dock toward Dru.

Problem was, Brock had been right earlier when he said I wouldn't have a fuckin' clue what to say if I found Dru. Because I didn't. Not the first damn idea.

But then, talking wasn't ever really my strong suit, was it? Maybe I should just play to my strengths, and *show* her what I meant.

# ELEVEN

# Dru

"Sorry, honey. No can do," the pilot repeated. "I told you, I'm gonna have a full load as it is, no space for passengers. And even if I did have the room, I couldn't possibly cart you wherever it is you wanna go without full payment up front. Get me the cash now, I could maybe wrangle something. But I'm leavin' in ten minutes, so you'd best hustle."

"And *I* told *you* I could get you more cash as soon as we land." I held up my cell phone. "One phone call, and I could have cash in hand the second we touch down. But there aren't any banks around here that'll let me withdraw from my savings account. *Please*, please…six hundred bucks for a one-way ride to Seattle? How much more do you want? Hell, even just get me *close* to Seattle! You'll get paid, you have my word."

"Words don't pay the fuel bill, sweetheart." He started flipping switches, and then the engines chugged, burped exhaust, and the props started spinning, ramping up to a deafening roar within seconds. He closed his door and leaned out the open window. "Try Bruce! Couple slips down!"

And then the seaplane was reversing out into the bay, and my last hope for getting the fuck out of here on my own was gone.

I glanced down the dock at the only other seaplane within sight. Single engine, tiny, with duct tape on the floats, visible rust in places and dirty streaks in others…the aircraft was obviously ancient, and well past its prime. And the pilot, sitting on the float with a fishing pole in hand…he looked like he was older than actual dirt, and as timeworn as his plane. Um… probably not. If I got drunk and desperate enough, *maybe*, but I didn't rate my chances very high of reaching Seattle alive. Thanks but no thanks, Bruce.

Shit. SHIT!

I was just gonna have to call Dad, I decided. I didn't want to, though. It felt too much like giving up, calling Daddy to come rescue me. I'd gotten myself into this mess, and the hell if I'd beg him to come pluck me out of it.

I stood on the edge of the dock, scrubbing my face and trying not to cry. I just wanted to go home and pretend none of this had ever happened. Drink a few dozen bottles of wine and eat a few dozen cartons of ice cream, and binge on *Real Housewives*.

Of course, my lease on *home* was expiring soon, which meant house hunting, or moving in with Dad. I knew for a fact my unit had been leased to someone else already, so I had no leeway there, and there weren't any units left in the building, since it happened to be a prime building in a desirable part of Seattle....which I'd given up for Michael.

A thought occurred to me, apropos of nothing. Michael had been in possession of the airline tickets for our honeymoon. And the all-inclusive resort reservation had been in his name, too. I checked the time on my phone: eleven-fourteen in the morning; our flight was scheduled to leave at eleven-forty. So I should be boarding right now. Obviously that wasn't happening, but maybe I could change my ticket in such a way to get me out of here...

I scrolled through my emails to the flight check-in notification, which I'd never gotten around to actually doing. Found a phone number, and after a few transfers got hold of an actual person.

"Delta Airlines, this is Felicia speaking, how can I help you?" a flat female voice said.

"Yeah, hi, my name is Dru Connolly. I have tickets for a flight leaving from Seattle-Tacoma in about twenty minutes, but I—"

"Flight number?" she interrupted. I read the flight number off to her, and I heard the sound of fingers on a keyboard, then she spoke again. "Yeah, I show that you're already checked in and on board."

"But I'm not, which is why I'm calling—"

"You'll have to ask the gate attendant. All I have is what my computer tells me." She rattled off a phone number and then promptly clicked off.

Nice. Customer service at its finest.

I dialed the number I'd been given, and after a few rings an exuberant male voice answered. "Delta Airlines, gate C20, this Kevin, how can I help you?"

"Has flight DL 743 left yet?"

"It's fully boarded, but it hasn't left yet, no. What can do I for you, ma'am?"

I struggled to find an explanation. "I have a ticket for that flight, but another Delta rep tells me someone's taken my seat. I'm wondering if you could help me figure this out."

"What's your seat number?"

"Three-C."

A few seconds of tapping, and then he hummed. "Oh, hmm. Interesting. What's your name, ma'am?"

"Dru Connolly."

"Ah, yes. Well, it seems the ticket was changed early this morning. The ticket holder is now one... Tawny Howard."

"*Fuck!*" I shouted, then immediately quieted. "Sorry, Kevin. I just—thanks. That's all I needed."

"Is there anything else I can do for you?"

"Unless you can make my ex-fiancé less of a cheating dickbag, then no, probably not. But thanks anyway."

"Men are pigs," he said, clearly commiserating.

"That they are." I sighed. "Well, thanks for checking."

"My pleasure, ma'am. Have a nice day."

I laughed bitterly. "Yeah, not so far." I hung up before subjecting the poor gate attendant to any more self-pitying awkwardness.

The bastard! He was taking *HER* on *MY* honeymoon? Motherfucker!

I wanted to throw my phone into the ocean, but that wouldn't actually help anything, so I didn't.

Instead, I cried.

Because apparently that was just what I did these days.

But then, being cheated on and then rejected

within forty-eight hours will do that to you, I guess.

I didn't hear the footsteps, didn't feel his approach, because I was bawling my eyes out.

He was just there, wrapping his arms around me, enveloping me with his heat, his strength, and I was so upset I didn't even question it at first.

Then it hit me.

And I shoved him away from me as hard as I could. "NO! Keep your damn hands off me, Sebastian!"

He recovered his balance and came back to stand in front of me, reaching for me but not quite touching me. "Dru, listen—"

"No, you bastard. You had your chance. It doesn't work that way. Not with me, not after everything I've been though. Hell, everything I'm *still* going through."

He was soaked, because even though the rain had slacked off, it was still coming down hard enough to soak you to the bone within a few minutes. And I had his raincoat.

Do NOT feel bad for him, I ordered myself. He was wet, not injured. He'd dry.

But he did have a shadow on his jaw, as if somebody had slugged him hard enough to bruise even his craggy jaw. And he did look suitably upset. He should, though, the asshole. He deserved it.

"Dru, please. Just listen to me for like ten fuckin'

seconds."

"Why should I?" I demanded.

He shifted from foot to foot, struggling for an answer, and he kept looking at me as if I'd take pity on him and explain his actions for him. Not likely, buddy.

"Look, this shit isn't easy for me, okay? I'm tryin' here."

I couldn't help a laugh. "What isn't easy, Sebastian? Talking to a woman? I'm sure you've had plenty of practice. Figure it out."

He growled, because that seemed to be the largest part of his vocabulary. "Yeah, I've *talked* to plenty. But this is different."

I kept my expression blank, even though hope was starting to germinate inside me. "Why?"

"Because—" He sighed, scrubbed his hands through his hair, flinging droplets of rain everywhere and making him look even sexier than he already did, what with the rain plastering his white T-shirt to his muscular body, highlighting his bulk and his ink and his everything being fucking stupid sexy...

No. NOPE. Do *not* go there, Dru. He's a troll. He's ugly. He's stupid. He's a man, and men are pigs.

*Yeah*, argued some other, stupider part of me, *but he's not Michael. Don't punish him for that. And he IS sexy as fuck.*

But he's still an asshole.

*Granted.*

Now that both parts of me were in agreement—sort of—I waited for Sebastian to come up with whatever it was he was trying to say.

"Because…?" I prompted.

"Because I feel things," he concluded, somewhat lamely, rubbing the back of his neck with one hand.

I rolled my eyes at him. "Wow. That was deep, Sebastian. You feel things? Could you maybe be just a *little* more specific?"

He growled again, turned away to glare at another man standing a hundred or so yards away, then back to me. "Tryin' here, sweet thing, but this shit don't come naturally." He let out another breath. "I feel things for you, Dru. I shouldn't've let you leave like that. I should've…I dunno. Done a lot of shit differently."

I sighed and shook my head. "As far as proclamations of love go, this one is rather…unique."

He didn't like that. "Maybe I don't know a bunch of fancy twenty-dollar words. You want that shit, go talk to Brock back there, he's full of 'em. All I got is what I got." He stepped closer, and I couldn't back away or I'd be swimming. I could only hold my ground and stare up at him, and god, even his scowl was sexy. Scary, but sexy. "And it's not a proclamation of love, because we just fuckin' met. I'm just sayin'…I feel shit for you, and maybe if we were to play this out, it *could* be. Meaning, I *could* feel that way for you. I know that's not some fairy tale poetry about my feelings or whatever, but it's the best I can do. It wasn't just fuckin', what we had earlier. I see that. I know that. I know you do too, and...I'd really like to see what that's like, long-term. I'm not promising I'd be any better at this feelings bullshit than I am now, because I haven't really had much practice with listenin' to what my heart has to say or however you wanna put it, but...I'd *try*. That's what I could promise you."

I blinked up at him, absorbing everything he'd just said to me. Which, despite the roughness of it, was incredibly sweet, and as honest and upfront as you could ask for. If he'd declared his undying love, I'd have laughed in his face, but that wasn't what he was offering. He wasn't saying he'd be able to change his nature, but he was willing to try. Because he "felt shit for me." Was that enough for me? Was it even what I wanted?

I didn't get a chance to reply, though.

"Now, what are the chances of you coming back home with me so we can continue this somewhere a little drier?" He jerked his head back toward the bar.

Apparently I didn't reply quickly enough, because he scooped me up in his arms and started walking back down the dock. I laughed and slapped him on the shoulder. "Put me down, you big idiot. I can walk."

"Will you be goin' in the right direction, though?" he asked.

"Yes, yes, I'll go with you. Just put me down. I'm not a fucking invalid."

"I'm wet and getting cold and you weren't answering," he muttered, setting me on my feet. "And I just put myself out there and you haven't said dick about it in return, so I'm getting a little antsy, here, you know?"

We'd reached the man whom Sebastian had said was Brock—one of his brothers, I assumed—and he heard Sebastian's last statement.

"Give the girl a minute to process, would you?" He extended his hand to me. "I'm Brock."

"Dru," I responded, shaking his hand, and hated how stunned I sounded.

Because holy mother of shit, if I thought Sebastian and Zane were hot? Brock was...Jesus. The man was *gorgeous*, in a neat, classical, lean-and-wiry sort of way. Similar features as Zane and Sebastian, the same rich brown hair and liquid, expressive brown eyes, but where Sebastian was rough and wild and rugged and Zane was cold and dangerous and brutal-looking in a scary sexy way, Brock was just...*beautiful*. Male, definitely, not at all effeminate, just truly beautiful. I had no idea what Brock did for a living, but if he said he was a model, I wouldn't have been surprised.

Which only made me wonder what the other five looked like. Holy hell, five more Badd brothers?

I elbowed Sebastian. "Are all your brothers this good-looking?"

He grinned down at me. "Nah. The rest are ugly."

I frowned. "That's what you said about Zane, and I wouldn't classify him as ugly by any stretch of the imagination."

Brock laughed. "Along with punching, insults are his way of showing affection."

"It's the only language you uneducated gorillas understand," Sebastian said.

And for some reason, Brock thought this was hilarious. "I'm surprised you managed all those syllables in the same sentence, Bast. I'm so proud of you!"

Sebastian growled. "I can still choke you out, you little prick."

Brock just laughed again. "Yeah, I'd like to see you try, you big macho fuckstick."

I watched their easy banter. Despite the harsh words, neither seemed truly insulted or angry. Weird. If anyone had said that kind of thing to me, they'd wake up in the hospital with false teeth and pins keeping their bones together.

Brock eyed me, apparently noticing my unfamiliarity with their brand of playfulness. "We're only kidding, you know."

Sebastian shoved Brock toward the water, and the younger brother barely managed to avoid taking a swim. "Speak for yourself, ding-dong. You'd still be unconscious if you hadn't spotted Dru."

"Excuse me?" Brock stopped and then took a step toward Sebastian. "I think you were the one about to pass out, actually."

And they were about to face off again. "Um, boys? Can we not?" I said, stepping between them.

Sebastian grinned at Brock. "By the way, in case you get any funny ideas...Dru here took Zane down in two moves."

Brock gave me a look of shocked surprise. "Damn, girl. Takes balls to go after Zane."

"Nah, just a knee *to* the balls," I said.

"How did this come about?" Brock asked.

Sebastian shrugged. "We didn't exactly start off on the best foot, you might say."

I snorted. "If by that you mean 'about to tear each others faces off', then yes, that would be an accurate statement."

"It wasn't that bad," Sebastian argued. "Just a... disagreement."

Brock shook his head. "You two argue more than

Corin and Canaan. It's pathetic."

"Wasn't my fault. He went in on me about the ten grand Dad left me."

"And let me guess, you said something about being stuck here in Ketchikan, and he took it personally, and then you were trying to beat each other into toothpaste like the muscle-bound ape-men you are?"

I laughed at that. "Pretty much exactly it. You're funny, Brock."

He winked at me. "That's me, the funny one."

"What are your other brothers like?" I asked.

Sebastian answered. "You've met Zane. He's serious, intense, and a little hard to get used to. But he's cool, if you can earn his trust. Brock here is the funny one—"

"And the smart one, don't forget," Brock put in.

"Nah, that's Xavier. He makes even you look like a numbskull," Sebastian said to Brock, then glanced at me. "Xavier is the baby. He's seventeen, national high school soccer all-star, got a full academic ride to Stanford and offers from a couple other Ivy League schools for that and soccer. Baxter is back at the bar already. He plays football, and that's really all you need to know about him. He plays in the CFL for now, but I guess there's been talk of going pro. Wouldn't surprise me, honestly. The kid is a monster."

Brock spoke up. "Well, there *was* talk of going

pro. This will of Dad's puts a crimp on that."

Sebastian sighed. "Yeah. It puts a crimp on a lot of shit for everyone."

Brock's teasing humor was gone, now. "Yeah, but Bax and the twins have the most to lose from this year in Ketchikan business. Bax basically has to put his career on hold, and the twins have to skip an entire year of touring. Zane took his discharge papers for this, in case you weren't aware, and who the hell knows what Lucian is doing. I can easily skip a year of air shows, so it doesn't bother me all that much."

Sebastian frowned at his brother. "Zane left the Navy?"

Brock snorted. "No shit. He *had* to. If all of us don't show up for this year of brotherly bonding, no one gets the money."

"I didn't think about that aspect of it," Sebastian said.

"That's why I'm saying something," Brock said, clapping Sebastian on the shoulder. "But I mean you *have* to know there's going to be some tempers flaring in the near future. But just remember, we're all doing it. For Dad, yeah, but for you too."

Sebastian stopped and glared at Brock. "For me? What the fuck does that mean?"

I felt like an outsider, listening in on this. It was obviously a very touchy, difficult subject.

Brock sighed, and took a minute to formulate his thoughts. "We should probably have this conversation another time." He glanced at me. "Not because of you, Dru, it's just…it's a tricky subject, for all of us. Dad's death is still fresh for us all, Sebastian. But none of us have forgotten how you stepped up, and that you've been running the bar alone since Dad died. We all took as much time off for the funeral as we could, but…" He shrugged, for once at a loss. "Then we got the call from that lawyer about the terms of the will, and we knew we had to come back. Not much choice. Not for any of us."

"Wait, wait…did you guys talk about this already?" Sebastian asked.

Brock hesitated. "Yeah, sort of."

"Of course you did." Sebastian pushed ahead, his long legs swiftly carrying him away from Brock and me.

"Not like you're thinking, though." Brock jogged to catch up. "Bast, you're not understanding. All of us have our careers. We don't really need the money. So we talked about doing the year and then giving Dad's payout back to you."

Sebastian stopped, anger on his face. "I don't need the fuckin' money, asshole."

"Yes, you do. But it's not about the money."

"Then what's it about?"

Brock grabbed Sebastian's shoulders. *"You."*

Sebastian shook his hold off. "I told you, all that bullshit about the way things were after Mom died… that was what I had to do. No more, no less."

"How *you* feel about it isn't the point," Brock said.

Sebastian threw up his hands and kept walking. "Then color me fuckin' confused." He jerked open the door to the bar and vanished inside.

Brock let him go, and turned to look at me. "He's a stubborn motherfucker, but he'll come around. You can't ever really take Sebastian's first reaction at face value. He tends to give in to knee-jerk reactions, and then after he has a chance to think things through, he comes around. So…you know, just give him a chance."

I nodded, but my mind was going a million miles a second. "Sounds like things are getting complicated for you guys."

Brock quirked an eyebrow up. "You could say that. Our dad passed away three months ago, and his will stipulated that all of his kids—meaning the seven of us who left home—have to return here for a full year to work in the bar with Sebastian before we get any of the money from his estate." He pulled the door open for me, and we went into the still-darkened bar. Sebastian was nowhere to be seen, which meant he was upstairs, I assumed. "Which, yes, complicates life for pretty much all of us. It's about time, though, if you ask me. Sebastian has had to deal with way more than his share of the burden around here for too long. So we all decided to come back and do what we had to do, for Sebastian's sake. Except he's too damn stubborn to accept that, so he's gonna be a grunty caveman about it until he decides to come around to our way of thinking.

"And yeah, all eight of us fully grown Badd brothers living and working in this little bar?" He chuckled with dark amusement. "Oooooh boy, it's gonna get *super* interesting around here, let me tell you. Between Zane and Sebastian posturing about who's the most badass, Baxter acting like his usual bull-in-a-china shop self, the cat-and-dog fighting of the twins…holy shit, man. The next year is going to be *fun*. Especially for me, since I'm the mediator most of the time."

"There's eight of you, right?" I counted off the names I knew. "Sebastian, the oldest, then Zane—"

Brock took over. "Then me, then Baxter, the football player, then Canaan and Corin the identical twins, who are currently in Germany on tour with their band, then Lucian, who's kind of a weird and mysterious guy, but cool if you can get him to open up, then Xavier the baby."

"And they're all coming back?" I asked.

He nodded. "I guess Lucian is going to take a while, since he was halfway across the world doing god knows what. Xavier should be here within a few days, and the twins in a couple weeks. They had a series of shows in Europe they were committed to, but they've canceled the rest. And that's the lot, as they say." He said the last sentence in a passable British accent.

I leaned against the bar. "And there's me, in the middle of it all, fucking with Sebastian's head."

Brock wobbled his head side to side. "I don't know, actually. I'm not sure I'd say you're fucking with his head. I mean, I've only been here an hour, but he's obviously hung up on you, and I've never known him to ever get hung up on a chick before. He needs a good kick to the status quo. He's been stuck in a rut, I think, and the only way he'll ever get out of it is if someone forces him out of it."

"And you think that's me?"

Brock just shrugged. "That's up to the two of you, whether or not he's willing to actually man up and let you in, and whether or not you have the patience to put up with his emotionally-stunted nonsense." He slapped the bar top with his palm. "And I, for one, hope you do, and hope he does."

"And if he doesn't?"

Another lift of his shoulder. "He'll asshole his way out of having to be vulnerable. I've seen him do it any number of times. He doesn't like it when things get real, so he puts up these spiky death rays of asshole behavior, to just sort of push people away. Doesn't work on us, of course, since we're his brothers and we see through it, but for women...? He's a bad boy, you know? Like, true-blue, down to the bone bad boy. Chicks love it, short term. But trying to push through the asshole to get to the truly decent guy lurking beneath it takes more than anyone's ever been willing to put up."

A big booming voice broke the skin of the quiet discussion. "Quit boring the lady with your girly psychobabble bullshit, Brock! Time to do shots!"

The man accompanying the voice must have been Baxter, according to Sebastian's description. Big, burly, thick, bull-necked, full of blustering thunder and power. Same as Sebastian, Zane, and Brock, Baxter had brown hair and brown eyes, but like each of his brothers, he wore it differently. His arms were so huge I found myself wondering how he even managed to wipe his own asshole, and his chest was actually some kind of tectonic plate, but his waist was a trim wedge hugged by a green and yellow University of Oregon T-shirt. He occupied a huge physical space, but as he left the stairwell and swaggered across to the bar, it was clear he was also one of those people who just dominated any room he was in, through virtue of sheer volume, bluster, bravado, and power of personality.

He slid behind Brock, trailing his fingers along the bottles of booze lined up on shelves. "Eeny... meeny...miney...mo!" He tapped a bottle of Johnny Walker, Jack Daniel's, Wild Turkey each in turn, and then at the word "mo" stopped on a bottle of Patrón Silver.

Brock whacked Baxter on the shoulder. "It's *noon*, moron. We're not doing shots of tequila."

Baxter ignored him, poured three overflowing shot glasses full of tequila, rummaged around under the bar for a tray full of sliced limes and a salt shaker. "It's always time for tequila, you little bitch!" He set a shot glass in front of me, grabbed my wrist, licked it, shook salt onto it, tossed me a lime. Held up his glass to me. "To my brother Sebastian—asshole extraordinaire, and owner of the meanest right hook I've ever fucking felt; and to you, Dru, for being woman enough to get even his tightwad panties in a hell of a bunch!"

He clinked my shot glass with his, spilling tequila all over my hand and his, and then he slammed his glass against Brock's glass who, despite his protest, was doing the shot with us. We licked the salt off our hands, did the shot, and then sucked the limes, each of us doing the requisite post-tequila shot grunt.

I noticed, then, that Baxter had a shadow on his jaw, too. "Wait, Sebastian punched you, too?"

Baxter poured another shot and downed that one, no salt or lime or gasp. "Yes, he did. The fucker. I always forget how hard that bastard can hit."

I frowned. "Why'd he hit *you*?"

Zane appeared, then, grabbed the bottle of tequila and stole Baxter's shot glass, did two shots in short order, forgoing the salt and lime. "Because the dumbfuck had the balls to ask Sebastian why he had his panties in a bunch."

"To which Sebastian replied 'not wearing any panties, cocksucker,'" Baxter said, rubbing his jaw, "and then he decked me."

I looked in turn at Zane, Baxter, and Brock, each of who bore some kind of mark from Sebastian's anger. "So he's clocked all three of you..." I grabbed the bottle and did another shot, but I went with salt and lime, because I clearly wasn't on the same level of hard-drinking badassery as the Badd brothers. "Which leads to tequila shots at...twelve-oh-nine on a Monday afternoon?"

Zane nodded. "Yep. I mean, I don't know about these fuckers, but I haven't been to bed yet. Took an overnight from London to LA, and then connected from LA to Seattle, and then from Seattle here, and that was the *short* leg of my journey. So for me, it's basically still Sunday, according to the ancient rules of staying up all night."

"And I got cheated on, on the day of my wedding," I said. "Which was two days ago—and then I met Sebastian and had him mess me up in all kinds of ways, so I feel a little entitled."

"And we've both been punched," Baxter pointed out, slugging Brock in the shoulder, "which gives us a good excuse. But you know me, I don't really need an excuse to get shitty, na'mean?" And then he promptly did a third shot.

I was feeling my first two, so I held off. "Why is Sebastian going around hitting everyone?"

"I told you," Brock said. "Because he's an emotionally stunted caveman."

"Oh," I said.

Baxter laughed. "And because he's an idiot. Thinks we're gonna just let him get away with hitting us because he's all pissy about things."

I glanced from brother to brother to brother in turn, once more, and noticed each of them had the same expression going on...and Brock was doing a second shot too, and then a third. They were all looking at each other, exchanging those meaningful glances in which men who know each other well have a tendency to do when they want to communicate.

"I'm guessing you're not planning on letting him get away with it?" I asked, warily.

Zane chuckled darkly. "Hell no."

Baxter corked the bottle of Patrón, replaced it, and then slammed his fist on the bar. "Ready, brothers?"

Zane and Brock answered in unison. "Ready."

All three swaggered off toward the stairs, Zane going up first, Brock second, and Baxter third. Baxter reappeared almost immediately, eyeing me. "Dru? If I were you, I would…um…duck."

I blinked at him, and then he was gone, and I heard his feet on the stairs. A few moments of silence, and then a wordless bellowing roar from Sebastian…

Thuds, bangs, the crash of something breaking, more thuds so hard and loud the walls shook…

And then several pairs of feet stomping on the stairs, more thuds, and then Sebastian's voice shouting and bellowing and cursing.

"LET ME GO YOU FUCKING ASSHOLES!" I heard him shout, and then Baxter and Zane appeared, each holding one of Sebastian's thrashing arms, and then Brock with his feet.

They carried him across the bar, and he was kicking and thrashing so hard they were obviously struggling to keep hold of him. Baxter had a bloody lip,

Zane's nose was trickling blood, and Brock's shirt was ripped...and they didn't even have him outside yet.

I waited until they got him through the door, and then I followed, tentatively, to stand in the doorway as the brothers unceremoniously tossed Sebastian onto his ass in the middle of the street, and then each of them jumped back a good foot.

Sebastian came up swinging, lunged for Baxter first, and that right hook of his connected with a sickening crunch that sent Baxter stumbling backward. Brock and Zane closed in, and the fight that followed was a brutal knock-down, drag-out bare-knuckle brawl between four massive, powerful men. And even though it was three on one, Sebastian was in such a horrific rage he held his own for a while, snarling, seething, cursing, roaring, lashing out with feet and fists and knees, taking nonstop hits from his brothers without slowing down.

It was still three-on-one, though, and Sebastian, even as powerful as he was, didn't really stand much of a chance. Eventually Brock got one arm in a lock and Zane the other, and Baxter followed in with a scything uppercut fist to Sebastian's gut, which took the wind and the fight out of him.

All four brothers were bloodied, by that point. I saw at least two broken noses, everybody's lips were split, jaws were bruised...

But Sebastian was subdued. They let him fall to the ground, gasping, blood oozing down his chin and nose, and from a cut over his eye. Zane flopped down to sit beside him, and then Brock, and then Baxter, each sitting facing Sebastian so they formed a ring of brothers. For long moments, nobody spoke.

And then, slurred by split, bloody lips, Sebastian spoke. "I miss him, goddammit." His voice was thick.

"Me too," Zane said. "I'll never get over missing his funeral."

"Nobody blames you for that," Baxter said. "Not like you had a choice."

"I lost my best friend that day." Zane's voice was quiet, low, rough. "Never told any of you."

Sebastian looked up at Zane. "You did?"

Zane nodded. "Marco. Took a stray round...it happened so fast—my head wasn't in the game, it was on Dad, on you guys, missing the fucking funeral... Marco shouldn't have had his head up and I didn't say anything to him. I've lost guys before, obviously, but Marco, man...we went through BUD/S together."

"Jesus, dude. I had no idea." Sebastian wrapped his arm around Zane. "That sucks."

"Yeah. I lost Dad and Marco within days of each other."

I was just standing there, in the doorway, hand over my mouth, full of so many conflicting emotions

I didn't know what to do about any of them. I wanted to smother Sebastian with kisses, wipe away the blood, take him inside and make him feel better, get him to talk about his dad, but I was a little frightened of how well he fought, how savagely. Of course, none of them were trying to really truly *hurt* each other, but they weren't holding back much either. Above all, I just wanted Sebastian to…let me in, I guess.

But this scene, with his brothers…it wasn't about me. It was about them; I was just a spectator.

I didn't understand, honestly. I couldn't fathom what kind of bond they had that could let them batter each other bloody like that, and then sit there sharing deeply personal thoughts, arms around each other.

"We all miss Dad," Baxter said. "You know how much fucking tequila I've put away the last few months because of it? Coach Baldwin nearly benched me a few times."

Brock spat a mouthful of blood, wincing. "None of us are really handling this very well, I guess."

"What, *you*? Mister well-adjusted psychology major?" Baxter said, his voice thick with sarcasm. "I don't believe it."

Brock shot his brother what I thought was an uncharacteristically foul glare. "Fuck you, Bax. You think I'm unaffected?"

Baxter held up his hands, unwilling to start

another brawl, apparently. "Just saying, you proba-bly sat in on therapy sessions every week instead of drinking your feelings away like the rest of us."

Brock reddened. "So what if I did? I don't care to pretend I'm not feeling things, and while I may have given in to the desire to numb the pain with alcohol more than I'd like to admit, letting go completely just wasn't an option for me. If I get in the cockpit hung over or still drunk, I'm gonna kill myself or someone else. I can't *afford* to drink my feelings away."

Baxter gripped Brock's shoulder and squeezed, shook it. "Yeah, well, somebody in this damn family has to be an adult, huh?"

Sebastian's shoulders shook, then, and my heart squeezed in my chest. "It's stupid…it's so stupid—"

"What's stupid?" Brock asked.

"I'm *angry* at him," Sebastian said, his voice break-ing. "At Dad—I'm so fuckin' pissed at him for leaving. Why'd he leave? He just fuckin' left me here alone, left the bar on me and, just like after Mom passed, I didn't have a choice but to fuckin'—to just do what had to be done. I didn't *want* it. I was gonna see if he could hire somebody else to fill in so I could—I dun-no what. Do something else for a change. But then he died, and I just—fuck. *Fuck.*" He shook his head, rubbed at his eyes as if he could rub away the pain. "Fuckin' hate this bullshit."

"When Marco died," Zane said, his voice thoughtful, careful, "me and Cody went AWOL. We took a Humvee and a bottle of some shitty booze and went off into the middle of fuckin' nowhere. We drank ourselves stupid and cried our eyes out like little bitches. You can't ignore this shit, Bast. You gotta let it out. It'll fuckin' eat you alive if you don't."

"Yeah, but I've just—" Sebastian shoved the heels of his palms against his eyes and rubbed hard. "I've just been so fuckin' *alone*."

"Not anymore, brother," Zane said, roughly grappling Sebastian into a hug against his chest, holding him there. "Not anymore."

"All'a you just fuckin' left me here. I know you had your lives to live, but—fuck, *fuck*—*goddammit!*" Sebastian's shoulders heaved again, and this time they didn't stop, and Zane just kept a harsh hold on his shoulders, refusing to let him go even though Sebastian was struggling, trying to get away, trying to deny the release of emotions.

My heart hurt, hearing the ache in his voice, the raw agony of loss and loneliness, and I understood then the reason for his walls, the reason for hiding behind the macho asshole façade. He was in pain, alone, and refusing to deal with it. Until now I think he'd refused to even acknowledge that he had a problem.

Brock and Baxter closed the circle, wrapped their

arms around Sebastian, and inside the safety of that huddle, I heard him finally let go, finally allow himself to grieve for the loss of his father and the months and years of loneliness.

I just stood there in the doorway of Badd's and watched, feeling like an outsider, but privileged to be able to witness the moment.

After several minutes, Sebastian straightened and stood up, grabbing the back of his shirt and pulling it off, wiping his face with it. Then he turned and helped each of his brothers to stand up.

He looked up and saw me standing in the doorway of the bar.

The look on his face in that moment made my legs shake and my core clench.

I was pretty sure Sebastian Badd was about to fuck me senseless.

# TWELVE

## Sebastian

I COULDN'T DENY HOW DAMN FREEING IT FELT TO GET THAT shit out. I felt as if a burden had been lifted off my shoulders, as if a crushing weight had been ripped out of my chest. Yet it all still felt raw, like a ragged wound. Despite the fact that I felt relief, Dad was not coming back. The bar was still my problem. The guys would eventually leave again, and I'd be alone all over again.

Shit, man, I hadn't cried since Mom died. But that had been by myself, in my room, door closed and locked, lights off, and I remember it had hurt like a motherfucker because I just couldn't keep it in anymore no matter how hard I tried. I hated letting it out, hated crying, but I couldn't physically stop it. Just like this moment on the docks with my brothers. I was powerless to stop it, and that was what they'd been after all along. The bastards had ganged up on me and physically forced me to confront my own emotions.

And they were right—I don't think I'd ever really truly let it all out or sorted through my feelings at all. Not after Mom's death, and not after Dad's, and I certainly hadn't confronted my deeply-rooted sense of abandonment. Irrational? Sure. I knew it was. But I couldn't shake it. Mom left me. Dad left me. All the boys left me.

But now they were back—under duress and temporarily, but they were back. And it felt good. Now I just need the other four to get here, and it'd feel complete.

I wiped the blood off my face with my shirt and held it in a crumpled ball in my fist.

And then I felt her presence.

I hurt all over: the boys hadn't taken it easy on me. They'd really gone in after me *hard*, and I was in a lot of pain. My emotions were still running on high octane, blasting through me hard and fast and merciless, and there she fuckin' was. Just standing there in the doorway of the bar, one shoulder leaning against the frame, still wearing my drab green raincoat. The hood was halfway off her head, revealing a portion of her auburn hair loose around her shoulders and framing her lovely face. And her eyes, goddamn, those eyes. So blue they fucking stunned me breathless from twenty feet away.

And the compassion on her face…holy shit. For me? That look she was giving me cut straight through me, digging deep and sinking barbed hooks into me that I knew would never be released. It was a look that said *I see you*. And those three words don't really do it justice. She *saw* me. Meaning, she saw past the front I put up. Past the tattoos, the muscles, the asshole player mentality, past all my bullshit emotional armor meant to keep everyone away…and to keep them from looking too closely.

But Dru? She saw. She didn't have to look past those things, because she saw them as part of me.

And that right there was what flayed me to the bone.

The bruises, the break in my nose, the achy ribs, the split lips…it all faded into nothing as I stalked toward her. She held her ground as I approached.

I stood over her, staring down, tasting the blood on my lips from my still-trickling nose. "I need you, Dru."

She just smiled up at me. "I know."

She reached up with both hands and placed them alongside my nose, hesitated a split second, and then swiftly and deftly re-set my nose.

"You've done that before," I said.

She grinned. "You don't spar with third and fourth dans and not get your nose broken a time or three."

"What you saw just now—" I started, even though I wasn't sure what I was going to say by way of explanation, or even ask how she felt about it.

She took my shirt out of my hand, dabbed at my nose, wiped at my lips, her expression soft and affectionate. "Shhh…"

I frowned. "But I—"

She lifted up on her toes. "Hush, Sebastian. Shut up and kiss me."

I shut up and kissed her. Wrapped my arm around her waist and yanked her flush against me, palmed her cheek with my other hand, and—gingerly—kissed her.

It's hard to gingerly kiss the ever-loving fuck out of someone, though, so I had to settle for long and slow and deep and thorough, tasting her lips, the line of her teeth, the slippery strength of her tongue. And then her hands were on me, sliding across my chest, my skin slick from the rain and sweat, and her hands were cupping the back of my head and tilting me down to deepen the kiss, to demand more from me.

I heard a motorcycle rumbling behind us, heard the engine cut off, boots hit the pavement. "Well hell, looks like I missed all the fun." The voice was muffled behind a helmet, but I knew who it was.

I pulled back, whispered against Dru's lips, "Xavier. Gotta say hi, and then I'm taking you upstairs."

"Make it fast," she whispered back.

I let her go, reluctantly, and pivoted just in time to see Xavier tugging off his full-coverage motorcycle helmet. The college boy had gone full hipster, apparently.

Of all of us, Xavier looked the most like Mom. His hair was closer to black than brown, curly and unruly. He was also the only one of us to get Mom's green eyes. He was a punk barely old enough to shave, but he sure as fuck had the Badd looks and swagger. Tight black jeans above half-laced combat boots, tight white T-shirt underneath a '50s style greaser leather jacket. The sides of his head were buzzed to the scalp with the top of his hair left long and messy in a wild curly mop. Triple-pierced ears, a series of geometric shapes tatted in interlocking patterns on his forearms...the boy was taking after me, it seemed.

That bike, though, that was new. Last I'd seen him he'd been driving some hoopty piece of shit beater-mobile, a '93 Topaz or some shit. Guess he'd saved for an upgrade, and I approved. It was a Triumph Adventurer, used, probably eight or ten years old but well maintained. A beauty, and I was a tad jealous. Not that I had time or money for a bike, but I'd been pining for one ever since I'd had to sell mine to pay off some debts I'd incurred while...intoxicated and impetuous, let's just say.

He grinned as I stomped toward him, grabbed him in a bear hug so fierce I nearly pulled him off his bike.

"Hey, you big fuckin' freak, let me go!" Xavier shoved at me in an attempt to fend me off, but I was ten years his senior and at least fifty pounds heavier, so he stood zero chance. Eventually he relented and gave in to the hug. "Fine, you goddamn ogre. All right, all right, you've gotten your hug, now let me go before I drop the bike. It's brand new."

It was fun to fuck with Xavier. He was a little standoffish, a bit stiff, and not really into physical touch. Meaning, he *hated* hugs, hated being touched by anyone. Just a quirk, I guess. Something to do with his freak of nature intelligence, I assumed. Perfect SAT score, 4.3 GPA, valedictorian of his high school class, college credits under his belt before he hit senior year, self-taught physics wizard, speed reader, voracious book nerd, master sketch artist, and in his spare time he also had this weird obsession with creating these odd little robots that did nothing useful, just sort of wobbled and gyrated and hopped around. He used watch gears and batteries and odds and ends and did some sort of genius magic and made them prance around like cute, freaky little living creatures. And, oh yeah, he was an insanely talented soccer player.

Go figure.

That kid got the brains Bax and Zane and I missed out on. Not that we were stupid, but Brock and Xavier were on a whole different level of smart, and Xavier then took that level and left it in the dust.

And damn the kid, but he was good looking as hell and had more fuckin' swagger than he knew what to do with. Just…don't touch him.

I let him go, finally, and watched him roll his shoulders and shrug and wiggle, as if trying to rid himself of the creepy-crawlies. "All right, you little punk. I got something I gotta do. I'll see you in a bit, yeah?"

Xavier's eyes went to Dru, then to me. He'd always been observant, and being the youngest had been around me longer than the others, so he'd seen me with an embarrassingly ridiculous number of different women over the years, none of whom I'd ever brought upstairs, never brought around the brothers, let alone Dad. I never saw them more than once, and never did anything to give them the impression it'd be anything other than a quick casual fuck. It meant no affection, no lovey-dovey bullshit.

Xavier, who'd had a habit of doing his homework sitting by the service bar, had seen me close up and go away with those girls, seen me take breaks to fuck them in the alley or the bathroom or wherever was close and convenient. He'd been a night owl, like me, and I'd just gone with it since he was always up in time for school without needing a wake-up call, so he'd seen things even my other brothers hadn't.

All of which meant he didn't miss the significance of the situation when I turned back to Dru, scooped her up with her legs hooked around my waist and her arms around my neck and kissed her as I walked with her toward the stairs.

"The hell happened to Big Bast?" I heard him ask as I was on the stairs.

Bax chuckled. "He got caught, little brother."

"Looks…uncomfortable."

"Yeah, well, you've still got your V-card." I heard Bax say. "You'll understand when you're older."

"I'll spike your whey powder with estrogen supplements if you ever bring that up again, Baxter," Xavier said.

"You wouldn't, you little rat."

"Think again, meat-head."

I lost the rest of the argument as I closed the door at the top of the stairs. Dru was chuckling against the side of my neck.

"He's a virgin?"

I laughed with her. "Yeah, he's an odd one. He's got the looks and the confidence, but he has this thing about being touched. I tried to set him up with a girl last year, this chick who was a friend of a friend's little sister, knew she was easy, knew she'd help a brother out, you know? But no, the little fucker wouldn't go for it. Said he'd wait for it to feel right."

"That's admirable," she said.

"It's dirtying the family reputation, is what it is," I grumbled. "Almost eighteen and still a virgin? The rest of us lost it years before that."

She huffed. "He's waiting for it to be right, Sebastian. There's nothing wrong with that. I think it's admirable and honorable."

"Yeah, well...for his sake I hope whichever chick he falls for feels the same way."

We were at my bedroom at this point, and I closed and locked the door behind us, then set Dru down on her feet.

"I have a question." She put her hands on my chest to halt me as I reached for her clothes. "Why do they call you Bast?"

I chuckled. "That was Xavier's fault. When he

was little tyke just learning to talk, he couldn't say my name. He'd say things like 'Sastian' and 'Sabashan', and he just couldn't ever get it. We tried short versions like 'Seb' or 'Bastian', but those never stuck. Then one day he called me 'Bast' and that was the one that stuck, and it's been my nickname ever since."

"Awww, that's so cute!" she said, in that high-pitched squeal girls use for adorable things.

I grabbed her wrists in one hand and pinned her up against the door. "I'll show you cute, wild thing."

She blinked up at me slowly, lazily, heat and mischief in her gaze. "Oh yeah?"

I kept her wrists pinned over her head with one hand and yanked her yoga pants down around her thighs with the other. "Yeah. It's so cute you won't even believe it."

"Does it live in your pants and resemble an anaconda in any way?"

"It might."

"Not sure cute is the right word for that monster you call a cock...*Bast*." Her voice was breathless as I slid my fingers inside the leg of her panties. "Oh... god, please touch me."

I dipped my finger inside her. "You're fuckin' soaked, Dru. Soaking fuckin' wet for me."

"Can't help that you make me crazy," she murmured.

"I love it," I said. "I love feeling you wet like this, knowing it's all for me."

I dragged my fingertips up her body, under the raincoat she was still wearing, the hood now fallen forward around her face.

"I'm hot," she breathed. "Take off my clothes."

I unbuttoned the raincoat slowly, pulling the edges aside while I released one of her hands and let her pull it free and toss it aside. Then I re-captured both wrists again and tugged her T-shirt up over her bra, working the cups down beneath her breasts to bare her nipples. She gasped as I bent and took one in my mouth, and now her hands wriggled and fought against my hold. I refused to let her go, though, liking her helpless under my touch. I teased her nipples until she was gasping and writhing, and then I slid my fingers inside her underwear and against her slit. Her head thunked against the door and she groaned out loud as I found her clit and started working my finger against it.

"Let me go, Sebastian. I need to touch you."

"Not quite yet," I murmured. "I'm not done."

I teased her pussy, fingering her, circling her clit, ramping her up and making her crazy but not letting her get near the edge of orgasm for her to really let go.

"I'm warning you, Sebastian. Let me go." Her

voice was low, and I wasn't really listening. Too focused on the taste of her tits, the feel of her pussy around my fingers.

I kept teasing her, and then—without warning—the world spun and my arms were wrenched behind me, and I hit the bed like a ton of bricks. Not sure what she'd done, even as I lay on the bed, dizzy and disoriented. She was sitting astride me, a feral glint in her eyes.

"Put your wrists above your head, Sebastian." She whispered the command, a hungry smile on her face.

Let's play this out, I decided. See what she does.

I just grinned back at her and offered her my wrists. Within seconds she had her T-shirt whipped off and was wrapping it around my wrists to bind them together, and then she tied the ends to the simple metal headboard.

She stared down at me. "Now it's *my* turn to make *you* beg." A shiver went down my spine at the sound of her voice, the look in her eyes. She shimmied down my body so she was sitting on my feet, reached up and unfastened the fly of my jeans, tugged down the zipper. "You're not wearing any underwear."

I just shrugged. "Knew I'd fucked up letting you go, didn't wanna take the time to bother with 'em."

She jerked my jeans down around my ankles,

swung off me, slid my boots off, then my jeans, and then I was naked and tied to my own bed, and the girl sure as hell knew her knots, 'cause there was no way I was getting out of this unless she let me; I'd been tugging and working at the binding the whole time, and had gotten nowhere.

"Well," Dru said, standing beside the bed near my face, "we're both here now, and you're at my mercy."

"No way in hell I'm getting out of this knot, so yeah, I'd say I'm at your mercy."

She leaned down and kissed the tip of my nose. "Sebastian, honey. One thing you need to understand about me is that I do *not* fuck around."

She kicked her boots off and climbed up on the bed beside me clad in nothing but a bra and her yoga pants, which were still down at mid-thigh, baring her underwear. She threw her leg over my chest and strad-dled me again, bringing her core near to my face.

"Now, you started taking my pants off, but didn't quite finish the job." She thrust her cotton-covered pussy against my face. "Finish taking them off, Sebastian."

"Hands are tied, honey. How you expect me to do that?"

Her grin was predatory. "Your teeth, dumbass."

"It's like that, is it?"

"It's exactly like that. You got me all worked up and left me hanging, so now we're gonna play this my way."

"What way is that?"

She pressed her thumb against my lower lip and pressed down until I opened my jaw, and then slid her entire thumb into my mouth. "Slowly, that's how. By the time I'm done with you, you'll be begging for my pussy." Her eyes went hooded as I sucked on her thumb, licking it as erotically as I knew how. "And make no mistake, I plan on giving it to you. But only after I decide you've learned your lesson."

"And which lesson is that, Dru?"

"*Off*, Sebastian." She pressed her thumb against my lower teeth to hold my jaw open, and then fit the waistband of her yoga pants between my jaws. "Which lesson?"

I clamped down and tugged, and Dru wiggled up, slowly working her way out of the tight yoga pants. When she was free of them, she reached up, unhooked her bra, shrugged out of it, and then, with a little giggle, set it on my head as if I'd decided to wear it like a hat. Like that crazy little blue fucker from the Disney movie. Xavier used to love that movie—which one was it? With the little blue alien critter and the Hawaiian girl? Whatever. Like that.

"Hysterical," I said, deadpan.

"I think so," she said, still giggling. "The lesson, my sweet, rugged, handsome Sebastian—" she paused to thrust her hips against me, encouraging me to take the elastic band of her panties in my jaws, which I did, "—is to never ever tease me unless you expect me to tease you back in kind, plus interest."

"Consider me taught, then," I said. I wasn't liking being tied up and helpless. Took my vulnerability to a whole new level, and I was still reeling from the scene with my brothers.

"Oh, I don't think so," she breathed. "Not yet. Not by a *long* shot."

"Dru…*please* untie me."

"Oh my…begging already?" She grinned down at me. "This'll be *fun*."

She writhed in front of me, on top of me, teasing me, draping her tits against my face and then pushing her core against my mouth, then pulling away, wriggling and writhing slowly, undulating upward, sashaying her hips side to side. She rose to her knees, the panties now below her hips. Spun around, pressed her ass to my face, and I took the panties in my teeth and tugged them lower, baring that beautiful ass of hers. Back to facing me, then, and now I had the upper few inches of her sweet pussy bared for me, and I stole a kiss as she thrust against me, urging me to finish removing her panties. When I had them between my teeth again, she undulated against me, pressing the sweet, desire-pungent slit of her pussy against my nose—I flinched at the twinge of pain, backed off a little—and then she was standing up on the bed, and the underwear was loose around her knees. She let them drop onto my chest.

She stepped out of them, snagged them, and sat down on my chest again. "You keep talking about how sweet my pussy is," she said, mischief in her eyes again. "Prove it."

"How?" I had a pretty good idea, and I was plenty eager to prove it.

She snagged her panties, sniffed them. "You got me all worked up, Sebastian." She leaned close to whisper to me. "Got me so worked up I was all wet and dripping because of you. You said it yourself...I was *soaked*."

"Fuck, Dru. I can smell you right now."

"That's right. I can feel it dripping down my leg." She brought her pussy close to my face, and I stuck out my tongue, eager for her juices on my tongue. "You want to lick me clean?"

"Fuck yeah, Dru. I'll lick every fuckin' inch of this sweet pussy."

"Show me."

She gripped the metal railing of the headboard and thrust herself against me. "Lick me clean,

Sebastian. I know you want to."

"Fuck yeah I do, Dru. I love this sweet, perfect cunt of yours."

"You do, huh?" I froze, stared up past her body to meet her eyes, realizing what I'd just said. She narrowed her eyes. "Is it just my cunt you love? What about the rest of me?"

"I—" had no fucking idea what I was supposed to say. Saying I loved her cunt had been a figure of speech, and I hadn't really been ready to say *those* particular three words just yet. "I meant—" Panic seized me, because she was going to expect it and I wasn't ready, wasn't fucking ready...

She laughed. "Relax, Sebastian. I'm just messing with you." She slid down my body and kissed my lips. "You don't have to say it. We've known each other less than what, three days? So I'm not ready to hear it any more than you're ready to say it. I was just messing with you. Relax."

"Not fuckin' funny."

She wormed back up again, writhing, as she placed her core against my mouth. "Sure it was. You should've seen your face." She gasped as I teased her opening with my tongue. "Yeah, just like that. Lick me so good, Sebastian. Make me come and I'll reward you."

"I like rewards."

"You'll *love* this one." She piled her hair on top of her head with both hands and writhed as I started eating her pussy with all the skill I had. "I have plans that involve your monster cock and my extraordinary lack of a gag reflex. And you…shouting my name so loud the neighbors will call the cops."

"Mmmmmmm?" I hummed my response, too busy trying to earn my reward to stop to reply.

"Oh yeah, it's gonna be so good for you, Sebastian…oh god, yeah, just like that, right there— oh fuck, fuck, *fuck*—that tongue of yours! My god, Sebastian…where'd you learn to do that? Jesus… never mind, I don't want to know. I'm just glad you learned, because god that feels so fucking good."

"How good is it gonna be for me?" I paused to ask, staring up at her.

She buried her fingers in my hair. "Less talking, more licking—I'm getting close." Pressing herself against me, she writhed as I gave it to her the way she seemed to like it best: slow at first, circling her clit with my tongue, and then as she got closer to orgasm speeding up and flicking her clit directly, and then as she started to come, sucking her clit into my mouth and going wild, tongue-thrashing her into a frenzy. "It's gonna be the best thing you've ever felt. I'm gonna suck you so good you'll forget your own name, and that's just to start. Oh god, oh god—yeah, yes…

yes—*YES!* Sebastian, fuck, you're making me come right now."

If I wasn't so utterly focused on bringing her to orgasm, I might've admitted something else: that I loved how fast she came, that it never took much to bring her to orgasm, and that I loved how she came, the way she let loose, just gave herself completely to the orgasm, the way her pale skin flushed and the way beads of sweat dotted her upper lip, and the swell of her tits, and the lines of her forehead.

I didn't say any of that, but I thought it. Which was scary enough as it was.

But then she was coming and it was all I knew, all I cared about, licking the hard nub of her clit and sucking it into my mouth and thrashing my face side to side and up and down until she was screaming past her clenched jaw and fucking my face with wild thrusts of her hips.

When she was finally done coming, after long moments of gasping and heaving and twitching and writhing against my face, she finally collapsed onto me, breathing hard, clutching my shoulders.

I gave her a few minutes to catch her breath, and then I shifted my weight beneath her, pushing against her. "You mentioned certain plans?"

She sat up, a sly grin on her face. "I did, didn't I?" She pretended to think. "What did I say I'd do? I don't seem to remember."

"You said, if I remember correctly, that you had plans which might involve my monster cock and your lack of a gag reflex."

She slid off me to sit beside me. "Oh, that's right—*those* plans." She gathered my cock in her fist, and gave it an exploratory stroke. "Now I remember."

She stroked me slowly, until I was fully erect. "A couple things I should mention, I suppose." She pulled her hair back into a ponytail and then a bun, and bound it back with a ponytail holder from her wrist. "Number one, I really don't have a gag reflex."

She pulled my cock away from my body, tilting it so it stood straight up from my groin. Stroked me a couple more times, slowly. And then she bent over me, keeping her eyes on mine. She opened her mouth, licked her lips seductively, and then—without taking her eyes off me—put her lips to the head of my cock.

Fuck, oh fuck, oh fuck.

An inch, two, three...she blinked at me, taking me deeper and deeper. Then backed away, licked her lips again, gave me a teasing little grin, and took me into her mouth again. And fuck, fuck, holy fuck, she wasn't kidding. *ZERO* gag reflex. I'd had some really great blowjobs before, but no girl had ever done what Dru was doing right then, namely, taking my entire cock in her mouth and down her throat.

It had never really mattered to me before, since the goal of blowjobs was typically just to get me off as fast as possible, so trying to make a girl deep-throat seemed kinda pointless. Just suck me dry and get it done, yeah? But this, what Dru what doing? This was...totally something else, something I'd never experienced before. This was...fucking erotic. Seductive. Teasing. She took me slowly, inch by inch, her eyes on mine, lowering her mouth around my cock, fluttering her tongue against my shaft as I slid in deeper and deeper. And then, fuck, she had all of me, every single inch of my cock down her throat, her eyes blinking over at me with a pleased, proud, eager gleam, her nostrils flaring, her throat working as she swallowed around my shaft, her nose against my belly.

And then she backed away as slowly as she'd taken me, unhurried, never looking away.

I swear to fuck I nearly came right then. That look on her eyes, the sight of my cock stretching her mouth wide, her lips sliding over my wet shaft...

She let me fall out of her mouth with a pop.

"Holy motherfucking hell, Dru..." I gasped. "What—um—what was the second thing?"

Almost idly, she stroked my cock with both hands, her saliva making me slick. "Oh. Just that I planned to make you enjoy it, but not necessarily make you *come*.

Or that it would be *quick*."

"What's that mean?"

She just grinned at me, and licked the head of my cock. "Oh...you'll see."

# THIRTEEN

# Dru

OH MAN, OH MAN, OH MAN. WHAT THE HELL WAS I doing? This wasn't me. Not anymore, at least. It *used* to be me, though.

Being with Michael had sort of chilled me out, taken the freak out of me. I used to like it kinky. Not, like, super freaky kinky like hardcore BDSM or anything, just...mild wild, if that made any sense. I was crazy. I was lonely, and horny, and had no reason to hold back. It wasn't Daddy issues, since Daddy was always there for me and was always amazing, but he was a busy guy as one of the better detectives in the

Seattle Police Department.

I ran wild, what can I say? I wanted attention, I wanted love, I wanted to be wanted. So I'd been a little crazy. Lots of guys, lots of hot and heavy nights and walks of shame the next day. I don't think anybody really knew the extent of my craziness during those years, because there wasn't anybody I'd have told. I never really had girlfriends, which was a direct result of Mom abandoning me at such a young age; I didn't trust women. Never had, probably never would. Which just meant I had no one to talk me out of bad decisions, like shacking up with Michael for four years.

Giving him the best of me and getting nothing in return.

Letting him flatten me, bore the actual personality out of me. His friends were boring, his job was boring, his life was boring...*he* was boring. *I'd* been bored. I'd been bored in my job, had no friends, and Michael, even though I loved him—or thought I had, which I was now beginning to question—I was starting to realize I'd been deeply unhappy. Michael hadn't even *begun* to satisfy me in bed. He liked it one way—missionary 'til he came, then it was done. He'd usually remember to work me up to an O before he started, so at least he had that amount of consideration as a lover, but there was no variety, no spice, no kink. Just…blah. Not bad, the sex was never *bad*—I wouldn't have stayed with him for so long otherwise—it was just…blah.

And I didn't like blah.

I think that was the entire point of my relationship with Michael: he'd made me feel normal. I'd grown up around cops, grown up learning martial arts from the time I could walk. I'd spent as much time at the shooting range as I had the library, as much time in the dojo as I had in the classroom. I could hold my own against three black belts at once, and could put an entire clip in a tight grouping dead center with a nine millimeter at twenty-five yards. I'd gone skydiving with Dad at eighteen, and did my first solo jump at nineteen. I could throw a knife and hit the target. I was on a first-name basis with most of the police officers in Seattle.

Not normal…at all.

Michael was normal. Even his family was the "normal" kind of dysfunctional. And being with him had sort of forced me to fit into a "normal person" pigeonhole.

But that wasn't me.

*This* was me.

Surrounded by a bunch of wild, dominant, alpha males who seemed to accept me at face value and weren't inclined to ask any questions. Men who weren't intimidated by the fact that I could go hand-to-hand with a Navy SEAL and hold my own, and were actually impressed by it. In bed with a big, hard, strong, powerful, bare-knuckle brawling tattooed bartender with a heart of gold—once you dug past the surly demeanor—and a monster cock. A man who let me tie him up and tease him. I had no doubt he could rip that flimsy T-shirt apart if he really wanted to, but he was content to let me do what I wanted, confident enough in himself to let me have my way and know it'd be good for him.

I hadn't left this tiny slice of Ketchikan, but even so I felt more at home here than I had my entire life in Seattle. The mountains in the distance, the constant squawk of seagulls and the crash of waves against the docks—it reminded me of Seattle in some ways, but there was a wildness to it that appealed to me.

Just like the man beneath me.

I had him hard as a rock, leaking pre-come. He was throbbing in my hands. His eyes were heavy-lidded with need, his hard muscles tensed from the effort to hold himself still. His cock was wet with my saliva, and he was already holding back, I could tell. And boy oh boy, I was just getting started. I knew all his tells, already. I knew he was close to coming and holding back, and I knew exactly when to back off so he didn't come before I was ready.

He'd made me come once already, and I was planning to get several more out of him before I let him come.

Sebastian growled and bucked his hips, and I realized I'd been spacing out, staring at him while lost in thought. "Dru? You all right?"

I plunged my fist down his shaft. "More than all right." Another slow stroke, then I bent and licked pre-come away as if I was eating an ice cream cone. "Just...coming to a few realizations of my own."

"What kinda realizations?" he asked, struggling to sound normal rather than breathless from pleasure.

I wrapped my lips around the plump head of his cock and swirled my tongue around him, then paused to answer. "Just that I never really belonged in Seattle. That was my dad's home, not mine. My life there wasn't what I wanted, it was just me making the best out of what I had."

He grunted as I put my mouth around him again and took inch after thick, throbbing inch of his cock. "And have you figured out where you—*shit, shit*, Dru, that feels so fucking good—where you *do* belong?"

I took all of him, swallowed to ripple my throat muscles around him. Backed away, then bobbed down again, backed away, bobbed down—taking him out of my mouth and then taking him deep again, teasing him, fucking him with my mouth until I had him grunting and bucking.

When I finally let him fall free from my mouth, I sighed in pleasure at the sight of his massive cock all glistening wet from my mouth, leaking pre-come, seconds from detonating. Such a beautiful cock this man had. I cupped my palm around the shaft and kissed the side of him. "I really love your cock, Sebastian."

He groaned. "My cock loves you back, Dru." I took him down my throat again, all the way, without warning. "Fuck, holy fuck! How the hell do you that?"

I grinned at him after I'd backed away. "Magic."

"I like your magic."

"I thought you might."

I stroked his length with both hands, slowly, rhythmically, until he was bucking into my fists and groaning and cursing between clenched teeth.

"Dru, shit—I need to come."

"Oh yeah?" I cupped his balls in my hand. "These feel pretty tight. Are they aching?"

He actually whimpered when I suckled those plump, sensitive balls into my mouth. "*Every*thing aches, Dru. So fuckin' bad. I need to come."

"I don't hear you begging, Sebastian," I said, then stroked his cock with one hand and massaged his balls with the other, licking up his shaft to the tip. "I think I need to hear you beg me to let you come."

"Please? Fuck, Dru, I'm dyin' here...I ache so

fuckin' bad. I need to be inside you. I need to feel your cunt, wild thing. Please. Please. Want me to beg? I'm begging. Please let me come."

I let go of him, straddled him again. "Hmmmm...I think you're *almost* desperate enough. But not quite. And I think I need another orgasm, first."

"I'm plenty desperate, Dru. I swear."

I slid up his chest, brought my pussy to his mouth. "Eat me out again, Sebastian."

"Fuck, Dru...I could spend every single fuckin' second of my life eating this sweet cunt of yours and never get enough." He was as good as his word, and he buried his face in my folds, tongue thrashing, lips suckling, stubble scratching.

Every single second of your life? Sounded an awful lot like love to me, Sebastian.

I thought it, but I didn't say it. No need. He'd get there, I'd get there. I didn't need the words, not yet, at least. I would, someday. But for now, knowing he wanted me this badly, knowing *I* wanted *him* this badly...feeling at home with him, in his arms, in his life, even around his crazy brothers...it was enough. More than enough.

I lost all capacity for thought, then, as his talented mouth pushed me to the edge and then over it, sent me crashing and thrashing to another orgasm so potent I had to grit my teeth from screaming out loud, and even then whimpers and groans and whining gasps escaped me, and even when I came he didn't relent, just kept devouring me until I was rocking against his face and grunting in time with my thrusts, fingers fisted in his hair, coming and coming and coming—

I wrenched myself away, gasping. I stared down at him; he had my essence smeared all over his mouth and chin. "I like you with my pussy juice all over your face," I said. "I think I'll keep you like this."

He exhaled roughly. "How about you just keep me, period?"

I slid my aching, throbbing, pulsating pussy down his chest to his belly, leaving a wet line of desire on his flesh. Then I nudged his cock against my opening, hovered there for a moment, my body flush against his, breasts flattened against his chest, my hands on his shoulders.

I impaled myself on him, took him to the hilt, gasping raggedly as he split me open. "Sebastian—"

"Dru?"

"What if I just never went back?" I asked it with his cock fully seated inside me, my pussy burning as he stretched me apart. "I kinda like it here."

He rolled his hips beneath me, pushing deeper yet. "I don't got much to offer. Probably never will. This bar, my brothers...shit, me, as I am right now...

this is what it is. It's all it'll ever be. I ain't the upwardly mobile type, sweet thing. Got no need for fancy houses and shit. You wanna stay here? Nothin' would make me happier, but it's gotta be what you want—Ketchikan, my grumpy ass, and my seven ugly, annoying, stupid brothers."

"Your seven gorgeous, incredible brothers, you mean?"

"Yeah…no. Ugly and annoying. But they're mine, and they're part of the package, I guess."

"We just met." I groaned as he rolled his hips again, filling me, moving inside me. "This is kinda crazy, you know?"

"Known your sexy ass less than three fuckin' days, but I'm hooked, Dru. That's all I know. Crazy? Sure. Whatever. Don't really care what you call it. Maybe shit'll change for one or both of us. No way of knowing. All I know right now is I can't get enough of you, and I like you here, and I like myself better when you're around."

I started moving, then. I couldn't take any more deep talk or emotional intensity. The whole point of this was to distract him from his pain, to help him get past the huge weight he'd let go of with his brothers. To show him that emotional maturity and vulnerability was sexy to me.

But it'd gone past that, somehow.

He was inside me. Literally, obviously, but meta-phorically, too. The moment I walked into this bar I'd felt calmer, I'd felt as if I was somewhere I belonged. It wasn't the bar itself, though, it was this man. Was I in love? Maybe. Getting there. If I wasn't, I was learning that what I'd felt for Michael hadn't been love at all. Affection, sure. I cared for him—at least, I had. Now I just hated him. But it hadn't been love. Because what I felt for Sebastian after something like forty-eight hours made everything I'd shared with Michael over four years pale in comparison. Made it seem stupid and paltry and flimsy and weak, like a tiny candle flame guttering from lack of oxygen. Sebastian was a wildfire, hot and majestic and dangerous and out of control.

There was no stopping this.

Not sure I wanted to…in fact, I knew I didn't.

God, god, god, he felt so fucking amazing in-side me. Heaven. Home. Perfection. Glorious. Words failed.

But words didn't matter, because Sebastian wasn't a man for whom words really mattered—actions mattered. He could tell me he loved me till he was blue in the face, but if he didn't act like it, it wouldn't matter, because it wouldn't be true; another lesson learned thanks to Michael. But because Sebastian wasn't a man of many words, he also would never say anything he didn't mean. He wouldn't waste his breath on bullshit.

"Shit, Dru, you're makin' me crazy here, wild thing." His voice barreled through me, that deep ursine rumble of his.

I'd lost myself in him, feeling him, thinking about him, which only served to tease him further, make him crazier. But it served my purposes. I wanted him crazy.

I propped myself up with my hands on his chest, rocked my hips forward to pull him nearly out of me, lifted up on my knees to angle him away.

"Making you crazy, am I?" I leaned in and bit his chin. "Sebastian, sweetheart—you have *no* idea what crazy is."

There's no better term for what I did to him then than to say I twerked on him. Bounced my ass up and down hard and fast in short little movements, so his cock ground in and out of my pussy in staccato machine-gun rhythm. After about thirty seconds of this, he started writhing, his spine going concave, his hips thrusting up, and he was yanking at the T-shirt trying to get away, grunting and snarling like a savage.

I bounced on him until he was riding the ragged edge of orgasm, tensed, arched, thrusting, groaning.

"Fuck, fuck—Dru, gonna come so fuckin' hard, Dru!"

I jerked my hips away so he flopped out of me. "I'm not ready for that quite yet," I said, then kissed him to take the sting out of losing my pussy.

"Fuck! Goddammit, Dru. I think you got your revenge already. Enough."

I bit his lower lip until he grunted in pain. "Not so sure about that, actually. I think I could tease you a while longer. Another...oh...hour or so?"

His snarl then was inhuman. He hauled at the twisted cotton of the T-shirt until his muscles bulged and his veins stood out. I heard seams pop, and then, after another roaring straining heave, the fabric gave way and his hands were free.

He was on me in a flash.

Curling forward, he snagged my wrists and jerked me against his chest. "Now you've done it," he rumbled.

I wriggled against him, leaned in to lick the tip of his nose. "Oh goody," I breathed.

He chuckled. "Why you dirty little minx! You were riling me up on purpose, weren't you?"

I felt myself being lifted as he caught me in his arms and rose to his knees. "Maybe."

"Tryin' to make me crazy?"

"I like you when you're wild," I said, going still in his arms, feeling utterly content and safe right where I was. "Plus, I hated seeing you upset."

He pressed his lips to mine in a brief, soft kiss—which felt like a wordless thanks—then bit my lip like I had his, hard enough to really hurt. "I'm always wild, Dru."

"Good," I whispered. "Tame is for pussies. Been there, done that, bought the wedding dress. No thanks."

His lips curled in a predatory smile, and then he tossed me to the bed on my stomach. He knelt behind me, grabbed me by my hips and hauled me backward toward him. I watched him over my shoulder, and I quivered at the sight of him. Tattoos covered his arms, shoulders, and chest in whorls and eddies of ink, turning his skin into a canvas, bright colors and bold images sheathing rippling muscles. He was huge and hard behind me, his hands smoothing over my back, caressing my ass, gripping my hips.

He gripped his massive cock in one hand, teased my opening with his fingers, and guided himself into me slowly, gently, until his hips were flush against my ass. A momentary pause, and then he pulled back, slid back in. Slow, deliberate.

Another slow, lazy thrust, his hands roaming my hips and ass, praising them with his hands, worshipping me with his touch.

Then he leaned forward over my back, gathered my hair in his fist. "That's all the gentle I've got patience for," he growled.

I writhed against him, shoving my ass against him, driving his cock into me. "Told you, Sebastian, I don't *want* gentle."

He let out a ragged breath, and then tightened the pressure of his grip on my hair, pulling me back with it. He drove his cock into me on a growl, and his palm smacked against my ass, setting it to stinging and quivering. "You're saying you want it rough?"

"Exactly what I'm saying," I gasped, breathless from the sting and the bliss of his touch.

He fucked me, then. Hard. Roughly. He drove into me hard and fast, his cock pounding my pussy mercilessly, skin slapping skin, our voices tangling in grunts and curses. Occasionally he'd slap my ass with his hand, but mostly...he just fucked.

And god, it was the most incredible thing I'd ever felt.

Because I'd glance back over my shoulder and his eyes would be blazing, raking over me, his body moving in perfect synch with mine, giving me exactly what I wanted, what I needed, what I'd never known I needed.

"Fuck, Dru. You feel so fuckin' amazing." He gripped both of my hips and jerked me hard back into him, thrusting forward to drive himself deep. "You're so beautiful, Dru. Need to feel you come around my cock, need to watch you come apart for me."

I slipped one hand between my thighs and tweaked my clit, and that was all it took, one little touch to set me on fire, the pounding beauty of his cock inside me and his words and his power, and then the light circling touch of my fingers against my clit—

"Sebastian! I'm coming, god—I'm coming!" I gasped.

"Fuck—I feel it, babe. I feel your cunt squeezing me…"

I clamped down even harder, shaking, trembling, torn apart by the orgasm. The fire of the climax was intensified by his wild thrusting, the unbridled lust of his driving cock.

"Fuck, babe. I don't ever want it to stop, but I can't hold out any longer. I gotta come, Dru."

That tickled something in my head, but I was so caught up in my own orgasm that I didn't pause to think about it. I just thrashed against him, gripping the sheets in my fists and slamming my ass back into his, taking his pistoning cock with breathless shrieks and gasps, and whispered curses, and his name repeated again and again—

"Sebastian, Sebastian, god yes, Sebastian!"

Then I felt his thrusts falter, and the thing that had been percolating in my head popped free.

"Shit! Don't come inside me, Sebastian!"

He growled. "Fuck—"

I felt him tense, and then he pulled out and I felt his fist moving.

I rolled over onto my back and he straddled my hips. I brushed his hand away, took his thick slick throbbing cock in my hands and smeared our essences all over his shaft, and then, on impulse, cupped his firm ass to guide him forward. He moved closer, his eyes on mine, wild, feral, desperate, jaw clenched as he teetered on the brink of orgasm.

I lay beneath him and took him into my mouth, tasted my own essence and his combined, tastes tangling, smoke and musk and tang and salt.

"I can't—fuck—Dru, *Dru*...I have to come, I can't fuckin' stop it this time," he said, his voice ragged.

I just moaned and fisted his length and cupped his balls, slid my finger along his taint and massaged the sensitive nerves there, fucked him with my mouth until his fist buried in my hair and he started pulling me against himself.

"Mmmmmm—" I moaned, and his eyes flicked down to mine. I let go of his shaft and cupped his ass, opened my throat, and then he understood what I wasn't saying.

He growled, tangled both of his hands into my hair and let himself go, let himself fuck my throat knowing I could take it, knowing I wanted it. And I did. I *did*. All I wanted then was to see him lose it, to feel him let go, to know he'd found what he needed in me. To give him the most pleasure I could.

He grunted, and his hips drove, and I tasted us, felt his girth between my lips and his length against my tongue.

"Fuck—I'm coming, Jesus...holy shit—Dru, god...Dru!"

I took over as he tensed on the thrust, backing away so his head was in my mouth. I sucked and hummed and flicked him with my tongue and tasted musk and felt his grip in my hair go painfully tight, and then he spurted and I swallowed; he groaned long and low as he came and came and came, his come salty and almost sweet and tangy and thick and warm in my mouth. I swallowed and swallowed, and still he came. And then finally he was done and I took him deep down my throat again until he shuddered and pulled away, collapsing onto his back.

After a few minutes of gasping silence, as we both caught our breath, he curled me into his arms and held me against his chest. "You're not on the pill?"

I shook my head against him. "Not on any kind of birth control. It messes with my hormones too much. Makes me all bloated and I gain weight. So no, no birth control for me other than condoms." I leaned up and kissed his jaw. "Sorry about that."

He brushed his thumb against my cheek. "Just glad you caught me before it was too late. I'm sorry, Dru. I didn't even stop to think about that." He sounded chagrined, thunking his forehead with his fist. "God, I'm such a fuckin' asshole."

"It's *fine*, Sebastian." I caught his hand and kissed his knuckles. "It's on me too. You're not an asshole."

He quirked an eyebrow at me. "You did sorta push my buttons on purpose."

I laughed, nuzzling his neck. "No regrets. Just can't forget the condom next time."

He played with my hair, rubbing it between thumb and forefinger. "You make me crazy like that, I can't be held accountable for how I react. Poke a bear, you're gonna get bit, sweet thing."

"I'll remember that," I murmured.

"Good. You better. 'Cause honey, you want wild, you're gonna get wild."

I reached down and toyed with his penis. "I think I proved fairly well that I can handle all the wild beast you've got."

He hardened in my hand, watching with glinting, hungry eyes as I fondled him to erection. "Think you fairly well did." He grabbed my hips and threw me on top of him. "But I think you might need to do a little more proving."

I reached over and took a condom from the

drawer, ripped it open and rolled it onto him. "I think I might be know a few more tricks."

"Oh yeah? Like what?"

I spun around to face his feet, slipped him inside me. "Better grab onto something, Sebastian. I'm about to rock your world."

"You just did, I thought," he said, taking hold of my ass.

I watched him over my shoulder as I rode him reverse cowgirl, starting slow. "That was just an appetizer."

"Then I can't fuckin' wait for the main course."

"It starts with a little something like this..." I swiveled my hips in wide, slow circles.

"Ho-*ly* shit—"

# FOURTEEN

## Sebastian

It'd be a damn dirty lie if I said Dru and I didn't spend the rest of the day fucking. And, sweet Jesus, the woman was absolutely *insatiable*. We fucked and we fucked and we fucked, and she'd be all over me for more as soon as my cock was ready, and Dru Connolly was so goddamn gorgeous I was always hard within ten or twenty minutes.

Finally, she passed out. We'd gone into my room at somewhere around one in the afternoon, and it was eight at night before she fell asleep in my bed, my flannel sheet draped low over her sweet round, juicy ass, the rest of her bare and so beautiful my breath caught just looking at her. When I knew she was asleep, I tugged on a pair of workout shorts and left my room. My brothers were all clustered in the living room around the TV, playing a video game.

But as I stood there and thought about it, a few things were different.

There was a new TV mounted on the wall, and it was HUGE. Like, sixty inches at least, probably closer to seventy—the old one was nearly four years old and less than fifty inches. The TV was goddamned enormous, but it was barely two or three inches thick, and it had a slight curve to it, and the picture was so crazy crystal clear it made my head spin. Also, a few hours ago I didn't possess a video game system, but I did now.

The game they were playing had the screen split into four quadrants, each showing something different. It was a shooter of some kind, but that was all I really knew. I'd never had time for video games growing up, although the twins and Lucian were addicted to them, and even Xavier to a lesser extent.

I stood in the hallway watching. Canaan and Corin had shown up apparently, so now the living room was a howling den of cacophony. Baxter, Zane, and Xavier were squished together on the couch with controllers in their hands. Canaan and Corin were standing behind them, and Cane had a controller in his hands while Cor stood beside him, shoving him and shouting directions: "NO, you fuckin' idiot, over there—*NO*, the other direction, yes, right there, now go down that hallway—"

Xavier was his usual quiet intense self, leaning forward with his elbows on his knees, tongue sticking out of the corner of his mouth, rocking slightly back and forth as he navigated the fantasy world of the game—HALO, it looked like, probably the newest version, but what did I know? Zane and Baxter were both shouting too, elbowing each other, cursing each other out, roughhousing even as they played. Brock was sitting in the easy chair, a beer in his hand, watching the game, a content smile on his face.

Then Brock saw me. "At last the wild creature emerges from his lair!" he said in a drawling, over-the-top Australian accent.

Which stopped the game as six pairs of eyes turned on me. Canaan and Corin both moved at the same time, in that freaky instinctive synchronization they had. They dropped their controllers and came over to fling their arms around me and crush me in bear hugs.

"BAST!" they shouted in unison.

Canaan and Corin looked the part of the rock stars they truly were. They had my height, both of them standing near six-three, but they carried it razor-thin and lean. Canaan wore his hair long and loose and messy, and it was constantly falling into his eyes, and he had the beginnings of a beard going. Corin was the edgier of the two, sporting a severe undercut with the top left long and brushed back over his scalp, the ends dyed virulent neon blue. They both had full-sleeve tattoos started, blank spaces showing where future tats were going to go, and they were both dressed in tight jeans that sagged around their waists with holes in the knees and thighs, faded graphic print T-shirts and Sharpie-decorated Converse All-Stars to complete their looks. Individual styles that still somehow managed to almost-but-not-quite match, enough individuality that you wouldn't ever mistake one twin for the other.

They'd played that game for a while, though, dressing alike and looking alike so you never knew which twin you were talking to. They used to fuck with the audience at shows, too, one of them playing lead guitar and lead vocals and the other doing bass and backing vocals, and then during a lighting change they'd switch guitars and mics. They even made a funny little gimmick out of it, tossing guitars back and forth while harmonizing, so you never knew which one was which. The label had cut that out of their act real fast, though. Which, in retrospect, had been for the best, as it had forced each of them to find their own niche as musicians, forcing them be more serious about the music rather than just showing off.

"Thought you'd never come out," Canaan said.

"She must be really something to keep you in there for seven fuckin' hours," Corin said.

"Or, rather, for seven hours of fucking," Canaan said, grinning.

I turned the bear hugs into headlocks on both of them. "Keep a respectful tongue in your damn heads or I'll rip 'em off, you little punk bastards." I punctuated this by squeezing until both of them started struggling and squawking.

"FINE! LEMME GO!" This was Corin, the more vocal of the two.

I released the headlocks then, but didn't let them go entirely. I spun them to face me. "Serious, guys. No bullshit about her. Got it?"

Canaan eyed me curiously. "Who are you and what'd you do with my real brother?"

I shoved him hard enough that he hit the back of the couch and toppled over. "It's really me, dumbass. I just found a girl I really like. Don't make big deal out of it."

"It kind of *is* a big deal, though, isn't it?" Xavier asked. "Didn't I hear you once say love was for pussies who couldn't haul down ass like a real man?"

I sighed. "Yeah, I think I did say something like that. But first, I was drunk when I said it, second, that was before I met Dru, and third, I was kind of an asshole back then."

Xavier's lips quirked. "That was less than a year ago."

"A lot can change in a year, kiddo."

Baxter laughed. "A lot can change in a single day, I think."

"Truth," I said, and then had a realization hit me. "Wait. If I'm here, and all of you are here, who's working the bar?"

Zane answered. "The committee decided to close the bar for a day. We've all spent the last several days traveling, and you were…otherwise indisposed."

Corin raised his hand. "Plus, minor point here… none of us know what the fuck we're doing down there."

"Who's the committee?" I asked.

Zane waved at the room at large. "All of us."

"And I'm not part of the committee?"

Zane laughed. "Well, you are now, I guess. But when we made the decision you were balls deep in the missus, so you missed out."

I growled. "Watch your fuckin' mouth, asshole."

He raised his hands palms out and shot me a look that said he was having as much trouble recognizing this new protective version of me as the twins were. "A joke, man, it was a joke. Relax. I'm the last one here that'll talk shit about that chick, seeing as my balls still ache from her foot."

Canaan and Corin swiveled on Zane and spoke in unison. "Wait...Bast's girlfriend kicked *you* in the nuts?" It was fuckin' freaky, how they could speak entire sentences in precise synch, including inflection and emphasis. I often wondered if they practiced doing it.

"She's not my girlfriend," I snarled. Then the events of the last day and the things we'd said and shared earlier today rifled through me, and made me rethink that position. "Well, maybe she is. We haven't nailed anything down. Point is, yes, she's a badass, so fuck with her at your own risk."

Zane shifted his weight on the couch and rubbed his crotch. "And I'm sayin' from experience...don't fuck with her. The kick to the balls was what laid me out, but the moves she pulled to get the kick out were as fast and precise as anybody I've ever sparred against."

I felt pride heat me up from the inside out, hearing a hardcore badass like Zane talk about Dru so highly. Zane didn't hand out compliments easily—he was hard to impress, and very sparing with his praise.

I gestured at the TV. "Where'd the monster TV

and the game system come from?"

Corin raised a hand. "That was us. We got here, saw your dinky little piece of shit TV from like the *nineties* or whatever, and the distressing lack of a PlayStation, and we had to rectify that poste-fuckin'-haste. That TV was so fuckin' tiny I don't even know why you even bothered. And no PS4? I don't think so."

"Who paid for it?"

Canaan answered. "We did."

"World tour opening for Rev Theory, remember?" Corin added. "We got'chu, bro!"

I rolled my eyes. "As long as it didn't come from bar funds, then whatever. It *is* a nice TV."

"*Nice?*" Xavier said, sounding incredulous. "Seventy inches of ultra high definition picture, and you call it *nice?*"

"Yeah, it's nice." I eyed the twins. "Is the tour done with, then? I sorta had the idea you had a few more shows left."

Canaan shrugged. "We were supposed to play a couple more dates...which cities was it, you remember, Cor?"

"Barcelona, Madrid, and Lisbon, I think. The original plan was to hook up with Beartooth in Paris and then do a double-headlining tour with them in the UK."

My gut sank. "You had a headlining gig?"

Canaan shrugged again; the kid had an entire language of shrugs. They could mean 'whatever', 'sure', 'why not', or 'who cares', plus a few more that were just sort of all around lazy *I-don't-give-a-shit*. This shrug was a *whatever* shrug. "Yeah. Not a solo headliner, though," he said. "Our manager was pissed at us for bailing, but family is family, right?"

"Fuck, man," I groaned. "You gave up a headlining tour to come back here?"

That had been their dream since they first organized a band when they were thirteen. They'd played gigs downstairs on Tuesday nights all through junior high and high school, and eventually those gigs had translated into playing at other bars around here in Ketchikan, and then in Anchorage, and then down along the Pacific Northwest in places like Seattle and Portland.

Eventually a scout had caught their act in a shitty dive bar in LA. Man, they'd been *so* proud to have booked a gig in LA, and for good reason. It had been a big deal. One fuckin' show in LA, and they'd gotten a contract. That was during their junior year of high school, when they were just barely sixteen. They quit high school to move to LA, spent a year recording a debut album while finishing their GEDs—that was Dad's stipulation for letting them go, they had to get their diplomas before they could start touring.

There'd been talk even then, before their first album was cut, of national and even international tours. They were destined for the big time, and always had been. A tour co-headlining with a fairly well known band like Beartooth could have really catapulted them into the spotlight.

And they'd bailed on that to come back here.

Brock's words from earlier came back to haunt me: *the twins have to skip an entire year of touring...we knew we had to come back...wasn't really much choice, not for any of us...*

Fuck.

The twins didn't need the money, they needed the touring experience and the spotlight on their talent.

Canaan was the more serious of the twins, and it was Canaan who leaned against me and wrapped a wiry arm around my shoulders. "Listen, big brother. We've been touring for more than two years. I've lost count of how many shows we've done, how many cities we've been to. Cutting the tour short wasn't just about the will. It wasn't even entirely about being here to help you out, so don't get all caught up in feeling like some kind of goddamn martyr, okay? We were approaching burnout."

Corin cut in without missing a beat. "We needed the time off. We recorded the album and then went right to touring and we haven't slowed down since. We needed a fuckin' break."

I shook my head. "Bullshit. You guys were on the verge of really breaking out big. You need another album. You need—"

Canaan interrupted me. "All respect, Bast, but shut the fuck up. Since when are you a music industry expert? You're not. This is *our* band, *our* career. And we choose to be *here*. If we're sacrificing a little momentum to be here, then so be it. We can get it back."

Corin leaned in on my other side, sandwiching me between the twins. "Also, we've got a buddy who specializes in building recording studios. He's coming up to Ketchikan some time in the next couple months and he's going to scout a good spot to put in a studio so we can record our next album ourselves."

"What about your contract? Doesn't that say when and where—" I started.

Canaan took over, interrupting me yet again. "When we bailed on the tour, we bailed on the contract. It was only for one more album anyway, and they wanted to take our sound in a direction we weren't cool with. We had to give back some of the advance, but it's all working out. It was just money, and we've made plenty of that the last two years."

"So wait, you broke your contract too?"

Corin blew a raspberry. "Try to keep up, bro—yes,

we broke the contract. The label didn't wanna let us go, and we aren't about to let some fuckin' suit and tie pussies in New York tell us what to fuckin' do with our lives *or* our music, so we told 'em where to shove their stupid contract, and then we came home."

I groaned again, and rubbed both hands over my face. "What a disaster."

Canaan, this time. "Bast, you're not listening to us. They were talking about our next album, how they wanted to us to sound more 'commercially approachable', meaning softer, closer to pop than hard rock."

"We're going indie, bro!" Corin shouted. "We get to make this album ourselves, make it exactly what we want rather than having to cater to the dumbfuck label execs. This is about us, now. Our music, our lives, our time."

"These days, there's just as much potential for recognition and gaining popularity by putting up videos on YouTube," Canaan said. "Our dedicated fan base doesn't give two shits about which label our music comes out on, they just want our music. We can do that here."

I sighed. "Sounds like you two have this thought out."

"We're not stupid, Bast," they both said at once.

"We have no plans to abandon our music

career—" Canaan started.

"We're just taking it in a different direction," Corin finished.

"Plus, family is family, and our brothers come first," they both said.

"Enough talk," Baxter said, shooting to his feet. "I need booze and food."

"I second that motion," Brock said.

The brothers all trooped downstairs to the bar, and I hung back to check in on Dru, who was still conked out hard, letting out a cute snuffling snore now and then. I left her a note telling her we were downstairs and to join us when she woke up, then jogged down the stairs to fix food for my brothers.

Bax was already playing bartender, pulling beers and pouring shots for everyone while Xavier was in the kitchen, firing up the fryers and the grill.

I joined Xavier in the kitchen. "Know your way around the kitchen, huh, kid?"

He dumped two full bags of fries into four of the six baskets, tossed several handfuls of my hand-breaded, locally-caught cod fillets into the other two baskets, and then started tossing patties on the grill. He shot me a grin while he worked. "I work midnights as a short-order cook at a diner back in Cali," he said. "I can only spend so much time studying, you know? And my electronics habit won't fund itself."

I did some mental calculating. "Hold up, X. You're in school full-time, on the varsity soccer team, work in the robotics research lab, *and* you work midnights? When do you sleep?"

He shrugged, a lot like Canaan's *why does it matter?* gesture. "I only need a few hours a night."

"What does 'a few' mean?"

"Four or five, max. I've never needed a lot of sleep, Bast, you know that."

"Yeah, but you're crazy busy, you can't—"

"All of the most successful, most intelligent people in history are the same way. Tesla, Einstein, Jobs, Edison, guys like that rarely slept more than a few hours at a time."

"Okay, I'll give you that, as I've heard similar stories. But why work a short-order job? With your brains—"

He gestured at a stack of plates. "Start plating buns and tartar, would you?" He flipped burgers and replaced the presses, checked the fries and the fish, and then started separating slices of cheese while talking. "I like the work. It's mindless, and fast-paced. It gives me time to think, you know? It's all automatic, I just kinda zone out on the rhythm and let the rest of my mind wander. I do most of my homework in my head while I'm working, and then I just have to go home and write the answers down later."

I laughed. "You do your homework in your head? How does that work?"

"Eidetic memory," he answered. "I read the problems and then I've got them in my head, and I can just...think them through and come up with the answers."

"What's—that thing you said...eidetic memory?"

"It's what most people are thinking of when they talk about a photographic memory. My brain basically takes a snapshot of everything I read—math problems, physics equations, books, sheet music, schematics, whatever. If I look at something once, I can bring it up in my mind with perfect recall."

"So that's why you're so damn smart?" I said, lifting the baskets from the fryers and shaking the grease out.

He tilted his head side to side. "It's more of a... symptom of intelligence, you could say. The fact that I have an eidetic memory isn't the *cause* of my intelligence, but rather is more of a by-product of it." He grinned a little sheepishly. "You know, just...clinically speaking, I mean."

"Hey man, as wicked smart as you are, I think you get to be a little smug about it sometimes."

He paused in the act of sliding a patty onto a bun. "Smug? You think I'm...*smug?*"

His expression was so concerned I couldn't help

laughing. "Dude, chill," I said. "No, you're not smug."

He went back to plating the rest of the food. "I can't rely on raw intelligence. If the smartest person in the world is a lazy bum with no drive or ambition, nobody will ever have heard of him because he won't have ever accomplished a single thing. It's wasted potential. I'm not going to waste my potential. Doesn't matter what my IQ is or what my SAT score was if I'm not pushing myself. That's all useless horseshit if I don't actualize my potential and turn it into real world accomplishments. Working as a short order cook just keeps my body busy while I'm unable to sleep, and lets me earn money while my mind is busy doing other things. I solved an equation in my head while flipping burgers that my professor was stumped on for six months—and that's less a brag on my smarts than my efficient use of time."

"I guess that makes sense," I said, feeling distinctly overwhelmed by my baby brother's intelligence.

I knew for a fact all of my brothers felt the same way if they spent too much time around Xavier. The brute force of his intellect tended to dominate everything. His mind was never at rest, ever, and neither was he. Even while studying, he'd be doing something with his hands. I remembered watching him read a history textbook for class once while he was standing up at the kitchen table idly tinkering with bits and pieces of electronics and a laptop. He finished the entire textbook in a single two-hour session, and when he was finished he'd built a four-legged robot that would totter around like a drunk dog, then stop, tip forward on its forelegs, then keep walking around doing handstands. It didn't *do* anything other than that little trick, but it wasn't meant to. He'd stuck pieces together to keep his hands and the rest of his brain-space busy while reading, and the robot was what he'd ended up with as an accidental by-product.

Honestly, it was hard *not* to feel a little inferior around him.

When all the food was plated up, we carried all seven plates out together. The others had shoved a pair of tables together and were playing some crazy drinking game that involved playing cards, and a lot of shouting, and a bottle of Jameson that had been new and unopened less than half an hour ago and was now nearly half empty. I had a feeling my liquor overhead was about to go up exponentially.

The game was cleared away and fresh beers were poured all around, even for Xavier and the twins since, as Brock—the only other brother with college experience—pointed out, even though they were underage here in Alaska it was obvious Xavier was going to drink at Stanford, and the twins would have constant access to booze while on tour, so pretending they didn't drink was kind of dumb.

We dug into our late dinner; it was well after ten by this point, but we'd always been a family to eat late. When I was the one in charge, I usually didn't get a chance to fix dinner for the boys until after nine or ten most weeknights, having been too busy cooking and waiting tables to take time for it until after the rush ended. Dad was always behind the bar then, and usually fairly well into a bottle of Jack by then anyway. He'd never gotten so drunk on shift that he stopped being a whirlwind wizard of a bartender, but it meant he was focused on the drinks and the customers rather than the rest of us. His way of coping, I guess. Easier to bury himself in booze and customers than to let himself give in to grief.

We finished eating and were working on a keg of beer and the bottle of Jameson, catching up, playing poker, just basically shooting the shit and reacquainting ourselves with each other.

Then there was a fist pounding on the front door, which we'd locked so people didn't mistake the glow of lights for us being open, just in case the neon *closed* sign wasn't enough of an indicator.

Brock jumped up. "That's probably Lucian," he said, striding for the door.

We all stood up, ready to crush our weirdest and most wayward brother under an avalanche of hugs.

Brock stiffened when he got the door open, though. "Sorry, man. We're closed for a private party."

A male voice came from the other side of the door. "I'm not here to drink."

Baxter was right behind Brock, as usual. "Good, since we're closed. Come back tomorrow."

"I just said I'm not here to drink. I'm looking for someone."

Brock turned to glance at me over his shoulder, obviously unsure how to proceed. I slugged the last of my beer and joined Brock and Bax by the door. The guy on the other side was probably a couple years older than me, maybe thirty or so. Medium height, fine blond hair slicked back. Not ugly, but not good-looking either. Just...average. Something about him made my instincts sit up and take note. He made me...uncomfortable, but for no reason I could pinpoint.

"How can I help you?" I asked.

"My name is Michael Morrison, and I'm looking for someone," the guy repeated. "A woman. About five-eight, reddish-brown hair. Her name is Dru Connolly."

Everything inside me went cold and hard and all sorts of pissed off. Brock noticed my reaction, and his arms went across his chest, and he shifted to block the door more completely. Baxter, always ready to throw down, cracked his knuckles and rolled his head on his thick neck. I heard chairs scraping across the wood floor behind me, and knew the rest of my brothers were there to back me up—not that I needed it, since I was fairly certain I could break this twerp in half without breaking a sweat. He was wearing pressed khakis and a pink polo, for fuck's sake, and the creases in his pants were as fresh at midnight as they would have been at noon. He even had a pair of Wayfarers hanging from the V of his polo. Jesus, what a dweeb.

"Get lost, motherfucker," I growled. "You ain't gonna find anything here but trouble."

"I'm not looking for trouble," he said, his voice calm despite the fact that I had a lot of inches and pounds on him—not to mention Bax and Brock standing there looking on. "I'm looking for Dru."

I actually snorted. "If you gotta go lookin', then maybe she don't wanna be found."

His brows lowered. "You know where she is, don't you?" He stepped forward, pushing to within a couple inches of me; ballsy sonofabitch, I'll give him that. "I spoke to the pilot who flew the airplane she arrived on, and he indicated that this bar was within walking distance of the dock where he'd tied up. I'd like to see Dru, please."

I crossed my arms over my bare chest; I'd never bothered putting on a shirt or shoes, so my build and tats were on full display. Most people tend to find me pretty intimidating, especially if I'm putting out the *I can bash your skull in without flinching* vibe, which I was doing right then. "All right, I'll say this as clearly as I know how: you have exactly thirty seconds to clear the fuck out, or you'll be eating your meals through a straw. You pickin' up what I'm puttin' down, shitstick?"

He paled a little, but held his ground. "No need for violence. I just want to speak with her."

"She don't wanna talk to you," I growled. "Twenty seconds."

"You're out of your depth, I'm afraid," he responded. "You've threatened me without provocation, and if you do physically harm me, my lawyers will sue you into the next century. Now. I will only say this once more. I *want...*to *speak...*to *Dru.*"

I saw red then, and started forward, ready to blast in his veneered fucking teeth.

Bax, however, got there first. His fist closed around Michael's throat, then Baxter's seventeen-inch biceps flexed and Michael left the ground. "You must be fuckin' stupid, yo," Baxter growled. "Get lost. Last chance. I squeeze just a little harder..." his fist tightened, and Michael's face went redder, nearing blue, "...and you won't be suing anyone. Got me, bub?"

A small, pale hand touched Baxter's biceps. "Bax...put him down. He's not worth it."

Baxter's head swiveled, and he stared at Dru carefully. "You sure? 'Cuz I can pop his neck like a pretzel."

Dru patted his biceps. "I'm sure. Let him go, please."

Baxter released Michael, who hit the ground like a bag of potatoes, gasping like a fish out of water. "If it ain't worth it for me to break him, then it ain't worth it for you to spend another second talking to his ass, yeah?"

Dru only smiled up at Baxter softly. "I spent four years with him, Bax. I deserve an explanation from him. I'll be fine."

"Yeah, well, we won't be going far." Baxter pivoted in place and whirled his hand in a circle by his head. "Let's go upstairs, boys. Hundred bucks says I can kick all of y'all's asses in HALO."

Canaan and Corin took the bet volubly, as did Xavier, but Brock and Zane were slower to respond. Eventually, Brock joined the younger three guys upstairs, leaving only Zane in the bar with me and Dru and her piece of shit ex-fiancé.

Zane, I noticed, had a nine millimeter in his fist held low next to his thigh, and an icy expression on his face. Dru hadn't missed that, either.

"Zane, it's fine. Really," she said.

Zane tucked the gun into the small of his back and went upstairs without a word.

Then it was just me, Dru, and Michael.

Dru pressed up against me, her hands on my chest. "Let me talk to him, okay?"

I noticed she was wearing my Badd's T-shirt... and probably nothing else. Fact was, I could see her nipples outlined by the T-shirt, and I was reasonably sure she wasn't wearing any panties either.

"So talk," I growled.

She backed away from me, her expression shuttering. "Alone, please?"

"Not fuckin' happening."

She shook her head. "Sebastian, it's *fine*, I promise. He's a cheating asshole, sure, but he's never hurt me. I'll be fine, I swear."

Not that he could, I realized. But even knowing she could handle herself if he got physical didn't make this any easier.

"Look me in the eyes and tell me you wanna talk to this douchebag."

She stared up at me. "I need to know why, Sebastian. So I can be done with him forever. It's just...closure, okay?"

My chest ached. This guy spelled money and he'd had four years with her. In that instant, seeing his dweeb ass gasping on the floor in his thousand-dollar outfit, I felt all the hope I'd just started to nurture begin to fade. What did I have to offer a woman like Dru

Connolly? I was a better man, sure, but did *she* see that? She wanted to *talk* to him? She wanted *closure*? She wanted to take him back, that's what she wanted.

I stepped back from her, feeling coldness wash through me. "Fine. Whatever you want." I pivoted and stalked toward the stairs.

But I only made it three steps when I felt her hands on my arms, felt her spin me around, and then she was pressed flush against me so I could feel every sweet perfect curve of her body against mine.

"Bast, wait."

Bast? Why would she call me that if she wanted this dickhead?

"What?" I snarled.

She smiled up at me. "You think I'm walking out of here with him, don't you?"

"Well? Aren't you?"

A flash of irritation shot through her features. "Really? Do I seem that wishy-washy to you?"

I let out a breath. "Guess not."

"No, I'm not. Not even a little. I'm going to give him a chance to explain himself, because I need that for myself, and because even though it ended the way it did, I still spent four years with him and that's not a small amount of time to invest in someone. I did care for him at the very least, and I'm going to give him a few minutes of my time. I'm not taking him back, I'm just hearing him out. Then I'm going upstairs." She rubbed my chest with her palms, and her eyes took on a hint of lust. "And after you feed me and get me drunk, you're taking me to bed and I'm going to show you a few more tricks I know."

"I like your tricks," I grumbled, feeling a bit reassured. "Sorry for my reaction. I just—"

She put her fingers over my lips. "Shush, you big macho fuckstick. I get it. We can talk about it later. Now go upstairs and play HALO with your brothers. I'll be up soon."

I nodded. "All right, but if he—"

She clapped her hand over my mouth, this time. "You forget who you're dealing with, Sebastian?"

"Yeah, yeah," I sighed. "Have your conversation. But I know a few tricks too, don't forget."

She grinned at me. "Oh *really*?" She drawled the last word, making it a lewd insinuation.

"I don't read much," I said, "But I have seen picture-book copies of the Kama Sutra …"

She giggled. "Oh my. This sounds promising."

"Got this one position I've been wanting to try out with you…"

She pushed me away. "Go, before I jump you right here."

Michael was on his feet at this point, massaging his throat and watching Dru and me with hate and confusion in his eyes.

"Got one thing I gotta do first, though, yeah?" I met Dru's eyes, and she saw the anger there. "Gotta prove a point real quick."

She stepped aside, and her jaw clenched, her eyes going hard. "Only *one* point, yes?"

I took two long strides across the floor, swung my fist, once, as hard as I could. People on the receiving end of my right hook have compared it to being hit by a twenty-pound sledgehammer…and those people are usually my brothers who I'm not really trying to hurt, so I'm always holding back. I didn't hold back, this time.

If his jaw wasn't broken, then he'd be missing a few teeth at the least. I didn't stop to check, though, just shook the sting out of my fist, kissed Dru as I brushed past her toward the stairs.

# FIFTEEN

## Dru

HOLY SHIT—SEBASTIAN HIT MICHAEL SO HARD HE went back down to the floor like a log. Michael just...*dropped*. Contrary to what TV and movies show, you have to hit someone *very* hard to drop them with a single shot to the jaw.

It was several long moments before Michael stirred again, and when he did it was with a lot of agonized groaning. More groaning and writhing, and he finally sat up, gingerly, slowly...and spat out a molar.

"Jesus," Michael slurred. "What a barbarian."

"Keep talking like that and I'll call him back

down here, Michael," I said. "That was Sebastian re-straining himself for my sake, so I'd watch what you say if I were you."

I circled around behind the bar and poured my-self a scotch on the rocks, leaned against the counter and waited for Michael to gather himself. He stood up, collected his tooth, examined it, and then tossed it in the trashcan standing beneath the service bar.

He indicated the bar. "Can I sit?"

I shrugged. "Go ahead. You won't be sitting for long, though."

Pulling out one of the high-backed bar chairs, he sat down and massaged his jaw. "How'd you get involved with that guy, anyway?" He frowned at me. "Or are you *involved* with all of them?"

I set my scotch down and leaned forward to get in Michael's face. "Have you forgotten who you're talking to, Michael? Keep talking shit, see where you get yourself. I don't need *them* to wreck your world."

He rubbed his temples with his index and mid-dle fingers. "Goddammit, this isn't how I envisioned things going."

"I don't know what you expected, but you'd bet-ter get any ideas about me forgiving you out of your head."

He peered at me, brow furrowed, sorrow in his eyes. "I had hoped, yes."

"Well, that's not happening. Not in a million years." I felt my eyes prickle, but refused to let it show. "It was our *wedding day*, Michael."

He hung his head backward on his neck. "I know, I know. I just…" He trailed off.

"You just what? This is what I'm waiting to hear. You what? And *why?*"

A shrug. "I don't know. I don't know, Dru. I fucked up."

"*Nooooooo*," I drawled, "you fucked Tawny Howard."

"I know, but—"

"On our wedding day. Less than ten minutes before I was going to walk down the aisle." I felt my rage and hurt boiling back up with each word. "A wedding *I* paid for—" That got my brain going, and I halted mid-sentence. "Wait a second. I thought you took Tawny to Hawaii with you…on *my* honeymoon, which *I* paid for, by the way."

"Actually, *I* paid for that, remember? That was the deal: you paid for the venue and catering, and I paid for the honeymoon. The airfare was included in the package." He waved a hand. "And I did. I mean, she's there now, but I hopped a flight here. I had to find you. I couldn't leave things like that."

"How did you find me, anyway?"

"Wasn't hard to narrow down which flight you

stowed away on, and once I had the tail number, it was a simple matter of getting the pilot's number and asking a few questions. Wasn't hard."

"Whatever, I don't really care. So you left Tawny in Hawaii to come here and…what? Nothing about this makes sense." I picked up my scotch and took a drink to fortify my nerves. "Like, I really, *really* don't get it. Four years. *Four years*, Michael. *You* proposed to *me*, and it wasn't like I was dropping hints about it. I wasn't even sure I was ready to get engaged, but you—you went to so much trouble making it romantic, and everyone in the restaurant was watching, and I…I didn't feel like I had a choice but to say yes."

Michel indicated my drink. "Can I get one of those?"

I shook my head. "No, you can't." I rolled my hand. "Explain, Michael."

He took a deep breath, let it out. "It's hard to explain. I did care for you. I do, I mean."

"Bullshit, but continue."

"I did, I swear. Like you said, we spent four years together. It just…I don't know. I wasn't happy." He wiped his face with both hands. "I thought if I asked you to marry me, it'd make us happier. I kind of felt like you were never happy with me either, and I hoped getting married would solve whatever the problem was, and that—that wasn't something I've ever been able to figure out, why you weren't happy."

"But you went through with the wedding anyway. Up until I caught you with your dick in Tawny, at least. And that begs the question...if I hadn't caught you, would you have married me? Would you have taken me to Hawaii and fucked me with Tawny still all over you?"

"I don't know—god, I don't know!"

"Stop saying you don't know, you fucking bastard!" I shouted. "You *do* know, you're just too much of a pussy to say what you really mean."

"Fine! I never loved you!" he shouted back. "I *wanted* to love you, I *tried* to love you, but I never did. And you were...you were always...I don't know how to say it. It felt like you were playing a role. Like you were trying to be someone else, or...like you were trying to fit into the persona of someone you weren't. Like an ill-fitting mask, perhaps. Sex with you was... never *bad*, per se, but...not enough. When I met you, you were this wild person with all these crazy stories, and the first few times we slept together you were... *fierce*, I guess. But then you changed. You got...*boring*. And I didn't know how to get you back to who you were, who you used to be. I thought, if we got engaged, you'd open up. You'd...that we'd—that something would change, I guess."

"*I* got boring?!" I shrieked, outraged. "It was

always the same old thing with you. You never showed the slightest interest in anything but the same thing every time! And I was trying to be what *you* wanted, to fit into *your* life, to fit into the box *you* put me in!"

"How the *fuck* did I ever put you into a box? I never *once* told you what to wear or how to act or that I wanted you to change. *You* did that on your own. I thought you'd...outgrown your wild ways, maybe. Like you'd settled down." He was standing up, now, visibly upset, more animated than I'd ever seen him about anything; he rarely swore, too, maintaining that cursing was the sign of a weak mind. "I always felt like I was missing out, like by getting the watered-down Dru Connolly I was missing out on the fun version you used to be. But I *never* put you in that box."

I staggered backward, hands shaking.

Holy fuck—he was right.

My eyes watered with tears I didn't dare shed. I turned away, set the rocks glass down on the back counter of the bar, struggling to get myself under control. I gripped the edge of the counter and leaned against it as if it alone was keeping me upright. And maybe, in that moment, it was.

I'd changed myself for him...but he hadn't wanted me to change. He'd wanted the person he'd met, and I'd put myself into a pigeonhole in some kind of effort to make myself into what I'd thought he wanted in his life.

Oh, the irony.

"Dru?" Michael's voice was soft, concerned.

I wavered, for a moment. I remembered when I'd first met him, how much fun we'd had together, how easy things had seemed. He'd been a little average, sure, and he'd never made my pulse thunder or my legs shake, but he'd been stable, easy to be around, decent in bed, and most of all...*normal*. I'd been so sick of feeling out of place and alone that I'd settled for someone I'd never loved, and in the process I'd changed myself, forced myself into being some kind of pathetic attempt at "normal", when I'd never be that; I *couldn't* be. I could never be in love with someone like Michael Morrison. And I should never have tried.

My eyes lifted, and I saw the mirror behind the bottles of Patrón and Sauza and Johnny and Jack and Beefeater, saw the name of the bar emblazoned in frosted letters across the top of the mirror: Badd's Bar and Grill. I saw the table where Sebastian had done such delightful, dirty things to me, and the door where he'd done other things...and then my eyes lifted to the ceiling, just beyond which were seven incredible men, one of whom could rock my world to the core without even trying. And when he tried? Holy hell.

I knew I could never go back to Michael. I didn't *want* to, first and foremost, for myself. Not because of Sebastian or any other reason than that I just didn't want that life or that version of myself. I wanted *this* me. The one who took a chance on a different life with a stranger in a bar in Ketchikan, Alaska. The one who wasn't afraid to kick some ass, fuck like the tigress I was, and never apologize for any of my sharp edges. Hell, maybe I'd get some tattoos. Take those edges and sharpen them, flaunt them for everyone to see.

I stood up, straightening my back. I turned around, took a deep breath, and let it out, feeling peace wash through me. "You're right, you know. I did change myself. That wasn't you, that was all me. And I guess I owe you an apology. It turned our whole relationship into something it wasn't, into something it could never be. So, for that, I'm sorry."

"Dru, wait, just listen—"

"I'm not done, Michael. Yes, you were right about that. I turned myself into a boring version of me, went to college and got a degree I didn't really want, took a boring job I hated, lived in a city I've never felt at home in, spent four years trying to convince myself I loved a man I couldn't ever really love and never had."

I jabbed a finger at him, let everything spill out.

"But that doesn't excuse what you did! If you weren't happy, you should have broken up with me! If the sex was boring, you should have—I don't know, tried to spice it up! Tried something different! Tied me up or put it in my ass or something. Anything! But you never did. So what if it wasn't enough? *I* wasn't enough for you? Fine, okay, whatever. Maybe we were both at fault, or maybe I'm the only one at fault for pretending to be something I wasn't, but you should've broken up with me if that were the case, not *proposed*! And just because I wasn't enough, just because I wasn't what you wanted, that doesn't mean you get a free pass to start fucking around!"

"I know, I just—"

"NO! There's no *you just*." I slammed a fist on the table. "Tell me *why*! Why her, why then?"

He deflated further, if that was even possible. "Tawny and me…we'd known each other before you and I met. We'd had a thing in college, just a brief fling, but—"

"Wait, *college*? Can she even read?"

His expression soured. "Don't be a bitch, Dru."

I seethed. "*What* did you just call me?"

He held up his hands. "I'm sorry, that was uncalled for."

"Damn right it was."

"Point is, yes, she went to college."

"And how do we get from you having a fling with her in college to you fucking her on our wedding day?"

He shifted, getting uncomfortable now. "I—she and I, we…"

"Spit it out, Michael."

A sigh. "That time you went backpacking with your dad?"

I gaped at him. "*Really*? We were gone *three* days! Not even!"

"Everybody came over for some drinks, and Tawny was the last one to leave, and we'd both had a little too much…" He shrugged. "And one thing led to another."

"That was two years ago." I was barely holding myself together, seconds from ripping him apart. "Two years ago. So all this time…?" I trailed off, waiting for him to fill in the rest.

And he did. "All this time, yes."

"I never even guessed."

"We were careful."

I struggled to keep some composure. "When? Where? How often?"

He sighed. "Does it matter?"

"YES IT MATTERS!" I screamed.

"The salon where she works." He was eyeing me as if I was a time bomb liable to go off at any second—which, admittedly, I was. "The tanning booths. Pretty much every day."

"I never smelled her on you. You never called her, never texted her."

He sighed again. "I'd go see her in the morning, on the way to the gym. We'd meet at her salon, and then I'd go work out, take a shower, and go to work." A wave of his hand. "She never called me, and I always deleted our text threads before I got home."

"So you've been seeing Tawny on the side for *two* years?" I nearly crumpled. "Two years. You've ben cheating on me for *two years*?"

"Yes."

I wobbled, and the room spun. Hearing it said outright took the earth off its axis. I collapsed onto my butt on the floor behind the bar. "And...the proposal, the wedding, everything...you'd have gone through with it, but kept seeing her on the side?"

"I don't know. It was sort of obvious that you were clueless, so I just went with it. Figured I'd just...I don't know what. Figure it out later, I guess. If things between us got better, I'd dump Tawny, but if not, she'd be there for me."

"And she was fine with this arrangement? Knowing she was the side chick?"

"It feels a little more complicated than that to me, honestly," Michael said. "She...*gets* me. I always...I've always sort of felt like...like you..." He hesitated again. "Like you were the side chick."

"That's..." I shook my head, palms to my forehead, heart pounding, gut clenching. "That's fucking batshit crazy, Michael. I'm the side chick, but you asked me to marry you and arranged a wedding..."

I stood up, then, because I was at the end of my ability to handle anything more. And that's when I saw it.

A thin, plain gold band on the ring finger of his left hand.

"You...wait, wait, wait...you—" I was about to vomit. "You *married* her?"

He stood up, pushed the bar chair in. "Yes."

"Saturday? After I left?"

He nodded. "Yeah. My family was there, the pastor was there, the rings were there, and I'd never signed or sent in our marriage license...and I knew how I felt about her, so I figured why not? Your dad and his cop buddies went after you, and that was the entirety of your side, so...it just worked. She was fine with it."

I had trouble formulating words for several seconds. "This is crazy." I blinked, tried to get my head to accept what he was saying. "Your family...they were fine with it?"

He chuckled, a little awkwardly. "They were kind

of confused, at first. But there was an open bar at the reception, so..." He trailed off, as if that explained it.

"You gave her *my* ring? The ring you proposed to me with? The wedding bands we picked out together? The pastor *I* interviewed, the catering company *I* hired, the venue *I* picked out..."

"It was all there and set up and paid for, so why not? No sense letting it go to waste."

I shook my head. "This whole thing is making my head hurt. I don't...it doesn't make any sense." I finally made myself meet his gaze. He seemed untroubled. "Why are you here, then?"

He shrugged and held both hands palms up. "I just...hated how you found out. You deserved more than that."

I choked. "I deserved—" I couldn't even finish repeating his words. "You're crazy. I don't even know how you're capable of craziness of this caliber. You're acting like this whole thing is perfectly normal."

"I know it's not. It's unusual, sure, but...it works for me."

"And what about me?"

He shrugged, and I was going to break his shoulders if he shrugged one more damn time. "You're a strong girl, I knew you'd be fine."

I circled around from behind the bar, opened the door to show him the street. "You need to leave."

He nodded. And that was it. A nod. A single bob of his head, and he was out the door, as if he'd said what he came to say.

"Michael?" I said, and he stopped just on the other side of the door. "Just one more thing."

He eyed me cautiously. "You're going to punch me, aren't you?"

I smashed my fist into his nose. "How'd you know?"

He staggered backward, blood sluicing down his chin. "Lucky guess."

He walked away, then, and I was finally alone.

And wondering how the hell I'd spent four years with the man and never knew he was capable of... whatever bizarre kind of craziness that was. Like...really? He married her? Instead of me? Who does that? I mean, if we'd broken up, or it had been a few months, or even weeks...but he literally just brought Tawny out and was like, *I'm marrying her instead of that other bitch.*

But yet somehow I deserved more than how I'd found out?

None of it made any sense. Had I fallen down a rabbit hole?

My head was spinning.

I heard feet on the floor behind me, and then felt Sebastian's arms go around me.

"Nice shot," he said.

"How much did you hear?" I asked, not quite ready to turn around and face him yet.

"All of it." He, apparently, had other ideas, since he spun me around and tucked my head under his chin, my ear against his chest. "I was on the other side of the door the whole time, listening."

"Asshole," I murmured, not really meaning it.

"Yeah, well, that's me. King of the Assholes." He touched my chin, so I was looking at him. "I know shouldn't've listened to your private shit, but...I wasn't ready to let you go through that alone."

"Meaning, at the first hint that he was going to get out of line you were ready to rip him apart?"

He grunted an affirmative. "Nearly came out when he called you a bitch."

"You do know I can handle myself, right?" I said, frowning up at him.

He just smirked at me. "Yeah, 'course. But now you don't have to."

I sighed, not minding it at all, if I was being honest. "So...can you believe all that?"

He rumbled a negative. "Not even close. I think he's gotta be one of those...whaddya call 'em, psychopaths, or whatever. Like, the ones who don't even really get the difference between right and wrong."

"I think that's a sociopath," I said. "And I think

you may be right. I just…it makes no sense."

"No, it doesn't." He scooped me up in his arms, set me down on the table nearest the door. "Now kiss me, so we can both forget that crazy fuckhead."

"Sounds good," I murmured, but the words were lost as he kissed me, and I realized that, from the outside looking in, this thing I had with Sebastian might seem just as crazy, just as unlikely as what Michael had done with Tawny.

I only met him the other night but I knew I wasn't going anywhere any time soon. Neither of us were claiming this was some kind of undying love, but we also both knew that was where it was going. How long would it take to get there? No way to know, and I didn't really care. A month, a year, five years? As long as it was *real*, both of us all in and honest about what we had and what we wanted…that was all I needed. Well, that and…

"You gonna take me upstairs and fuck me or what?" I whispered.

He laughed. "Wild thing, we've fucked like eight times today."

"So? I'm ready for number nine." I cupped his hardening cock over his shorts. "And from the feel of it, so are you."

"Yeah, always. But I got brothers you ain't met yet."

The door to the bar opened then, and Sebastian swiveled to put me behind him, but then when the figure stepped over the threshold and into the light, he immediately let me go.

"Lucian!" He took an eager step forward. "You're here! Wasn't expecting you for a while yet, from what I was hearing."

Lucian Badd...dear god. Whatever magic had gone into the creation of these eight brothers hadn't spared the beautiful gene. Lucian was—like the twins I'd only barely seen and the youngest brother, Xavier—tall and thin, rangy, corded with lean muscle, more of a razor than a burly bear. He had the same rich brown hair as the others, but his was so long I wondered if he'd ever cut it. It was bound low on his nape and hung to mid-spine. He had a bit of everyone's features, the sharp nose, the strong jawline, the deep-set dark eyes, the perfect symmetry, but where even Brock, the most classically handsome of them all, was still handsome in that rugged, masculine way, Lucian was...

I struggled to put a word to it.

Ethereal. Otherworldly.

Something like that. All of the brothers I'd met were larger than life and could easily dominate a room with their loud, brash personalities, and the quieter ones like Brock were still fascinating, people you couldn't ignore. But Lucian just…sucked you in.

It was hard to explain, honestly.

He was gorgeous, freakishly so. Sharp-featured, hard-eyed, tall, emanating a quiet strength. His presence was…unnerving, in a way. He hadn't said a word, but his gaze was taking in me, Sebastian's shirt on me, Sebastian's protective posture, and he'd probably seen Michael outside with his bloody nose. Lucian's gaze missed nothing.

Finally, Lucian stepped forward, slammed his arms around Sebastian. "Good to be home, Bast."

"How'd you get here so fast? I thought you were in the Philippines?"

Lucian tilted one shoulder upward. "Red-eye from Honolulu."

"Hawaii?" Sebastian asked.

A nod. "Some sick waves on the North Shore."

"So were you ever in the Philippines?"

A shake of his head, ponytail bouncing. "Not for a while. A few months ago? Got the call from the lawyer in Honolulu. Been there a few weeks."

Sebastian chuckled. "Never could pin you down. What were you doing in Hawaii?"

"Surfing. Fishing." A sly wink. "And…*fishing*, na'mean, brah?" He held out his hand to me. "Lucian."

I shook his hand, still trying to get a read on him. He was chill, quiet, and terse even, but I could see a whirling, dizzying depth boiling beneath his placid exterior. He just…gave away little of what he was thinking or feeling. But you just knew it was deep, and that he was seeing and hearing everything, missing nothing, and you couldn't help but wonder what he was thinking, if only because he was so hard to read.

"I'm Dru Connolly," I said. "Welcome home."

"Home?" Lucian asked, and it was just one word, but the inflection he lent that one syllable put a dozen questions out in the air.

Sebastian clapped his brother on the back. "Yes, *home*. For you, for all the others…" he curled me against his other side, "and for her, if that's what she wants."

A lifted eyebrow, and a single nod from Lucian. "Gonna be crowded, then." He let go of my hand, and even offered me a small smile. "If Sebastian likes you, then pleased to meet you."

"I more than *like* her, punk."

This got Lucian's attention. "No shit?"

Sebastian seemed to be able to read Lucian a hell of a lot better than I could, and they obviously had that silent guy-communication going on. "Yeah, no shit."

Lucian nodded and shrugged. "All right then." He had a huge backpack on his back, the kind people who hike the Appalachian Trail for weeks and months at a time use. "I'm hungry."

And, just like that, all the Badd Brothers were home.

And, it seemed, so was I.

# EPILOGUE

## Zane

I FUCKIN' HATED SUITS. PUT ME IN GHILLIE SUIT IN THE goddamn desert and I won't complain, but when I stuff my ass into a tuxedo I'll bitch till the cows come home.

Dru didn't seem to give a shit. "It's for like twenty minutes, Zane. Soon as we start the reception you can take the coat and tie off."

"I want the goddamn tie off *now*," I growled.

She just patted my chest. "But you're the best man. You *have* to wear the tie. Plus, if you don't wear the tie, none of the other boys will. And then all hell will break loose, and my wedding will be ruined. You wouldn't want that, would you?"

I frowned at her logic. "The stupid fuckin' ties aren't what's keeping them in line, Dru, it's the threat of violence and the promise of booze."

She gave me her patented freeze-your-balls-off glare. "*Wear* the goddamn motherfucking *tie*, Zane Badd."

God bless Sebastian and may he have a long life and a happy one with Dru Connolly, but god, it took balls to parlay with this woman. She was something else, that was for damn sure.

I held up my hands in surrender. "Fine, Jesus. But the second that service is over—"

"Then I'll take the tie off for you, if you're so worked up about it," she cut in. "Just *please* quit bitching about it."

"I can't breathe wearing the fuckin' thing," I started.

Dru just hissed at me. "You're a Navy SEAL, Zane. You can hold your breath for, like, ten minutes."

"That's beside the point," I said. "Doesn't make the goddamn monkey suit any more comfortable."

She just shook her head. "Pussy."

She turned away from me, then, because Baxter was rolling up on his Harley. The bastard had gotten one look at Xavier's bike and had decided he needed one too, but of course he needed the biggest, baddest, loudest one ever made, so you could hear the stupid gorilla coming from a mile away. He wasn't wearing a helmet, being absurdly vain about his hair, and he wore his tux like he'd been born in one. But then, he went to a lot of players' dinners and such, so he wore one more frequently than I ever had.

Dru, wearing her wedding dress, gathered up the back of her dress and swung onto the bike behind him. I was pretty sure only Dru Connolly could pull this off. She'd taken her old wedding dress, the one that douche-canoe Michael hadn't ever even seen her in, and went to town with a pair of shears and a needle and thread. A joke, a joke—I'm just kidding.

She'd taken it to a qualified seamstress and had it professionally altered. I'd never seen the original version, but this dress looked pretty good to me. I'd heard she'd had the top part loosened so she could breathe in it, and had the skirt part cut away up to her thighs so she could walk it in while leaving the back long enough to be a real train. I don't know how the seamstress had managed it, but she had, and Dru looked fuckin' bangin'. Classy, sexy, and regal all at once.

This being Dru and Bast, the wedding was anything but traditional. The service was being held on the docks outside the bar, and the reception was on the street outside the bar...during normal business hours. It was seven p.m., and Bax was only taking her around the block so she could make her grand entrance on the back of a Harley. No aisle, no "Here Comes the Bride". Well, actually, I think Cane and Cor were planning on surprising her with an impromptu version of it.

We'd blocked off the entire street around the bar, and the catering company had set up a buffet of food outside and a bunch of white-cloth-covered tables in the street and on the docks. Canaan and Corin had a stage off to one side and planned to play all night long, taking breaks for food and booze, of course.

The twins, being the twins, could play covers of just about anything, plus their catalog of a hundred or so original songs—including dozens of songs they'd written while touring but had never got into the studio to record. They'd never told their old record label about them, and there were only the twelve songs from their debut album that they weren't allowed to play without permission.

The whole wedding was open to the public, with the interior of the bar open for business as usual, the wedding and reception all taking place outside. We'd hired temporary staff in addition to the catering staff to run the bar for the evening so all of us could hang out and party all night.

There were something like two hundred people gathered already, more in the bar, and yet more streaming in from all directions. Might have been Canaan and Corin's rambunctious cover of "Stairway to Heaven" they were currently playing, or it could have been the lights and the crowd and the smell of food...or just the air of a rippin' party that had infused this entire section of Ketchikan.

In the four months since Dru had drunkenly crash-landed in Badd's Bar and Grill, things had gotten a little crazy. Word had spread that all eight of us Badd brothers were back in town, and that we all were around in the bar on a regular basis, which had brought in the ladies in droves...and their boyfriends and husbands had stuck around because of the kick-ass music provided on a nightly basis by the twins and the stiff drinks poured by Bast and Bax. Business had turned around, you might say. Xavier had proven to be as talented a chef as he was at anything else, which meant we had a killer menu, and Dru provided a smiling, beautiful, happy face for the crowds which pushed in to max capacity every night. That's right, the chick had torn up her law degree to play hostess at a dive bar...and seemed well and truly happy with the decision.

Lucian, Brock, and I took turns helping out as needed in the kitchen, behind the bar, and on the floor, and Xavier took it upon himself to take care of the books, since he could do the requisite math in his head blind-drunk. Things were…amazing. We were busier than ever, and all of us were pretty content with the way things were.

I hadn't shot a gun in months, which was the longest I'd gone without spending hours on the firing range or in combat since I was eighteen.

Not all of us fit in the apartment above the bar, obviously, so some of us brothers had pitched in funds to buy and renovate an old storefront and the apartment above it a block away from the bar. The storefront had been turned into a recording studio for the twins, and the apartment above provided living space for them, Lucian, Brock, and Bax, while Xavier and I had the other two bedrooms above Badd's. None of us spent much time in any of the bedrooms except to sleep, so it didn't really matter, as we all tended to spend every waking moment at the bar either working or drinking.

With Dru and Bax making their circuit around the block, it was time for me to take my place beside Sebastian at the altar—which was a microphone stand and a rented white archway decorated with roses—with the brothers lined up on either side. Since Dru didn't have any real girlfriends and no family except her dad—who was performing the ceremony—the brothers had taken it upon themselves to be her "bridesmen" as well as Sebastian's groomsmen. Lucian, Xavier, Bax, and Brock were her bridesmen, and the twins and I were Bast's groomsmen. Technically I was the best man, but that just meant I was tasked with carrying the rings.

Sebastian, standing next to Drew, seemed more nervous than I'd ever seen him.

I nudged him. "You're not nervous are you?"

He scowled at me. "Fuck yeah I am. Gettin' married, man. Of course I'm nervous."

"It's not like she's gonna back out or anything, you know that, right?"

He snorted. "Well, fuck, dude, I hope not, but that ain't why I'm nervous."

"Then what is it? Never seen you look so green around the gills about anything."

He shifted his weight from foot to foot, peering over the heads of the crowd, watching for Dru's approach. "My vows. I wrote 'em myself, but..." He shrugged uncomfortably. "Putting what's in my head into words ain't ever been my strongest suit."

I struggled for something useful to say. "I'm not much better at it than you, bro. But just...be you, I guess. That's what she loves, and she'll be happy with it."

Drew Connolly, wearing his full dress uniform

from his Corps days, clapped Sebastian on the shoulder. "Listen, kid. It ain't all that complicated. Your brother hit it on the head. Trick is, don't try to say what's in your head. Say what's in your heart. My Dru doesn't care much for fancy words, never has. I raised her to pay more attention to what people do, 'cause that's what really tells you their character. You try to put your vows in iambic pentameter or some shit, she'll just stare at you like you've lost your damn mind. Just tell her how you feel, and make her heartfelt promises about the future."

Sebastian pulled a face. "The hell is iambic whatever the fuck you said?"

Xavier spoke up:

"'Let me not to the marriage of true minds
Admit impediments. Love is not love
Which alters when it alteration finds,
Or bends with the remover to remove:
O, no! It is an ever-fixed mark,
That looks on tempests and is never shaken;
It is the star to every wandering bark,
Whose worth's unknown, although his height be taken.
Love's not Time's fool, though rosy lips and cheeks
Within his bending sickle's compass come;
Love alters not with his brief hours and weeks,

But bears it out even to the edge of doom.

 If this be error and upon me proved,

 I never writ, nor no man ever loved.'"

Everyone just kind of stared at him for a moment, until he shrugged. "What? That's Shakespeare. Sonnet one-sixteen, in iambic pentameter. One of the most iconic poems about love ever written."

Sebastian stared at Xavier blankly for a minute. "Well that's real pretty, but what the fuck's it mean?"

Xavier blinked rapidly, which meant he was thinking through his response. "Depends on if you read it on its own, or in context with the other sonnets in the series to which it belongs. If you read it by itself, out of context, it's about the perfection of true love, and how love is eternal and immalleable."

Sebastian laughed. "You lost me, bro. I only know what like four of those words mean."

Xavier sighed. "Never mind." He frowned at Sebastian, then. "You know, I actually think you're a lot smarter than you give yourself credit for."

"Thanks for the vote of confidence, punk, but I'll leave the fancy words and poetry to you and Brock."

"Hey, leave me out of the poetry, thanks," Brock said. "I'll take Kant and Nietzsche over Shakespeare and Marlowe any day of the week."

Xavier opened his mouth to argue, probably some off-the cuff doctoral thesis on the intersection of poetry and psychology or some fancy bullshit, but the rumbling snarl of Bax's Harley interrupted him. The crowd parted for the big bike, and when Bax was parallel with the altar and the line of Badd brothers, he halted, flipped down the kickstand, swung off, and held out his hand to help Dru dismount. She swung her leg over, flashing an almost indecent amount of leg in the process, smoothed her dress over her hips and stomach, and then let out a deep breath.

She stood there for a few long moments, just breathing and smiling and staring at Sebastian. The twins, right on cue, began playing "Here Comes the Bride", although I've never heard a version that included a howling guitar solo or a thudding bass riff. It worked, though, somehow.

Gathering her train, she approached Sebastian, holding onto Bax's arm.

Drew took her hand and Sebastian's, and joined them between both of his. "None of us are much for ceremony or tradition around here, so I'm gonna do this quick and simple."

He looked at his daughter. "Dru, baby-cakes, my baby girl—I'm the happiest man in the world, next to Sebastian, here. Seeing you happy, seeing you find a man who's worth his salt? Makes this old soldier's cold, hard heart soften, just a little. Never woulda thought something so good could have come from that shitty day four months ago, but here we are, hitching you and Sebastian in what they call holy matrimony."

He looked to Sebastian, then. "Sebastian, my boy. Not much I need to say to you. Love her, take care of her, be the man she deserves. I know you will, and I know you are. You asked me a month ago for my girl's hand, and I gave you my blessing in private then, and I'm giving it to you again now, publicly. You're a damn good man, and I'm proud as fuck to have you as my son-in-law."

Dru smacked her dad's arm. "Dad! You can't swear when you're marrying us!"

Drew just chuckled into the mic. "Sure I can. We're not in a church, are we?" Dru sighed, conceding the point, and her dad continued. "So, without further speechifying, here we go."

He looked at Dru.

"Dru Connolly, do you take Sebastian Badd as your husband, and do you promise to love him and him alone with everything you've got for as long as you live and for whatever comes beyond this life?"

Dru took a deep breath and let it out. "I do. Forever, and beyond."

Drew looked at Sebastian next. "And Sebastian, do you take this woman—my precious daughter and my only family in this world—to be your wife, and to love her and her alone with everything you've got for as long as you live and for whatever comes beyond this life?"

Sebastian nodded. "I do."

Drew's gaze went from one to the other. "You have vows to exchange, before I do the honors?"

Dru let out another breath. "Sebastian...sometimes I have trouble accepting that I'm here, that this is real. That *you're* real. But you are, and...I love you. So much. And your brothers, all seven of them, they're all the family I've never had, and I'm thankful for you, and for them. I promise to love you with all the crazy I've got—which is a lot. All I can say is, I'm so glad I wandered into your bar that night."

Sebastian laughed. "I'm glad you did, too. I had this whole big speech written out, but the cards I wrote it on are all crumpled now and I can't make out my own handwriting—" he held up a pair of 3x5 cards covered on both sides with illegible scrawl, then stuffed them back in his tuxedo pants pocket, "so I'm just gonna have to wing it. When you stumbled into my bar four months ago, you were wearing that same wedding dress you've got on now, but you were soaking wet, your makeup was running, your hair was a tangled mess, and you were heart-broken and hammered. And, honey, my first thought the moment I laid eyes on you, was that you were an angel. You took my breath away then, and you've taken it away every single damn day since. I didn't know what I was lookin' for, but I found it in you. So here we are. I love you. And thanks for taking a chance on me." He glanced at Drew, then. "And Drew, now that I've married your daughter, you've got eight of us as your family. So on behalf of my brothers and me...welcome to the tribe."

Drew let out a deep breath, cleared his throat and blinked hard. "Thanks, Sebastian. That means more than I can say. Now, if you two don't have anything else—" he looked from Dru to Sebastian and back, and they both shook their heads, "then all there is left to say is...by the power vested in me by...what's it called...the Universal Life Church—and the great World Wide Web...I now pronounce you husband and wife. Kiss her, kid."

Sebastian wasted no time laying one on Dru and, holy shit...it was a scorcher of a kiss. Made a few people more than a little uncomfortable, but hell, you couldn't miss the love between them.

Sebastian threaded his fingers in Dru's, and they held their joined hands up, and the crowd, a mix of Ketchikan locals and tourists, plus the small but rowdy knot of Drew's cop buddies, all wearing loud Hawaiian tourist shirts and Crocs with socks—they especially howled and clapped like crazy, but nobody made as much noise as us Badd brothers.

Sebastian let it go on for a while, and then leaned into the mic. "Thanks, everybody. Now that the ceremony is done, let's party! Have fun!"

The twins hopped back up behind their mics and instruments and kicked off a rousing rendition of the Beastie Boys classic, "Fight For Your Right To Party", and wouldn't you know those two knuckleheads could even do the back and forth rap?

The party was on then, the drinks flowing and the food line forming.

As soon as Dru and Sebastian left the altar and the mic, Dru stepped in front of me and untied my black bowtie. I shrugged off the coat, took the tie from her and stuffed it into the pocket of the coat, which I then tossed over the back of the chair I'd be sitting in. After I'd rolled my sleeves up to my elbows, I felt a good bit better. Tie off, coat off, sleeves up...I could breathe again.

The crowd was getting wild, which wasn't doing my anxiety any favors. After countless missions in Iraq and Afghanistan and a few in South America going after drug lords, being around large groups of people wasn't exactly super awesome. They tended to make me nervous, antsy and uncomfortable. The crazier things got, the more my nerves turned into anxiety, until eventually I'd have to remove myself from the noise and activity and find somewhere quiet so I could breathe again.

None of my brothers knew about my anxiety attacks, because I'd be damned if I'd ever admit weakness to any of them, even though I knew logically they'd never say shit about it except to support me. Still, I couldn't admit it. No way, no how.

For now, though, I was doing okay. I had my brothers gathered around me, and Sebastian was happy as fuck, grinning ear to ear and refusing to let Dru get more than a foot away from him. I grabbed a beer from the ice bucket at the head of the food line, piled a plate high with grub, and took my seat next to Lucian at the head table near the stage.

God, Lucian. The kid was back, and just as opaque as he'd ever been. I always thought I did a good job of keeping my internal bullshit to myself, but Lucian just...the dude let out *nothing*, so even for those of us who knew him well he was nearly impossible to get a read on.

Yet here he was, leaning his chair back on two legs, sipping a beer out of a red Solo cup, a sly, amused grin on his face.

"What's funny, Luce?" His nickname was pronounced *loose*, even though his name was pronounced *LOOSH-yee-an*. Go figure, right? No accounting for familial nicknames, I guess.

He just shrugged at me. "This." He waved at the

proceedings with his beer. "Bast, gettin' hitched."

I shot him a warning side-eye. "Why's it funny?"

He shook his head side to side. "Eh, not funny stupid or funny like it ain't serious." He paused to take a drink, probably because he'd reached the limit of how many words he could say all at once. "Just... funny weird, I guess. Bast...*married*? Never thought he'd be the first of us to do that, is all. And it's weird. And kinda funny."

I couldn't help a chuckle. "Yeah, I hear that." And thus we spent the next few hours, Lucian and I, sitting at the table and sipping beers, neither of us real big into hard drinking. Oh, don't get me wrong, I'm inclined to get black-out drunk from time to time, I just do it in private. Not sure about Lucian, but I suspected he rarely let himself get so far gone he lost control.

Brock and Bax, however, had no such inhibitions. A party was a party, especially for Bax. He was well on his way to getting wasted, and unless things had changed while he was in Canada playing for the Calgary Stampeders in the CFL, Bax always provided an interesting time when he had too much to drink.

Case in point. I just looked up and, yep, here we go. Bax was standing with one foot on his chair, one up on the table, a bottle of Jameson upended, chugging straight from the bottle. The crowd was chanting "CHUG! CHUG! CHUG!" and Bax, being Bax, looked like he was gonna try to polish off the whole bottle in one fuckin' go…and goddammit, that would NOT end well. At all. For anyone.

So I hopped up, snagged the bottle from him and said, "Bax, don't be a dumbass."

He peered at me blearily, angrily. "Hey, fucker. I was about to win a bet." He winked, a little unevenly, at a couple of girls, who tittered and giggled coyly. "I kill a whole bottle of Jameson at once, they'll take me back to their hotel with them."

I chuckled, despite my irritation. "Bax, buddy. Listen. You slam this bottle of whisky, won't be nothin' happening with either of 'em, *or* both of 'em, even as fine as they are, since you'll have a wicked case of whisky dick. So, this is me doing you a big-bro solid. Be smart, yeah?"

Bax reached out faster than I'd have expected him to be capable of given his state of intoxication, and snagged the bottle from me. "I…*don't*…get whisky dick…*bro*." He shot me a dirty look, stuck out his tongue, and polished off the bottle in half a dozen long swallows. "I mighta shared this, but now I ain't."

He was still standing in his Captain Morgan pose, one knee up, one foot on the table, so I shoved him, half as a knee-jerk reaction to him being a dumbass, and half because I was pissed at him. He toppled backward, arms wind milling, bottle flailing, and then just before he went down, he got a grip on my shirt and hauled me down with him. He hit hard, and I slammed down on top of him, and I heard the sound of glass breaking. Bax rolled over, throwing me off, and I felt something sharp gash my ribs, and then I was on my back, the wind knocked out of me, ribs screaming fire and pain, and people were shouting, and Bax was cursing.

I sat up, pressed my hand to my ribs and it came away red. Lifted up my shirt, checked the cut; not too deep, might need stitches, but not sure. Nothing too terrible. I grabbed a handful of napkins and pressed them against the cut, clamped them there as hard as I could, and then turned to check on Bax.

Fuck.

FUCK.

He was in a bad way, a jagged piece of the smashed bottle deep into the meat of his upper thigh. An inch in, if not more. I knew basic battlefield triage, which meant I knew to put pressure on a wound, how to improvise something to keep the pressure on, and I knew to not attempt to remove something impaled into the body.

"Don't move, Bax," I said, working to keep my voice calm. "We need to leave it in there for a hot minute, okay, bro? I know it hurts, but we gotta leave it in."

"Why?" He spoke through gritted teeth, glaring at me. "Fuckin' hurts. Get it out."

"Can't, not yet," I said. "Might cause worse damage if we take it out. And it's high up enough, it might be near your artery. We pull it, it could sever that artery, and you'll bleed out before we can do shit."

He was lying down on his back, struggling now and then to sit up and look at it, hands hovering around his thigh as if fighting the urge to just yank the shard out.

"Fuck, man."

"I'm sorry, Bax. I shouldn't have pushed you."

"No shit, asshole."

The blood, the pain in his eyes, the tension, the guilt...it put me back. "MEDIC!" I shouted forgetting, momentarily, that I was in Alaska, and not on a mission.

I heard commotion around me and looked up to see someone shoving their way through the crowd. "Lemme through. I'm a medic." I heard a woman's voice, with that brusque snap of someone used to being listened to. "Move the FUCK out of the way, assholes!"

People were shoved aside, and a woman stepped through the gap she'd created, kneeling beside Bax. I shifted aside to give her room, and she quickly took stock.

"Ah, not too bad. Not pretty, but you'll be fine. Just hold still, okay?"

"I am holding still!" Bax whined. "You're the one who's wiggling."

She glanced at me. "Pin his leg down for me."

"Yes ma'am," I said, because she had that voice of authority, and I'm a soldier trained to listen to that. I grabbed Bax's thigh up near his groin and his knee and pinned him down. "Now what?"

"Now I yank it out, and hope he hits you instead of me." She said this with a lopsided grin that knocked the air out of my lungs.

Fuck, damn, and holy shit, this girl was gorgeous. On the shorter side, but curvy as fuck. Blond hair braided tight against her head, the tail hanging over one shoulder, bright green eyes the color of grass with the summer sun shining on it, and that grin, fuck, that grin. Lopsided, cute, confident, sexy, a hint of white teeth, her lips expressive and done in bright red lipstick. That grin knocked me the fuck out.

And she was handling this with the calm ease of someone who'd seen much, much worse.

"Won't it hurt him worse if you take it out?"

She shook her head, the braid swinging against her shoulder. "Nah. Not where it is. No danger of nicking his femoral. Just muscle and blood in there. He'll be fine. It'll *hurt* him worse when I take it out, but it won't *damage* him worse. Key difference there." She glanced at Bax. "You need a belt to bite down on, big boy? Or can you take the pain?" She was baiting him, I realized.

"I can fuckin' take it, okay? Just get it the fuck out of me," Bax growled.

"Grab onto me, Bax," I said. "Break something if you have to."

"Oh I'll be breaking something," Bax snarled at me. "Just you fuckin' wait."

"I need you to keep his leg pinned down," the sexy medic said. "So he doesn't thrash and make things worse."

"Gotcha," I replied. I heard sirens in the distance, which meant someone had called 911. Keeping a firm grip on Bax's leg, I braced for the moment she'd pull out the jagged shard of the bottle. Bax was braced too, teeth gritted, both of his hands clamped down on my shoulder, his grip brutally powerful. I deserved it, so I allowed it. But it fuckin' hurt, and along with the cut on my ribs, which was still bleeding, I was in a world of hurt.

But Bax had to be hurting worse, so I pushed the pain aside and focused.

The medic shot me a look. "On three, all right? Ready? One... two...," and then she yanked it out in a quick jerk of her hand, lightning fast. "Three."

"Ha ha," Bax grunted, sounding distinctly faint and unamused. "Very fuckin' original. Oh fuck... fuck, it hurts."

The medic glanced up at Brock, who was hovering over us. "You. Need your shirt and belt."

Brock complied immediately, shrugging off his coat, ripping off the tie, and unbuttoning the shirt. In less than thirty seconds he gave her his shirt and belt. The medic wrapped the shirt around Bax's thigh, keeping a thick wad of fabric bunched over the site of the wound, and then wrapped the belt around it and cinched it tight. The ambulance arrived and the EMS crew took over, the sexy medic filling them in, and then Brock was climbing into the ambulance after Bax who was on the stretcher. And then they were gone and I was left standing there, hand pressed to my side, with the medic next to me, her hands bloody.

She eyed me. "Military?"

I nodded. "Navy SEAL. Well...ex, now, I guess." I returned her gaze, found myself lost in that green. "Combat medic?"

"Army. Three tours, one in Iraq and two in Afghanistan."

"Thanks." I held out my hand, the one not pressed to my ribs. "Zane Badd."

She held out her hand to take mine, but then hesitated. "I'd shake, but my hands are messy."

"Not the first time either of us has had blood on our hands." I closed the space, took her hand in mine. "What's your name, darlin'?"

She shook my hand with a firm, strong grip. "Mara Quinn." Both of our hands were slick and sticky with blood, hers with Bax's, and mine with his and mine both.

I'm not a talker, like some of my brothers, and I'm also not quite as taciturn or grunty as Lucian or Sebastian, but I've never had any problems talking to women. Mainly, I'd guess, because my looks typically speak for themselves, and the fact that there's not usually much talking necessary after I say, "I'm a Navy SEAL." But, for some reason, Mara Quinn left me tongue-tied.

"So." I felt like my tongue was stuck to the roof of my mouth, words lodged in my throat.

"Small talk sucks, and I need a drink." She gave me that lopsided grin again, and something fluttered inside me, as if there were a colony of bats inside my chest. "Happen to know somewhere...quiet...where we could get one?"

I grinned back at her. "I might. There happens to be this bar named after me..."

"The bar's named after you, or you after the bar?"

"Same difference. It was our dad's, and now it's ours," I said, gesturing ahead of me for her to go into

Badd's.

"When you say 'ours,' who is that, exactly?" Mara asked.

"Me and my seven brothers," I said. "Sebastian, the one getting married, is the oldest. Then me, then Brock, whose shirt you put around Bax's leg. Bax is next, then Canaan and Corin, then Lucian, then Xavier."

Mara's eyebrows lifted. "Damn, that's a lot of brothers."

I nodded. "Sure is. But that just means it's never boring around here."

We took two stools at the bar, and the temp bartender came over immediately. "What can I get you, Mr. Badd?"

I frowned at him. "Name's Zane. Mr. Badd was my dad and he's gone. Bourbon on the rocks for me." I glanced at Mara. "For you?"

"Same as him."

"Any particular bourbon you'd like, sir?"

"Maker's Mark is fine," I said.

"Good choice," Mara said, smiling. "Although I'm usually more of a Blanton's neat sort of girl, but not everyone has Blanton's."

When we had our Maker's, we sipped in an oddly companionable silence for a couple of minutes, and then Mara swiveled on her chair to face me.

"So, um…" she looked at me over the top of her rocks glass, a small, sly grin on her lips, "when I said somewhere quieter, this isn't exactly what I meant."

The way she was inching closer to me, letting her knees brush mine, told me what she likely meant, but I'm not one to play games or mince words. I like to know exactly what I'm getting into, and I like the girl to be clear about what she wants from me. I've brushed too close to Death too many times, seen too many buddies' lives cut short to bother fucking around playing mind games.

"Oh. Well…what *did* you mean, then, Mara?" I slid closer to her, half standing now, framing her knees with mine, and I slid a palm up her thigh. She slugged the last of her drink in one go and then stood up, pushing closer to me. No hesitation, no games.

"You, me, and somewhere private with a bed," she said. "Or a couch. Or a counter."

"I have all three of those at my disposal, and everyone else will be down here for the foreseeable future."

"Lead the way, then," Mara said, slipping her hand into mine. I led her upstairs to the apartment and showed her into my room. As soon as I had the door closed behind her, Mara jumped at me. Literally, she leapt into the air and crashed against my chest, letting me take all of her weight, her mouth slamming against mine, her tongue seeking mine.

For a long, breathless moment, then, we kissed. I had both hands on the plump, juicy peach of her denim-clad ass, squeezing it, holding her aloft with that grip. I shifted her higher, and she wrapped her short, powerful legs around mine.

I held her there, backed away from the kiss enough to whisper against her lips. "Damn, girl. You don't waste time, do you?"

She shook her head. "Fuck no. You've seen the same shit I have, Zane…you feel like wasting time when we both know what we want?"

"Fuck no," I echoed her words back to her.

"But, to be clear," she murmured, that sweet, sexy, mischievous, lopsided grin gracing her lovely mouth, "just because I don't want to waste time with stupid games doesn't mean I want to skip any of the good stuff."

"I'd never skip any of the good stuff," I said.

"Good, because foreplay is half the fun."

"At least half," I agreed.

"Glad we're on the same page, then."

"Me too."

She slid down to her feet, pushed my shirt up and let me rip it off, then she tossed it aside. As she reached for the fly of my tuxedo pants she stopped, seeing the cut on my ribs. "The fuck is this, Zane?"

I glanced down at it, having forgotten about it. "Oh, that? It's nothing."

She pulled at the paper napkins, which were sodden through with blood and sticking to my skin. "It's not nothing. Jesus, why didn't you say anything?"

"Bax was hurt worse, and then I just sort of... forgot."

She shot me a baffled look. "How can you forget about a six-inch cut across your fucking ribs?"

I shrugged. "I mean, it doesn't exactly tickle, but you sort of...distracted me." I grinned, knocking her hands away, reaching for her shirt. "I'm fine. We can deal with it later."

She ignored my attempts to put her off, and continued to gently peel the blood-wet wad of napkins away, then examined the cut. "You might get away without stitches. It's not all that deep, just long. And it's already congealing." She glanced up at me. "Got any super glue?"

"Super glue?"

She nodded. "Yeah. Works great for things like this. Medical glue would be better, but plain old super glue works in a pinch."

"There's some in the junk drawer in the kitchen."

"Well, show me the way. I can't just ignore this, you know. Not in my nature. So the faster you show me the glue, the faster we can get back to the fun stuff."

I led her out of the bedroom and into the kitchen, found the glue and the first aid kit with the bandages and tape. She ripped off a giant wad of paper towels, filled a cup with water, and poured the water across the cut to clean it, and then when she was satisfied it was clean she dabbed it dry and carefully applied a thick strip of super glue along the cut, then knelt and blew on my skin to dry the glue faster. Within a minute, the glue was dry and I was as good as new.

Well, mostly.

She stood up, washed her hands, and then leaned a hip against the counter, standing facing me. "Your pants are wet. Oops." She said this with a grin that told me everything I needed to know.

"Guess they'll have to come off," I said, and led her down the hallway to my room, closed and locked the door behind us.

"Guess they will." She unbuttoned the fly, unhooked the clasp, and lowered the zipper. "Is this where we were? I'm having trouble remembering."

I felt my gut flipping, my cock hardening, my head hammering. "I think we're on the same page, about how foreplay is at least half the fun of sex."

"Oh, yeah," she murmured, tugging my tuxedo pants down. "That page."

"That page." I toed off my shoes, stepped out of

my pants, and stood in front of a fully clothed Mara in nothing but a pair of tight black briefs.

"God, you're fucking gorgeous, Zane, you know that?" Mara's voice was low, a hum of sincere appreciation. "But you're still wearing too many clothes."

I let her tug my underwear off, and then I was naked, and she still had every last article of clothing on, a situation I intended to rectify ASAP. She stood in front of me, her gaze raking blatantly up and down my body. I let her look, because I worked my ass off to look this way. "Mara, honey, you're plenty gorgeous too, but I think I need to see more of you. Just...you know...just to make sure we're on the same page."

She grabbed the hem of her shirt in preparation to peel it off, but I caught her wrists in my hands.

"Ah-ah-ah," I said, "that's for me to do."

Mara let me peel her shirt off, toed off her shoes like I had, let me work those tight jeans off. And then she was, gloriously, in nothing but her bra and underwear, a matching set of green lace and silk that covered just enough to be, you know, functional, but still left little to the imagination. I took a moment to take in her beauty; she was, as I already knew, fucking incredible. Five foot five at most. Muscular arms and legs, toned abs, a taut round ass that told me she did a shit load of squats at the gym, and tits that would be just slightly more than a handful. She wasn't what

I would call ripped, but she was clearly no stranger to the gym and clean eating, yet she still had hints of softness and flesh where I liked to see it on a woman. Fucking perfect is what she was.

I popped her bra clasps with a pinch of one hand, tossed the garment aside, and then knelt in front of her, running my nose across her belly to one hip, then across again, a little lower, giving her plenty of warning as to my intent in the next few moments. She didn't demur, and I didn't expect her to. She let me shimmy her panties off and, sweet goddamn, her pussy was waxed bare except for a thin, closely trimmed landing strip. Plump, thick pussy lips, damp, glistening.

"Fuck, Mara. You're perfect," I growled.

I slid my hands up the backs of her thighs, cupped that firm but juicy ass, bare for my hands now, and as soft as the silk I'd just stripped off her. I brought my hands around, traced a finger up the slit of her pussy, getting a low moan from her.

"Can I taste you, Mara?"

She scraped her hands over my scalp to clutch the back of my head. "I'll be pissed if you didn't."

I slid my tongue up her slit, tasting her juices.

"Oh fuck, Zane, fuck that feels so good."

"I'm just getting started, babe."

She watched me lick her pussy, and with each

slow lick she moaned louder and her hips flexed and pushed, telling me she was getting closer and closer to orgasm. And then, just when I was sure she was seconds from coming, she pushed my face away. "Wait. Zane, wait."

I stopped immediately, but frowned up at her. "I thought you wanted that?"

"I did—I do." She didn't try to pull me to my feet, just stared down at me for a moment. "I just need to make sure we're on the same page about one other thing."

"What's that?"

"That this is...no strings. Just for tonight. That neither of us will make it weird in the morning."

My heart squeezed at her words. That wasn't what I wanted. I wanted weird. I knew, from the few short moments I'd had with her so far, that this one night wouldn't be enough, no matter how many times we fucked. I'd want more. But I wasn't about to lose my chance at what I had in front of me, so I squashed my hopes.

I slid two fingers inside her channel, and flicked my tongue against her clit.

"No strings, no weirdness," I agreed.

But I wasn't sure I was telling the truth.

Or maybe I was just making a promise I wasn't planning to keep.

That wasn't honest though, but right now I didn't care.

I knew I would do whatever it took to keep Mara in my bed for as long as I could.

*BADASS*: A Badd Brothers novel

COMING SOON!

# Jasinda Wilder

Visit me at my website: **www.jasindawilder.com**
Email me: **jasindawilder@gmail.com**

If you enjoyed this book, you can help others enjoy it as well by recommending it to friends and family, or by mentioning it in reading and discussion groups and online forums. You can also review it on the site from which you purchased it. But, whether you recommend it to anyone else or not, thank you *so much* for taking the time to read my book! Your support means the world to me!

My other titles:

**The Preacher's Son:**
*Unbound*
*Unleashed*
*Unbroken*

**Biker Billionaire:**
*Wild Ride*

**Big Girls Do It:**
*Better (#1), Wetter (#2), Wilder (#3), On Top (#4)*
*Married (#5)*
*On Christmas (#5.5)*
*Pregnant (#6)*
*Boxed Set*

**Rock Stars Do It:**
*Harder*
*Dirty*
*Forever*
*Boxed Set*

**From the world of *Big Girls* and *Rock Stars*:**
*Big Love Abroad*

**Delilah's Diary:**
*A Sexy Journey*
*La Vita Sexy*
*A Sexy Surrender*

**The Falling Series:**
*Falling Into You*
*Falling Into Us*
*Falling Under*
*Falling Away*
*Falling for Colton*

**The Ever Trilogy:**
*Forever & Always*
*After Forever*
*Saving Forever*

**The world of *Alpha*:**
*Alpha*
*Beta*
*Omega*
*Alpha One Security: Harris*

**The world of Stripped:**
*Stripped*
*Trashed*

**The world of *Wounded*:**
*Wounded*
*Captured*

**The Houri Legends:**
*Jack and Djinn*
*Djinn and Tonic*

**The Madame X Series:**
*Madame X*
*Exposed*
*Exiled*

**Standalone titles:**

*Yours*

**Non-Fiction titles:**

*Big Girls Do It Running*

**Jack Wilder Titles:**

*The Missionary*

To be informed of new releases, special offers, and other Jasinda news, sign up for Jasinda's email news-letter.